Praise for
*The Best of Evil*

"With *The Best of Evil,* Eric Wilson reveals himself as *the* author to watch. His writing sizzles; his characters grab you and won't let go; his story intrigues, entertains, and makes you think. This is a page-turner you'll talk about with your friends."

—ROBERT LIPARULO, author of *Germ*
and *Comes a Horseman*

"The world through Aramis Black's eyes is mysterious, rich, and brewing with surprise."

—BRANDILYN COLLINS, *Seatbelt Suspense*

"Eric Wilson masterfully weaves together mysteries from past and present in this gutsy thriller. Wilson is an extraordinary writer with one of the freshest voices in fiction today. *The Best of Evil* is first-rate suspense."

—GINA HOLMES, Novel Journey/Novel Reviews

"A work of amazing maturity and skill."

—JAMES BYRON HUGGINS, author of *Cain,*
*The Scam,* and *Sorcerer*

"*The Best of Evil* is riveting reading—Eric Wilson at the top of his game. He combines suspense, history, a reality game show, full-blooded characters, and, yes, palpable evil into one addictive read. You'll love his flawed but charismatic protagonist, Aramis Black, a man prepared to live by the sword and die by the sword. Quite simply, *The Best of Evil* is the best of fiction."

—RANDY SINGER, author of *The Cross Examination of Oliver Finney*

"In *The Best of Evil,* you get the best of Eric Wilson—the only novelist I know who can make you wish you'd paid more attention in your seventh-grade history class. Wilson manages to make Meriwether Lewis into a figure of contemporary fascination in this intriguing tale set in modern-day Tennessee. Aramis Black is serving up hot coffee and sarcasm when a customer gets shot dead, propelling us into a story with all the twists and turns of a Smoky Mountain road. A stolen hanky, a pretty girl, a lock of hair, simmering family tensions, and a complicated hero with a dark past—this mystery has it all."

—MELANIE WELLS, author of *When the Day of Evil Comes* and *The Soul Hunter*

# THE
# BEST OF
# EVIL

# THE
# BEST OF
# EVIL

A NOVEL

## ERIC WILSON

### WATERBROOK
PRESS

THE BEST OF EVIL
PUBLISHED BY WATERBROOK PRESS
12265 Oracle Boulevard, Suite 200
Colorado Springs, Colorado 80921
*A division of Random House Inc.*

10-Digit ISBN: 1-57856-911-7
13-Digit ISBN: 978-1-57856-911-3

Library of Congress Cataloging-in-Publication Data
Wilson, Eric (Eric P.)
  The best of evil : an Aramis Black mystery / Eric Wilson. — 1st ed.
     p. cm.
  ISBN 1-57856-911-7
  1. Restaurateurs—Fiction. 2. Coffeehousees—Fiction. 3. Murder—Fiction.
4. Family secrets—Fiction. 5. Nashville (Tenn.)—Fiction. 6. Psychological fiction.
I. Title.
  PS3623.I583B47  2006
  813'6—dc22

                                2006017541

Printed in the United States of America
2006—First Edition

10 9 8 7 6 5 4 3 2 1

*Dedicated to*

*my mother, Linda,*
*for loving me through the rough days*
*even when your own love had been depleted*

*and my father, Mark,*
*for showing me the grace in my adolescence*
*that you never found in your own childhood*

Don't let evil
get the best of you;
get the best of evil by doing good.

—ROMANS 12:21

# PART ONE

# SINGLE SHOT

*Aramis…while seeming to have no secrets,*
*was actually steeped in mystery.*

—ALEXANDRE DUMAS, *The Three Musketeers*

# ONE

f she had lived, I know she would be ashamed of me.

I'm trying to change that.

My mother adored her morning coffee. I imagine her in my espresso shop, quiet, unimposing, lifting her drink and winking at me the way she did when I was a little kid in Oregon. A few months back I started the place with her in mind. She would love the mahogany counters, the polished brass rails and gleaming Italian machinery, the rich aroma.

Black's—that's what I call my shop, in honor of the family name.

Mom was always busy, they tell me. A dutiful housewife with a set jaw and silky, raven hair twisted back in a bun. She bore secrets no one should have to carry alone, and when at last she did seek support, she found only hostility and greed and a cup of conspiracy that spilled over into the lives of her family.

Dianne Lewis Black. Despite her weariness, her eyes sparkled. That much I remember and hold on to.

She'd still be with us if not for Uncle Wyatt's mistake, and I still hate the carelessness that stole her life away.

I was six when she died. I watched her fall, a stone's throw away. For two decades, that one moment held me in its grip. I wallowed in its rage through my young adult years, courting violence and a nasty drug habit. I tattooed my cynicism onto my forearms.

*Live by the Sword* on one. *Die by the Sword* on the other.

Despite all this, I've never stopped believing that we are created with the ability to soar. But then circumstances slash at us and pluck our feathers, and we get entangled in our sins. We fight to get free. We struggle, flapping our wings, beating at the air. Exhaustion leaves most of us numb.

Thirteen months ago I decided to break away. I packed a U-Haul and left Portland to live with my brother in Nashville, Tennessee—a place to start over, start clean. A safer world, I thought.

This morning proved me wrong.

Sitting here at my desk, putting it on paper, I hope to gain a glimmer of understanding. This is my way of processing, I guess. Not that it'll change things.

My shop is in shambles, and a fellow human being is dead.

Two and a half hours before the shooting at Black's, I was barely out of bed and shaking off my nightmares. I stumbled from the bathroom toward the kitchen, feeling cheated of sleep, quiet, and a general sense of sanity. My brother's guitar strumming in the living room did little to improve my mood.

I wouldn't think of asking him to stop, though. Music is Johnny Ray's love, his life, his very breath, wrapped up in a three-minute, three-chord, country music ditty. The man has his dreams, and with a name like Johnny Ray Black, how can he fail? I'd do anything to make it happen for him.

"Sounds good," I said, pausing in the doorway.

His eyes jerked up. "Aramis? Don't scare me like that!"

"Jumpy, jumpy."

"I thought you were long gone, kid."

"Should've been. I'm running late."

Cross-legged in his Tabasco boxers, surrounded by sheet music and scribbled notes, Johnny Ray shifted his guitar and tucked a section of yellowed newspaper under his knee. "Guess you better get movin'. Listen, grab yourself a muffin on the way out. Should be one left on the table."

"Another of your bran concoctions?"

"You got it. All natural, from scratch, and still warm."

"Ahh. That explains the smell."

"Hey now."

I pointed at his folded edition of the *Nashville Scene,* a weekly rag full of local news, events, and divergent viewpoints. "You hiding something from me, Johnny?"

"We'll talk later."

"I know. You're looking to get me tickets to the U2 concert, aren't you?"

"Don't go gettin' your hopes up."

My brother pressed his knee down on the paper and shifted his attention back to his guitar, golden brown hair falling over his shoulders, bronzed skin glowing—evidence of his weekly tanning bed routine. He believes "you've gotta look the part, gotta be video friendly," blaming his music aspirations for his obsession with health and appearance. Truth is, he's always envied the fact that I got Mom's Mediterranean coloring. I joke with him that he got the talent and I got the looks.

"How can you sit like that?" I asked. "Doesn't your butt get numb?"

"As a rock."

I slipped into the kitchen, scowled at the lone muffin, then rummaged in the cupboard. "Hey, what happened to my Froot Loops?"

"You finished them yesterday," my brother called back.

"I did not."

"You did too."

"Did not."

"Well, it wasn't me," he said. "I wouldn't touch the stuff, and you know it."

"Fruit, Johnny. It's good for you."

"Very funny."

Knowing that I lack any culinary skills, Johnny Ray gets a chunk of my change each month and does our grocery shopping and cooking; Froot Loops and Dr Pepper are his two concessions to my dietary needs.

He asked, "What would you do without me, little brother?"

"Spoil myself rotten."

"Honestly, I worry about you. You can't survive on caffeine forever."

"It's better than the stuff I used to do. Cheaper too."

"And legal, Aramis. I'll give you that."

I went to the table, hefted the muffin, and took a bite. Yum, yum. Lots of fiber.

"Still, there's something not right," my brother said as I returned to the living room. "You've stayed clean for a year now—which is a good thing, don't get me wrong—but I can see it in your eyes. You're still on edge."

"On edge?" I snorted. "I'm dog-tired. Drop it, okay?"

"You've always got a reason to avoid the issue."

"What issue?"

"Uncle Wyatt. And the way Mom died."

"What? Where did that come from? It was over twenty freakin' years ago. Why keep dredging up the past?"

"See now, that's your pain talking."

"Dude." I pulled on my jacket. "I know you're trying to help me, but it's too early in the morning for psychoanalysis. I have to get to work." I took another bite.

"It's come full circle—that's all I'm trying to tell you."

"Sure. If you say so." With my mouth full, my words were pebbles rolling in wet gravel.

"I'm not sure you're ready for it."

"Gotta go. My customers will be lining up soon."

"I'm probably gonna regret this, but…Aramis, does this look familiar?" My brother's question brought me to a halt.

In his hand, waved into view from the folded newspaper, he held a silk cloth with Mom's initials embroidered on it: DLB. Hours after my mother's death, after the police had come and gone, I'd realized this memento was missing. She'd given it to me in confidence, saying that it held secrets, and then someone had stolen it away. I'd always wondered if the thief had known its significance. He must have.

"Is that…?" I took the cloth from my brother, cradling the soft material. I felt like a boy again. Six years old. Choked with emotion. "It's Mom's handkerchief."

"I found it last night." Johnny Ray gestured toward the front door. "On the steps, in a FedEx envelope."

# TWO

Numbed by this link to my mother, I kneaded the handkerchief with my fingers. In the last year I've been trying to pull things back together, honoring the convictions Mom once held dear. Not an easy task. Certain questions never go away, and I've come to the decision that faith is all about believing even when you don't understand.

Which is a good thing, because there's a lot I don't understand.

According to my brother, the envelope arrived with the sender's name left blank. The originating address: the Oregon State Penitentiary.

What was it doing there, at a prison? Who'd been keeping it all these years?

And why send it back now?

Still gripping the memento, I trekked on foot through Centennial Park's morning fog toward my espresso shop. By leaving my car in the brownstone building's lot, I do my part each day to protect the environment, and it gives me time to wake up, clear my head, sort my thoughts.

Against my will, my mind replayed clips of my mother's final moments.

A gun barrel pushed into her hair. Fright on her dignified face. Refusing to speak. Dropping to her knees, then plunging into the river below as a madman pulled the trigger.

The day Mom died, she gave me a small ebony box containing this handkerchief with its intricate embroidery. Her whisper was full of urgency: *Hold on to this for me, okay, Aramis? I have secrets wrapped in here. Someday it'll show you the way.*

I still have that box. Sitting on my bedroom windowsill, polished, visible to all who enter, it's a statement that Mom's still with me. Sometimes I run my fingers over the smooth ebony and imagine I catch her scent. Just a whiff.

Inside my shop, I stabbed a finger at the alarm code. Installed for insurance purposes primarily, the alarm gave a confirming beep, and I left the door unlocked. It's a habit. My route through the park has helped me befriend two or three homeless people, and they know they're always welcome to come in for warmth and a few kind words. Free coffee too.

Of course, I had no idea that today my shop was to be the site of a homicide.

Five thirty. Black's remained in near darkness for my half-hour opening routine. I folded and tucked my questions away with the handkerchief in my chest pocket. I operated on autopilot, grinding espresso, brewing coffee, straightening chairs and tables, putting a till into the register.

Music City USA…home of the Grand Ole Opry, Chet Atkins, and Minnie Pearl. These names call forth a parade of down-home stereotypes: banjos and fiddles, rhinestones and whiskey, cowboy hats and boots, and some country yokel spittin' tobacco juice into the dirt. But they're preconceived ideas, mental ticks that latch onto your thoughts and suck away your objectivity.

I won't lie. I arrived here with a few ticks of my own.

This morning, however, looking out my shop windows, I was reminded once again how far such caricatures are from the truth.

Situated at 2216 Elliston Place, in Nashville's West End, my shop caters to the newest generation of java junkies. Many of Davidson County's estimated one million residents commute to work in some of our nation's most respected halls of medicine and learning. New condos and high-rises are sprouting throughout the area. BMWs, Hummers, and Lincoln stretch limousines are common sights, and the hills boast mansions befitting the Vanderbilts.

Of course, the Vanderbilts helped build this city. Vanderbilt Hospital, Vanderbilt University, and a cluster of historic churches rub shoulders—or parking spaces—while the music and publishing industries grope for success. The War Between the States may have failed to change certain things, but the almighty dollar has proven mighty indeed, and the Southern way of life is crumbling beneath the demands of big business.

No wonder some call it Cashville.

Here's a sobering fact, though: last year the Metro Police recorded one hundred homicides. Count 'em: one-zero-zero. Considering that, maybe I should've seen it coming, should've sensed trouble.

Without the usual morning sun, my espresso shop seemed drab and dull, and I had the feeling I was back running that mom-and-pop store on Portland's east side.

*Need a bag for that booze? That magazine? The hair gel?*

*You don't see what you want on the shelves? Well, tell me what you're lookin' for. I know how to...find things, if you know what I mean.*

No. That life was behind me. Thirteen months ago I'd had my *Fight Club* moment, staring hell in the face at the business end of a lowlife's Glock, my nose shoved down into the error of my ways. But it was no movie, and I was convinced I was a goner.

Then a miracle…out of nowhere. A wake-up call.

Since then I've been holding on to the belief that I'm turning a new page, discarding the past, and putting things right. No more trouble.

Yeah, right.

As of today, it's a documented fact: Black's—site of this year's homicide number seventy-nine.

A phone call broke through my mood. I answered it to stop the racket.

"Black's. Can I help you?"

"Aramis, you sound tired."

"You sound…perky."

"Don't I always?"

"Sammie, it's always good to hear your voice." And I meant it.

With her considerable wealth and corresponding business sense, Samantha Rosewood had agreed last year to join me in this financial endeavor. We had picked the location after extensive research and a couple of conversations with the Elliston Place Merchants Association. They felt that, yes, another espresso shop could fly. Or maybe they just wanted our membership dues. Either way, Black's would still be on the drawing board if it weren't for Miss Rosewood's money.

Simple facts: I needed more than my savings could provide, and she had more inheritance than she could spend. Poor Sammie.

No complaints, though. She's a savvy woman, with old money and Southern manners. Sure, I've imagined the romantic possibilities, but we're different people from different worlds, and it'd never work between us. Not that she'd even consider it.

"Checking in on the hired help?" I asked.

"Actually—"

"Caught you spying, didn't I?"

"May I finish my sentence, Mr. Black?" Sammie's playful tone didn't ease the sting of her reprimand.

"Sorry. Go ahead."

"Actually, I *am* calling about the hired help. Not to stick my nose into operating affairs, but I have a friend—the daughter of a friend, really—who's looking for employment. I told her she could see you for an application. She strikes me as intelligent and determined. When she heard me talking with her father about the espresso shop, she was quick to ask if there were any job openings."

"Have her come by."

"She's planning on it."

"Today?"

"If it's no inconvenience." Sammie's demure tone implied I had a choice in the matter. Which I knew I didn't. Not really.

Tucking the phone against my shoulder, I shook dark Sumatran into a filter. "Hope she's better than the last two." A pair of students from Belmont School of Music—heads in the clouds, chips on their shoulders. I'd done the hiring.

Sammie, with typical Rosewood restraint, left that point unmentioned.

"I think this girl could do well," she said. "This is just an FYI. I didn't want you thinking I'd maneuvered behind your back."

"Not at all."

"Her name's Brianne. She's a doll and—"

"Oooh. Sounds promising, for a single man such as myself."

"Aramis, honestly, this is business we're discussing. The customers will love her—that's all I meant to imply."

"Ahh. Too bad."

Sammie sighed, and I smiled at the thought of her touching a finger to her temple in practiced patience. She and I have regular dinner meetings—usually on the company tab, at places of her choosing—and I always enjoy them. Sammie Rosewood knows how to engage in conversation and how to make me feel like…well, like a gentleman. Like I'm capable of something more.

I can't help it, though; I still enjoy ribbing her, driving a wedge into the cracks of that well-mannered veneer. Once or twice I've caught glimpses of something underneath, a little girl wanting to break loose, to run free.

"Brianne should be by early," Samantha said to me. "Let me know your impression of her, because of course you'll have the final say. As you well know."

"I do."

"Have a nice day, Aramis."

Her practiced courtesy brought a smile to my face. A nice day? I certainly planned on it.

# THREE

All of us want to believe we would recognize a killer if he or she were on the other side of the counter sipping a double mocha with whip.

But I didn't.

My morning started with the usual rush of the caffeine-deprived, and the customer in front of me looked mundane enough in an Old Navy shirt and painter jeans. A coat hung from his left arm. Over a slightly crooked nose, he studied his drink, then scooped a finger of cinnamon and whipped cream into his mouth.

As he turned to find a table, his gaze landed on a bright-eyed girl in a Vanderbilt sweatshirt near the window. She dipped her head and looked away.

He took another sip and pointed at the change I'd set on the counter. "Put it in your jar," he said.

My tips go in an orange ceramic mug that reads: "Tip your barista…and he won't poison your drink." It's a joke, and it works.

Male customers read the mug and respect it as a flexing of muscle, a testosterone indicator, while the ladies see it as the playful side of a man who could be mysterious and naughty if given the chance—a perception I'm willing to allow. Growing up without a mother's nurture, Johnny Ray and I learned early on to find female attention by any means necessary.

"Thanks." I gave the man a thumbs-up, but he was already settling into a seat with his coat folded over his lap.

I glanced at the change, almost two dollars' worth.

Not bad for a three-dollar drink. Not bad for a man about to draw a gun and point it in my direction.

—⊏⊐—

On the side streets of Portland, my old stomping grounds, anything could serve as a weapon. Knives and elbows, two-by-fours, and crescent wrenches. I've seen them all employed to gruesome effect.

The last time a gun was pointed at me, the fault was my own, really. I should've known to keep on my own side of Burnside Avenue. In that urban environment, you leave a circle of friends, and they become mortal enemies. There's no in-between.

But I was desperate.

I'd discovered my girlfriend was cheating on me—a rumor I'd tried to shrug off, yet one she'd confirmed in the heat of our yelling match the evening before. Felicia was the first woman I'd ever entrusted with my heart, and we'd been together three years.

After a rough night, I went out early, looking for something to take the edge off. A little pick-me-up.

I found myself on the sidewalk at the dividing line, eying the other side of the street where a previous supplier of mine still plied his trade. Fog hovered over the pavement, stirred and torn into shreds by a passing vehicle.

Then, just as easy as that, I crossed Burnside.

I was low on cash, but in my state I didn't care if someone put a bullet through my head so long as I could shove a straw up my nose.

A familiar face watched my approach while others floated nearby. Maybe they would find it in their hearts to step up. A short-term loan from my old ICV pals.

ICV is a group of anarchists that claim to be on the side of the environment—at least that's how they hooked me originally. I left when I realized their anarchism was more an excuse to indulge nasty habits than a stand against government corruption. The initials come from the Latin phrase *in cauda venenum*. Translated, it refers to a scorpion: "in the tail is the poison."

"Well, if it ain't Aramis Black."

"Hey, Striker." I reached out a hand, but he ignored it.

"You got some nerve, wandering into our zip code." Striker pushed away from a telephone pole. A short man, a compact slab of muscle. Shaved head. Tattoos coiling around his neck and down into his puffy Blazers jacket. He's never been the brightest bulb in the pack, but he's more than capable of delivering pain in high wattage.

"One favor," I said. "That's all I need. For old times' sake."

"A favor, you say. A *fa*-vor."

"Ain't nothin' free around here," said his companion.

"Felicia left me last night. Just a little help, you know what I'm sayin'?"

Striker shook his head. "You cut yourself loose, left us high and dry. And a funny thing happened right after that. The cops came down on us, hard and fast."

I started backing up. It'd been a mistake to come here.

"Now, now," Striker chided. "Not so quick."

The blow to my back caused an explosion of pain in my head, but it was the tire iron across my shins that brought me down. I hit the concrete and felt blood fill my mouth.

Within seconds, a door slammed and darkness followed.

I groaned. Tried to open my eyes. To focus.

"You thought you were a free man, huh, Aramis? Thought you could escape your history?" Striker crouched near my head, tapping my nose with the cold barrel of a Glock. To someone behind me, he said, "Get his hands."

I was on my knees, bent forward. The sound of a zip tie accompanied the cinching of my wrists. I winced. With my eyes adjusting, I could see we were in an empty warehouse.

Striker said, "I'll take it from here, boys. Watch those doors while I teach our narc a lesson."

"No. You got it wrong. I never—"

He backhanded me, his knuckles cracking the bridge of my nose. I watched my blood spray the concrete floor.

"Move!" he yelled at his companions. "This isn't free entertainment."

Their footsteps echoed between support beams, old crates, and around a torn sofa in the corner. Once they'd taken up outside positions and the warehouse had fallen silent, Striker shoved his arm forward so that the Glock's mouth gnawed at my forehead.

Wild guess: a leisurely stroll home wasn't in the cards for me.

"Aramis, Aramis. Look at you, all trussed up."

I didn't respond. I'd been an idiot, my common sense bulled over by a moment of need. Of weakness. Now I was a scapegoat for the trouble ICV had experienced with the authorities. Striker was nothing but a favored minion of the group's upper echelon. He did as he was told, which meant the group must've already fixed me in their sights.

I was a goner. Today, tomorrow, or the next day. But a done deal.

Striker was twisting at my forearms, studying my tattoos. "Those're the words you live by, ain't that right? Isn't that the reputation of Aramis Black?" He read from the banners, which wrap around dark green, double-edged blades: " 'Live by the Sword. Die by the Sword.' So now it's come full circle, eh?"

My shins were still pounding in pain, my thighs cramped, my hands bound. With little chance of escape, I had images run through my head of a funeral procession, a sparse gathering of friends and family gazing into my freshly dug grave.

It hit me then. Harder than expected.

My mother, if she were alive, would be disappointed in me. Could she see me now? Was she looking down, heart torn by this scene? This wasn't what she'd hoped for me, what she'd tried to instill in her sons.

Tears of shame clouded my eyes.

"Mighty Aramis. Not so tough *now*, are you?"

I didn't care what Striker thought of me, the lowlife.

"Thought you could wedge your way back in? Get our trust so you could betray us again? Well, listen up: you tromped into the wrong backyard."

A tear burned a salty trail along my chin.

"Ah, you're breakin' my heart. How 'bout you say you're sorry for what you've done?"

I refused to waste words on him. I wasn't worried about myself; I was begging God's mercy for my mother: *One favor, that's all I ask. If you could convince my mom I made it through the pearly gates, for her own peace of mind, I'd sure appreciate it.*

"Can't do it?" Striker said. "You don't got it in you to apologize?"

Another backhand. The edge of a ring carved across my cheek.

I gave a bitter chuckle, sending up years of regret in a split-second prayer: *End of story, on my way down. And how often did I tell myself I was having 'one helluva time'? How ironic.*

Another blood-burbling chuckle.

*God, I've blamed you for what happened to Mom, been ticked off for years. I still don't know why she was taken from me, but this…this one's my fault. Straight up. Tell her I'm sorry, would you? What can I say? I'm a sinner, Jesus—and a good one, at that! Thought I could turn things around. Well, look at me now…*

"Ticktock, Mr. Black." He gave a shrill laugh and nudged my neck with a steel-toed boot. The Glock bit into my temple. "Time to meet your Maker."

*Bye, Mom.*

Through narrowed eyes, I saw a pool of red on the floor. I waited. I wondered if there'd be any awareness between the sound of the shot and the bullet's brain-scrambling arrival.

Instead of an explosion, I heard a whoosh of air, a shattering of glass, a burst of breath. Metal clanged. The Glock and the boot eased off in the same movement, and my ears filled with a dull ringing. Ten yards away, at eye level with my prostrate body, concrete exploded in a fan-shaped field of shrapnel.

A wild gunshot. It deafened me momentarily.

I maneuvered into a sitting position and saw Striker laid out on the ground, the weapon loose in his palm. His black jeans were baggy, cinched with a belt low on his hips, and a necklace glistened against the red T-shirt beneath his jacket. Rammed down onto his head, looking like a spaceman's dome-shaped helmet from a fifties comic book, was a beveled industrial lighting fixture.

I glanced up at the corrugated roof and spotted a frayed cord thick as a fire hose.

Sounds cheesy, but there it is. In that exact moment, in that precise spot, I'd been saved by a light from above. Coincidence? Well, that's easier, isn't it? Easier than accepting that good and evil exist in personal form. Easier than believing that, on occasion, the physical and spiritual realms collide.

Believe what you will, but a second later or a few inches in either direction and that fixture would've done me no good. With my own eyes I saw the results, and I wasn't about to stick around waiting for Striker's antiestablishment friends to verify my story.

Already a door behind me was screeching open.

I brought my knees to my chin and pulled my bound hands under my feet so I could grab the Glock. I rolled behind Striker, let the piece settle into my grip, and fired at the first man in the opening.

A corner of the doorway burst into splinters. The man spun away. Cursed. A shaft of wood had wedged in his thigh.

Beside me, Striker moaned. His eyes opened and found mine.

I jabbed the gun barrel into his cheek, pushing upward, filled with a sudden desire to do away with this man. He'd intended to kill me. It was me or him. Rage and adrenaline coursed through my limbs, then subsided.

*Mom, I'm sorry.*

I withdrew the weapon. Ejected the clip and kicked the gun across the floor.

Bound and bleeding, I stumbled toward a broken-out window. I sawed the zip tie against a shard of glass, then jabbed with my elbow to clear the remaining shards and rolled through the opening.

I landed outside on a pile of crates. My kidneys still ached from the blow to the back. My wounded nose was dripping, and my lungs felt like deflated balloons. I couldn't get air, could hardly breathe.

I straightened, looked left and right, checking the length of the alley. Clear for the moment.

Hugging the shadows and the side streets, I hobbled home, a bundle of nerves, spooked by every sound. I locked the deadbolt on my door before taking a shower.

Later, alone on my couch, I weighed what had happened.

I'd been spared.

My mom looking out for me? God's hand of protection?

I saw it as a sign to leave the streets behind. Felicia was gone, and my life in that neighborhood was on borrowed time. It wasn't a matter of running from trouble so much as running toward the things my mother had tried to deposit in me.

Within hours I was on my way to Nashville—to my brother's apartment. He took me in, stood by me. And the move had seemed to do the trick.

Until this morning, when memories came flooding back—in my mother's handkerchief and in the words of a dying man.

When I slid a cup of Sumatran to the next patron at the bar, I had no idea he would be the victim. "A buck seventy-five," I told him.

"Quarters okay?"

"All spends the same."

Pewter and beads ringed his neck, and a tattered sweater hung

like a third-world garment on his narrow frame. His hair was dusty
blond, scraggly. He glanced past me into the storage and roasting area.
Then, like the customer a few minutes earlier—the one with the Old
Navy shirt and the slightly crooked nose—he jerked his head toward
the skinny girl in the Vandy sweatshirt.

*Could you be any more obvious?* I wondered.

A moment later I was sniffing at my own armpit, despite the fact
I'd rolled the area with a liberal dose of deodorant. Come on. I must've
looked like an idiot, preening and checking for body odor.

Near the window, the girl scooted over in the booth to make
room for her shoulder pack. The table lurched, forcing spume from
the lid of her drink. Was she aware of our attention? Distracted? Earlier, while ordering a mocha, she'd looked at me as though working
up the nerve to say something.

Maybe I did smell.

The guy at the counter was still staring at her. Then he looked
back at me. He seemed to be on something—jumpy, hollow cheeked,
his neck raw on one side from habitual scratching. I'd seen it all before.

"Cream and sugar's over there," I said.

Behind the guy, metal glinted. I tried to look around him, but he
still wanted something.

"Dude," he said, "listen to me." He had one hand shoved deep
into his front pocket; the other twirled a thread on his sweater that
was thick as a rolled joint. "Are you paying attention?"

No use arguing with a meth user. "What do you need?"

"Need the whip, that's what. You know where the whip is?"

"However you like it." I held open the refrigerator door with my
foot and found the can of whipped cream. Gave it a shake. Anything
to please this tweaker.

"You even listening? Look at me. Do you know where it is?"

"Where what is?"

"I need the whip."

I set the can on the counter. "All yours."

His fingers locked on my wrist, his eyes bursting with fear and determination. I would've written off this drug addict's next statement except it was an echo of the words my mother had said to me the morning of her death.

"Spare your soul," he ranted, "and turn your eyes from greed."

My throat tightened. "What'd you say?"

His bead necklace dangled as he leaned toward me and repeated himself. Despite the fair number of customers in the shop, I was transfixed. My pulse pounded in my ears. What were the odds of someone speaking these same words to me? And within hours of Mom's memento reappearing on my doorstep? I reached up and pressed my free hand against the handkerchief folded in my pocket.

Past the man's shoulder, sunlight again flashed along metal. I glanced up and saw the customer in the Old Navy shirt lifting an object from beneath his folded overcoat.

I knew that shape.

A revolver.

Oblivious to danger, the tweaker continued mumbling, his fingers still tight around my wrist. I twisted my arm from his grip, my bewilderment shoved aside by a sudden desire to stay alive.

*Down! Get down!*

I dropped behind the bar and crammed my body against the wooden cabinetry as the roar of a gun shattered the tranquillity.

The mahogany reverberated against my ribs, and through ringing ears I heard customers' screams and chairs screeching against the tile floor. I imagined businesspeople and students jarred from their news-papers and laptops, scrambling for safety. On the metal door of the ice machine behind me, cream, coffee, and blood formed a violent collage.

Someone had been hit.

# FOUR

**C**alm settled over the shop, an eerie pause. Even the red, black, and white droplets on the ice machine seemed to hesitate—wobbling, swelling, before throwing themselves onto the bar mat with a squishy splat.

A blink of an eye—that's all it was. Eardrums flinching. Heart thumping.

I pivoted to glance around the counter, and in the moments that followed, things sprang back into action. Some customers spilled out the door while others crouched in quivering balls beneath the front windowsill; cups toppled from tables and broke into myriad pieces; coffee gathered in shimmering lakes on the floor, then branched into the tile grout.

Only the victim remained motionless.

He was still alive, still breathing.

I tried not to notice the weird angle of his body, the way a primordial shadow filled his pupils and spread outward. I'd seen that look before. Years ago. Almost killed a man. Would've done time for it if Johnny Ray hadn't pulled me off.

Was I getting what I deserved? Violence back in my lap?

I met the victim's eyes, offering support and empathy. Tweaker or not, he was a fellow human being, and I tried to assess the damage without telegraphing the worst of my fears.

His mouth moved. Gurgling sounds. "Aramis?"

I recoiled. "How do you—"

"Turn your eyes from greed," he told me again.

I couldn't wrap my head around it. The guy would've been a toddler when my mom was still alive. How did it fit? Did he know about the silk memento in my pocket?

I needed to understand.

"Who sent you?"

"You need—" He winced. On his mouth, blood mixed with saliva. "You need the whip. They're coming for you next."

"Who?"

"Mary—" A cough cut off his answer, and his eyes locked shut.

"Who?"

"Lewis."

*Lewis?* My mother's middle name.

I rested a hand on the man's shoulder, willing him to hold on long enough to provide the details I needed, but he was already gone—his mouth slack, his eyes dark. Watching for broken glass, I pulled myself to my knees, a sense of responsibility propelling me. This was my shop. I had to call the cops, get help. An ambulance.

Who'd shot this man? *Who?*

I recalled the flash of metal, the man with the slightly crooked nose. He was nowhere to be seen, his chair on its side. A pang of fear that he might still be around gave way to logic. He'd already taken down his intended victim. No reason to loiter. Plenty of reason to run like the devil.

I staggered to my feet. Customers beneath the window flinched at my movements, only their eyes relaxing as they saw me in my green apron, confused and shaken—just like they were.

I spoke out loud, I think, throwing out reassurances fished from my subconscious. Distinct in my mind was the feel of the phone in my hand, the numbers spongy beneath my fingers as I punched 911.

"Come over and sit down."

I looked up to see the blond girl in the white Vanderbilt sweatshirt. She was one of the few remaining in the shop.

"Here, take a seat," she said.

I was about to protest, but she led me by the arm to a booth with padded black leather seats. Her fingers were warm.

"Thanks."

"You look pale."

"I get like that," I told her. "Trapped indoors all day."

"That's not what I meant. Are you all right?"

"Yeah. I'll be fine." Inside, I was shaking.

"The cops'll be here in a few minutes," she said. She averted her eyes from the man in the sweater, from the dark, stained section on his back. Her eyes were grayish blue, bright with fear, and she faced me in the seat, her fingers on my forearm. "Did you see who did it?"

"I saw…this other guy. In an Old Navy shirt." I pointed at the table a few feet away. "He had a coat folded over his arm."

"You saw him shoot?"

I shook my head. "I hit the deck as soon as the barrel pointed my way."

"It's so…horrible. I mean, why would anyone do such a thing?"

"Wish I knew."

"Did the guy at the bar say anything, give any indication he was in danger?"

I shook my head, too overwhelmed to go into detailed explanations.

She pinched the bridge of her nose, lost in her own thoughts. "Why this morning of all mornings?"

"Why what?"

"I could've avoided all this." She took a deep breath. "All I wanted was a job."

"You're the one who was coming by for an application?"

"I'm the one."

"Brianne?"

One shoulder lifted as her eyes met mine. "That's me."

"I'm Aramis Black."

"Hi, Mr. Black." Brianne gave a valiant smile. "This job sounded like a perfect match, like it was meant to be. I really need this, and now…now look at what's happened. I can't imagine what's going through *your* head right now."

"You don't wanna know." I gazed around the dining area. "Something's not right with this picture."

Brianne's eyes followed mine toward the dead man, and she broke down. I watched my hand slip across the table to cover hers, then sat frozen while she cried for both of us.

*Live by the Sword…Die by the Sword.*

For reasons beyond me, my past had paid a visit and claimed its first victim.

By the time the authorities arrived, my head was a mess of guilt and questions, anger and disbelief. Police lights lashed the building. Sirens warned of an approaching ambulance. Less than a half minute behind, a Channel Two news van screeched to a halt at the opposite curb. While two officers began a cautious advance, a third addressed the gathering crowd and issued media instructions.

"Metro," announced the first one through my door.

"How long does it take to drive a couple of blocks?" I barked.

"You're upset. I understand—"

"Upset? One of my customers got shot."

"Please lower your voice, sir. We arrived as quickly as we could."

While the first officer bent to examine the victim, the second came toward me with hands lifted in a show of nonaggression. "Sir, are you the owner?"

"I'm Aramis Black. I'm sorry for sounding angry. It's just—"

"Fully understandable, Mr. Black. Why don't we step outside for some fresh air and go over what happened?"

I followed him outside, my thoughts as scattered as the carnage at my feet.

"You're going to be all right, Mr. Black."

"Yeah." I cupped my hand to the back of my neck. "It was all just so…crazy. I should've tried to stop it."

"And become a victim yourself? I'm sure there was nothing you could do."

I was unconvinced.

Psychologists say it's natural to take the blame. Guilt transference, I think they call it. Okay, so some cold-blooded killer pulled the trigger, but I was still at fault. I had to be, in some way. Why hadn't I called out a warning? Could I have thrown my body over the counter as a shield?

I had failed to act, and now a man was dead.

What about his last mutterings? Was there any chance of deciphering them? From Mom's lips so long ago, the same words had sounded like parental guidelines and unfathomable truths. In the months that followed, I'd asked Dad and Johnny Ray for an explanation, but they were equally clueless.

So I had let it go.

Until now.

# FIVE

ramis? I don't think you've ever called my work number before."

"Tried your cell. It wouldn't go through."

"Can't get service in this building. What's wrong?"

"Sorry, Johnny. I should've waited till you were off the clock."

"What are you talking about?"

"I'll fill you in when you get here."

"Here?"

"Home."

"You're at home on a Thursday afternoon? Now I'm really worried." Johnny Ray lowered his voice, and I imagined him cupping his hand over the receiver while his thin-as-a-rail boss approached the Ryder Transportation dispatch desk with suspicious eyes. "Is it your anarchist pals from Portland? Don't tell me they've tracked you down…"

"Nothing like that. When do you get off?"

"Right now, if you need me. Spill it."

"Someone got shot."

"Who?"

"Don't know. Some guy. Took a bullet in the back and died right there on the floor of my shop. Black's is closed for investigation till

Saturday. It's a mess. I just finished talking to the cops, the insurance people, Samantha Rosewood."

"Is she okay?"

"She's Sammie. She's calm. She did sound worried about me, though."

"In your dreams."

I tried to think of a humorous response, came up empty.

"I'm clockin' out," Johnny said. "When you have nothin' to say, that means you've got lots to talk about."

"I don't wanna talk about it."

"See what I mean?"

"I'm fine."

"You're a liar. I'll grab a six-pack and then swing by Michelangelo's for some pizza. You stay put."

Yeasty dough? Cheese and beer? For my brother, that was a major investment in my psychological well-being.

"I'll pay you back as soon as I can," I said.

"Don't insult me, idiot. What are brothers for?"

The homicide led the evening's local news, with a full report on the victim and possible motives for the attack. They're referring to it as the "Elliston shooting." By giving it a name, they create distance, a subliminal buffer.

Johnny Ray and I watched with morbid fascination. I'd already told him everything that had happened, but it was a whole different matter to see it shoved at us through the TV screen.

There was my face, filling the picture, talking to the officer. Emergency lights cycling in the background.

The victim: Darrell Michaels.

Mr. Michaels looked younger in his photo, in which he was wearing the same pewter and beads around his neck and a scrunched-up, close-lipped smile beneath his dusty blond hair. He was a twenty-two-year-old Caucasian parolee, a drug addict, and a small-time dealer. Memphis police had a long rap sheet on Darrell. Nashville's finest had nothing on him but a traffic violation.

The news anchor reported that Darrell's parole officer, a Mr. Leroy Parker, claimed Darrell's death was brought about by feuding drug dealers who wanted to keep Darrell in the game. "They'll be brought to justice for this senseless tragedy," Parker was quoted as saying. "Darrell was trying to turn a new leaf, but his past caught up with him."

I knew that struggle all too well.

Despite having three grown kids and four youngsters, Darrell's mother lamented her son's demise as though he were her only child. She was a heavyset woman, her face weighted by sorrow. "My boy, he was a survivor," she said. "Weren't barely four pounds when he was born, but the kid just never gave up. Darrell had heart."

Her grief stuck in my throat. That mother-son thing.

Johnny Ray popped the top on another beer for me, slid more pizza onto my plate. He'd ordered my favorite—supreme, extra cheese, deep-dish. He was nibbling on a salad with sprouts.

Phone calls started spilling in after the newscast, and I listened to the concern through the message machine: "Oh, it's just horrible, Aramis…" "What's this world coming to…" "I can only imaaagine how hard it's been on y'all."

With not even twelve hours between me and the Elliston shooting, I was already tired of the sympathy. Didn't deserve it. I could feel the shame settling inside me, and I was pretty sure it wasn't pepperoni causing the ache in my gut.

Guilt transference. There it was again, as if I'd personally pointed the gun.

What about denial? Don't the headshrinkers claim that comes first? So far I'd experienced nothing of the sort, which meant either (a) the shrinks were wrong—an assumption I was willing to make—or (b) they were right on the money, and my denial was using guilt to block the true horror from my mind.

I chewed through another heap of sauce and dough.

A woman's voice on the machine caught my attention. "Mr. Black? I hate talking to these things, but I'm sure you've been inundated with calls. Sorry to bug you. This is Brianne…from the shop this morning."

"Brianne?" Johnny Ray lifted an eyebrow.

"I was given your number by Samantha Rosewood," she went on. "Just thought you'd like to know I've reconsidered."

"Sounds cute. Haven't been holding out on your older brother, have you?"

I shot him a withering look. Although I knew he was trying to leaven my mood with humor, it was the wrong time.

"I'd still like to apply for the job, assuming the position's still open."

I fumbled for the receiver.

"Will you be at Black's tomorrow? Maybe we could talk it over and—"

I slapped at the buttons, and the message machine deactivated.

"Brianne? Hi."

"Oh. Mr. Black?"

"Yeah, don't hang up."

"I was just leaving a message."

"I heard."

"You remember who I am?"

I thought of her blond hair, the white Vandy sweatshirt, the warmth of her hand on my arm as she found a seat for me—the big, bad dude with tattoos and a list of priors. Of course I remembered. It was humiliating.

I said, "You're the one Sammie sent over."

"Samantha, that's right. You're on intimate terms with her, by the sound of it."

"Not really. I mean, yes, we're friends. But the relationship's mostly business."

"She's a nice lady."

"Listen, Brianne. Thanks for hanging around this morning."

"I couldn't just leave you there, not after everyone else had bailed. Plus, I still need the job and the money in a big way. That is, if you're still taking applications. You're not closing down the shop, are you?"

"No," I said. "Definitely not. I'll be back up and running before you know it."

"Which means you're looking to hire?"

"I can always use reliable people."

"Great," Brianne said. "I'll take it."

I chuckled. "You're a brave woman. Considering what you saw today."

"Sorry I lost it, Mr. Black, crying and all."

"Aramis. Just Aramis."

She rolled the sounds off her tongue. "Air-uh-mis. I like the sound of that."

Behind me, Johnny pretended to serenade the night, batting his
eyelids. I sneered at him. When he held up fingers, trying to guess her
attractiveness on a scale of one to ten, I growled at him to leave me
alone.

"Hello?" Brianne said. "Did I lose you?"

"I'm still here."

"She's cute," Johnny whispered, "or you would've let the machine
get it."

"Was it wrong of me to call you at home, Aramis?"

"Not at all," I told her. "Please, don't hang up."

"You really *do* need the help, don't you?"

"It's a bit much to handle on my own."

"I'll help you get things turned around."

She'd been there with me at Black's, gone through the same con-
fusion and terror. Now the softness in her voice sent my heart on a
wild scamper around my rib cage, and I turned away from my brother
to hide any reactions he might latch on to. He pulled his Martin guitar from its stand. Time to end this quickly.

"So, Aramis, you want me to come by tomorrow to fill out an
application?"

"Actually, the shop'll be closed. An official crime scene, under
investigation."

"I can drop by your place," she offered, "if that'd be easier."

"Uh, no. Got stuff to do. Let's meet at the shop on Saturday."

"Okay. What time?"

"Would seven in the morning work? Come ready to do some serious cleaning."

"Bright and early, you can count on me."

"Thanks for calling, Brianne."

"Try to get some sleep," she said. "Don't let what happened get you down."

"Good-bye."

"Bye for now."

I set the phone down and found Johnny eying me.

"Spill it," he said. "A solid eight from the way you're acting. Or even a nine."

"Good night, Johnny Ray."

At my window, with twisted tree-branch shadows across my chest, I stood in the wash of an amber-tinted moon. I watched a car leave our brownstone's lot. Trying to turn my thoughts from the day's disaster, I lifted Mom's handkerchief to my face and let the silk play along my cheeks.

My mind gave way to unnerving questions. Who'd returned this to me? Why now? How did the sender know my address?

Although the mysteries loomed large, I was thankful for anything bridging my memories to my mother.

Only as the moon faded into a cold, gray disk did I decide to call it a night. I lifted the lid of the ebony box on my windowsill and, for the first time in more than twenty years, laid the handkerchief inside.

Back where it belonged.

# SIX

Voices echoed through my mind, tugging at my thoughts from the land of the dead. The swish of toothpaste and water failed to drown them out. I spit into the sink, rinsed with a handful of water, then braced myself on the porcelain and stared into the mirror.

My mother and a total stranger. Both had spoken the same words before being gunned down before my eyes.

Dianne Lewis Black's gentle tone: *Spare your soul…*

Darrell Michaels's urgent warning: *…turn your eyes from greed.*

It was 6:02 a.m. Too early to be thinking about this stuff.

I pushed away from the mirror, returned to my room, and curled up in my bed. Even there, chills lifted the hair on my arms as I thought back to yesterday. Michaels had told me something else, something ominous.

*You need the whip. They're coming for you next.*

Who was coming for me? One of my anarchist rivals? Or maybe the same person who'd stolen Mom's handkerchief in the first place, ages ago? Did the original thief send it back, hoping I'd reveal its mysteries?

Like I even knew Mom's secrets.

With his final gasps, Michaels had tried to provide me a clue, through blood and saliva and a death-rattle cough.

*Mary... Lewis.*

Who was she?

Johnny Ray was repeating a guitar riff in the other room, layering the sound with impromptu vocals, pausing at infrequent intervals—probably to scribble lyrics on his pad. That's his way. Spur of the moment. Chisel and sculpt.

I'd watched him go through the routine many times, and I admired the man, believed in his dream, supported him. I'd scheduled him to be on stage at Black's in the coming week.

Six in the morning, though? I thought these musician types didn't get up until happy hour.

The strumming stopped, and footsteps warned of Johnny's approach.

"Aramis, you awake?"

"Nooo. You think?"

"There's some food keepin' warm in the oven. Figured you could use a good breakfast after what you've been through."

My desire to roll over and wrestle sleep from the morning gave way to my stomach's demands. I pulled myself to the edge of the mattress. "Sounds good. Be right out."

I yawned. Groaned and scratched. Popped my neck.

Five minutes later I plopped into a chair at the dining table. Spying my brother's handiwork, I lost my enthusiasm. Should've known we'd be eating whole-wheat waffles, turkey-bacon strips, and unsweetened grapefruit juice.

No complaints. But I would have preferred blueberry Pop-Tarts.

Johnny was wearing his boxer shorts, with a dishtowel flung over the shoulder of his bathrobe. He served me a plate of food still toasty from the oven and topped off my juice glass. "I already ate, but there you go, kid."

"Thanks." I chased down a bite of waffle with juice. "Why so early?"

"I was worried you'd curl up in bed and sulk the day away."

"Me? It's not my style." I chewed on a bacon strip. "I am kinda stuck, though. The cops told me to stay away so they could sift through the mess at the shop."

"Music City's finest—they'll get it all squared away."

"Hey. Did you know Chief Serpas served in the Northwest? Seattle, I think."

"That doesn't exactly make him a local favorite."

"Bunch of rednecks. What do they know?"

Johnny raised an eyebrow. "You're one to talk. Been in Nashville just over a year, and you're already pointin' fingers. Kid, you've barely earned the right to switch lanes on I-40."

"Like people here know how to merge."

"Eat your food."

"Just kidding. Nothing personal."

"And you wonder why some Southerners dislike Yankees."

"Easy. Because they're always winning the World Series."

Johnny Ray cleared his throat, cracked his knuckles. "This is my chance to live out my dream. Nashville's my home now, even if the skies don't part for me, even if the industry reps keep slappin' me down till I'm shorter than Little Jimmie Dickens. I like this place. It's more of a home than we ever had in Portland." His voice faded, and his Adam's apple bobbed once. "Dad was too busy working, and you and I lived separate lives."

"Well, we're here now. Right?" I said through a mouthful of waffles.

"You've cleaned up, I'll give you that."

"After what happened in that warehouse, I knew things had to change. That was the first time in years I felt like…like Someone was watching out for me. I was this close to dying."

"Here we go." Johnny rolled his eyes. "The way I see it, we're best off trusting ourselves to make the world a better place. Oughta help each other instead of waiting for some cosmic being to put everything right."

"You said it yourself, though. I've cleaned up."

"And found some of that old-time religion, by the sound of it."

"You know me better than that."

"Hallelujah, brother." Johnny Ray's voice lilted into a church campfire tune. "You've come to the right place, smack-dab on the buckle of the Bible Belt."

I kept my mouth shut.

The last time I darkened a church doorway an usher slipped an offering plate into my hands while, from behind a pulpit, the minister said, "If you've been spiritually fed, don't you owe it to God to pay for the meal?"

Judging by his girth, the man looked plenty well fed already.

I don't know about you, but if church services are all about motivation and the next emotional fix, I'd rather attend a good rock concert. Same group dynamics. A good show. And a better high. U2's live show—now that was a spiritual experience.

"Okay." Johnny Ray brought me back to the point. "So you're walking the straight and narrow now—which is a good thing, don't get me wrong. Drugs, bad. Drunk driving, bad. But you've gotta live a little. Like last Friday night. That girl, the brunette with the belly ring—she was into you, and you *blew* it."

"That was a tough one to pass up, believe me."

"How 'bout that girl on the phone last night? Brianne."

"Hey. I'm not saying it's easy."

"I know the way you used to be."

"I don't need the distraction right now."

"Well, if women don't do it for you anymore, I'd like a heads-up. Coming out of the closet's one thing, but sleeping under the same roof with me—"

I slugged him in the arm.

He grunted. "You…you are my retarded little brother. You should know that right now."

"Work it into your first big hit."

"Very funny." Johnny changed the subject. "So, any plans for the day?"

"With the detectives scouring my shop? Not really. I hate it that I can't do anything about that mess inside."

"How about we take the day off, go exploring?"

"You and me?"

"And my six-string." He pointed to his guitar.

"Lousy two-timer. You just like her for her curves."

"Not to mention she smells better than you."

"Hey."

"I'm just saying."

"No. That's definitely you. Go take your shower."

"Twice a day, Aramis. All part of keeping up my image." He ruffled his hair. "Seriously, I've got a place in mind for us to go."

"Anywhere. So long as I can't see the Batman building."

The tallest building in the state of Tennessee, the marble-and-glass BellSouth Tower stands on Third Avenue and Commerce in downtown Nashville. Visible from all over Davidson County, its twin peaks taper like bat ears. I like it. I do. But the sight of it reminds me I'm not far from the hubbub of neon lights and honky-tonk bars.

"And we've got to be outdoors," I stipulated.

"Here's my suggestion." Johnny said it so casually. "We take a drive along the Natchez Trace, maybe follow the trail down to the memorial near Hohenwald."

"The memorial?"

"It's just over an hour from here. I've told you about it."

"Oh. The site where that guy's buried."

"That *guy*?"

"The one from Lewis and Clark. The explorer dude."

"Aramis, you're in dire need of a history lesson. Didn't you listen in school?"

"Just tell me the guy's name."

"I'll give you a hint. It's not William Clark but the other one."

"Do I have to beat it out of you, Johnny Ray?"

He took a seat across from me and spread out the same yellowed section of the *Nashville Scene* I'd seen him tuck under his knee yesterday. "Clear your dishes," he said. "I'm going to need your full attention."

"What's this about?"

"Dishes." His finger jutted toward the sink.

Only fair, really. He makes the meals, and I clean up. The clinking of plates and cutlery nearly covered my brother's next words, yet something brought me to a halt.

"What'd you say?" I set the stuff down and faced him.

"Meriwether Lewis."

"Meriwether." I rolled the name in my mouth.

"I wasn't mumbling," he said. "That was the other explorer's name. We're talkin' *the* Lewis and Clark, the Corps of Discovery. These guys, they shaped our country's future—crossing the Plains and Rockies, making friends with Indians, killing bears. This was two hundred years ago. They were the real deal, and we can't remember their names? Kinda sad, don't you think?"

"Not everyone's a history buff like you."

"It's our country, our heritage."

"To most people it's old news."

Johnny tapped the newsprint. "Old news is what got me interested in the first place. See this article? It's about four years old, and the title alone got me curious. 'The Strange Death of an American Hero.' Most historians believe Lewis committed suicide on the Natchez Trace back in 1809, but there've always been rumors of a murder. So I've been poking around, turning up a few surprises, but only recently started connecting it to Mom."

"Come on." I faced him, hands planted on the table. "What're you getting at?"

"Well, don't know for sure. Not yet."

"Just say it."

Johnny squared his shoulders. "I believe Lewis was a blood relative."

"What?" I laughed. "How does that make any sense?"

"Think about it. Our mother's name?"

"Dianne?"

"Middle name...Lewis."

"In honor of her grandfather. That's what I heard."

He hesitated. "Something like that. And you know where he was from originally? Virginia. Same place Meriwether Lewis was born. I've done some checking, researched the genealogies, and it seems to pan out—a matter of public record."

I scratched my head. "I find all this hard to believe."

"Consider this. Mom's handkerchief reappears the night before a man gets killed in your shop, and what does the man say to you? 'They're coming for you next.' Isn't that how you told it to me?"

"Yeah."

"And what'd you ask him?"

"Who was coming for me."

"And his response?"

"Mary," I said slowly. "Lewis."

"Meriwether Lewis. That's what the man was trying to tell you."

"Oooh. So a two-hundred-year-old dead guy's coming after me? I'm so scared."

"Might have reason to be," Johnny cautioned. "You ask me, there's some kind of evil at work here. Don't know how yet, don't know why, but I think it's all linked to the reason our mother died."

# SEVEN

**E**vil, I believe, is a choice. We embrace or reject it. It comes at us in insidious guises, and we make decisions that push it back or let it edge closer. It never tires and never sleeps; it's there every day—crouching on our doorsteps, hoping for a cozy place to shack up.

After a while, it seems easier to give in. Just a little.

Years ago my mother took a bullet and tumbled into a river.

Yesterday, Darrell Michaels's life spilled across the tiles in my espresso bar.

Would another human fall today? Was there some malevolent presence lurking, waiting, with insatiable hunger and greed? And where was God in all this?

My thoughts turned to my responsibilities at Black's and to Samantha's financial investment in the place. Tomorrow, Brianne will meet me, and we'll get the place back in order so I can get on with life.

As for today? Two choices. Turn my back on what happened, or track down and face the truth.

Hours earlier I might've called Johnny Ray a liar had he told me Mom's and Darrell Michaels's murders were dots on a time line leading from Meriwether Lewis to me.

But ignoring the coincidences seemed as crazy as accepting them.

Johnny accused me of avoiding the issue of Mother's death, and when it comes to our uncle's involvement on that horrible day, he's right. I've been trying to change, to let go of my bitterness, but I still tense at the mention of Uncle Wyatt's name. His actions precipitated his sister's death. From twenty feet away, hidden and helpless in the tall grass, I watched it play out as hot tears clawed down my face.

I needed the truth now. No matter how painful.

My brother's voice brought me back to the present.

"Are you just going to stand there?"

"I'm coming." I set our cooler of meat, chips, and cold drinks in the bed of his Ford Ranger and climbed into the cab. "So how's this brush with Lewis's ghost gonna help us figure things out?"

"I'm fixin' to tell you on the way."

"You're 'fixin' to,' Johnny Ray? Nashville really *is* your home now."

He buckled in beside me. "Only since you arrived, kid, and I mean that."

I set my foot on the dash, staring out the window as we headed west.

The morning was gorgeous, a typical October day in Middle Tennessee. A spike in humidity gave the air a leafy, moldering scent.

Wearing his black Stetson, Johnny Ray drove us—me and his Martin guitar—along I-440. His trusty pickup then carried us southwest, away from the headaches of the concrete jungle. No more snarling traffic, sirens, or screeching trains, no Wal-Marts, Mapcos, or Dollar Generals.

Flanking the parkway, sugar maples waved red leaves in the breeze against a waxy green backdrop of magnolias. Ginkgo trees shot golden flames through the foliage, catching and intensifying the rays of autumn sun.

"Look at these colors," I said.

"Pretty spectacular."

"Think your boss'll be mad?"

"He'll get over it. This is my first sick day in three years."

"Ah," I said. "But that's how it starts. A day here, another one there, a couple in a row. Dude, it's a gateway drug."

My brother played along. "I can quit anytime."

"You want me repeating that to your boss?"

"Watch it now." Johnny slid a guidebook across the seat. "Here, this'll keep you quiet. It's history-lesson time. Read up on the trace and its origins. You'll also find some bits about Governor Lewis."

"Governor? An explorer *and* a politician?"

"In St. Louis and the surrounding area. Which makes his death that much stranger. He was a genuine American hero, but when he died, the first official report didn't show up until ten days later in Nashville's *Democratic Clarion*. The man changed the face of the modern map and couldn't get a proper burial for months. There wasn't a single government inquiry into his murder."

"Suicide, you mean."

"I mean it just the way I said it."

"Maybe he took his life but they wanted to spare his family more shame."

"He was found with multiple knife *and* bullet wounds." Johnny raised an eyebrow at me. "And guess where he was headed when he died—to the capital to clear his name of some rumors and to Monticello to see his friend Jefferson. For years Lewis had been working on his journals from the expedition, and he was finally ready to publish them. Funny time to kill himself, don't you think?"

"I've got to admit it sounds fishy."

"The man was an icon and smart too. While in St. Louis, he helped set up their first publishing house and post office—"

"Maybe he went postal."

"This is serious, Aramis."

"Sorry. That wasn't right."

"I'm telling you, there's some shady activity behind the scenes." Johnny flipped on the AC to combat the rising humidity, then draped an arm over the steering wheel. "I believe the same secrets that gunned him down also came after Mom. Now they're coming after you."

"What secrets?"

"I'm still trying to figure that out." He pointed to the guidebook. "Read up."

I opened to the first page.

━━━

With my head against the truck window and my thoughts mulling over what I'd learned from the book, I let my eyes follow yellow wild-flowers along the curve of the hills to a limestone edifice.

I know virtue and honor played roles in our country's birth. I guess it's no surprise that treason and greed also got involved. Rising from the American Revolution, Thomas Jefferson, Aaron Burr, Meriwether Lewis, and James Wilkinson became household names. Yet conspiracies and lies knotted their destinies.

And some of those shady scenarios played out along the Natchez Trace.

More than four hundred miles long, the trace stretches from

Nashville to Natchez, Mississippi. Originally a buffalo trail, it drew Choctaw and Chickasaw hunting parties, who later used it as a warpath. In the 1700s, French traders, settlers, even itinerant preachers trod the same ground, giving it names such as the Devil's Backbone and the Old Chickasaw Trace. By 1800, it had become a federal road.

President Jefferson was at the country's helm, and the republic was booming. Despite rampant threats—including Spaniards stationed in the Florida territories and Napoleon on the march through Europe—the government sought to expand its territory.

The Louisiana Purchase swiped nearly a million square miles between the Mississippi and the Rockies from beneath Napoleon's prominent nose. Jefferson pushed Congress to ratify the purchase quickly. He knew the territory could become a jackpot of trade and industry. If a northwest passage—a water route connecting the Atlantic to the Pacific—could be found, the young United States would become a political dynamo: self-sufficient, wealthy, poised to fend off all foes.

Jefferson called upon his one-time personal assistant, Capt. Meriwether Lewis, to form the Corps of Discovery. Lewis chose William Clark to join him in command.

It's all there in the schoolbooks. The corps found success conquering unknowns, mapping huge territories, establishing Fort Clatsop—a site that still stands near the shores of the Pacific, on the Oregon side of the Columbia River. Reputations and fortunes were made, and our nation would never be the same.

But when power and wealth share the same bed, they always produce corruption.

In those early years, one man embraced such corruption with gusto.

General Wilkinson, commander of the U.S. armed forces, served as governor of the Louisiana Territory and throughout his career spewed lies to three presidents, directing their decisions while consorting with the Spanish, as confirmed by papers found a hundred years later archived in the courts of Madrid. A disgruntled defense counsel once commented that Wilkinson "instilled as much poison into the ear of the President as Satan himself breathed into the ear of Eve."

The general was cunning. No doubt about it. With numerous disloyalties, Wilkinson was always in need of a scapegoat, and when suspicions mounted, he was quick to throw Aaron Burr to the wolves.

Later, rumors of treason circulated again. He needed another scapegoat.

Meriwether Lewis had previously made accusations about Wilkinson, so it was no surprise when the general started pointing fingers back, planting seeds of suspicion. In a letter, Lewis insisted, "My Country can never make 'A Burr' of me…she can never sever my attachment from her."

In 1809, Lewis departed for the capital to defend his honor. He also planned to turn in his journals, reminding the nation of his contributions to her legacy.

He never reached his destination.

---

"Johnny, this is all fascinating. But how do you know it's connected to Mom?"

My brother lifted his Stetson, ran his hand through his hair.

"There're a couple of things I can't say, things you'll have to find out on your own."

"Like what? Since when do you hide stuff from me?"

Johnny stared straight ahead.

"Hey. I'm talking to you. What's going on?"

"Listen, I'll do my best to point you in the right direction. But you've got to trust me on this. It all starts with Lewis's murder. Someone wanted to shut him up—of that I'm convinced—but his secrets couldn't be contained."

"Maybe it was just a robbery gone bad," I said.

"No, even back then no one bought that theory. There at the scene, among his belongings, they found his watch, decorative pistols, knives, cash. It doesn't wash."

"Okay, so let me get this straight. Lewis was killed…"

"Uh-huh."

"…somehow he passed on secrets through his descendants…"

"Uh-huh."

"…and Mom, being a Lewis, paid for it with her own life?"

Johnny Ray nodded. "That's how I see it."

"Two hundred years of secrets and multiple murders? That's some story. But if you're right and Darrell Michaels was killed as part of all this, then we could be in serious danger too."

"That's what I've been trying to tell you."

I cupped my hand to the back of my neck. "How much longer?"

"To the monument? Couple miles. You're not backing out now, are ya?"

"You kidding? If there's any chance of understanding what happened to Mom, I'm there."

Johnny grinned. "You said it, Aramis. Let's get 'er done."

# EIGHT

With shirt sleeves rolled up and buttons undone, I stepped down from the Ford Ranger and headed for the stone obelisk that commemorates Meriwether Lewis. There's some dispute whether his bones are actually buried here, and a few years back there was a push to exhume the remains for DNA testing.

The plan dissolved, and that mystery still simmers.

I was doing my own simmering—succumbing to the day's unseasonable heat. Hair clung to my temples, and my shirt was plastered to my back. Settled among the ridge-backed hills and deep glens, the humidity had the bees humming among the scented dogwood and persimmon trees.

"Let's go have a look," Johnny said.

I waved off a pair of mosquitoes, filled my lungs with wet oxygen, and followed him to the grave marker where an elderly couple stood in contemplation.

Crafted in 1848 by a local sculptor, the stone rises twenty feet with unpretentious grace. The top is broken, symbolizing Lewis's abrupt departure from this world. On a marker, I found these words: "His life of romantic endeavor and lasting achievement came tragically and mysteriously to its close on the night of October 11, 1809."

"It's ridiculous," Johnny murmured.

"What?"

"The man risked life and limb for his country, and this is all he gets."

The elderly couple backed up a step, joined hands, and left.

My brother adjusted his hat, sighed, then let his eyes wander to the obelisk's jutting tip. "The whole thing's a pity. The man died on his way to Washington, DC—"

"Federal City back then. Check the handy guidebook."

"Which means," Johnny Ray pressed on, "he never got to deliver his writings to his publisher, never got to swing by Monticello to defend his reputation. And the worst thing is, no one seemed to notice."

"Mass communication wasn't what it is now."

"I'll give you that. But get this: a coroner's inquest was never even filed. Up till 1814, papers like that were the personal property of the justice of the peace, but these just disappeared."

"You really have been researching this."

"It's got me hooked." Johnny set his hand on the monument, bowing his head as though bestowing a benediction.

"So what happened to these papers?"

"Hard to say."

"Some sort of foul play, though, right?"

"Mmm, not necessarily. Whoever had them could've just thrown them in a box and stuffed them in an attic. Who knows?"

We crossed the gravel and grass to Grinder's Stand, the site of Lewis's death.

A man with slumped shoulders, wrinkled gray slacks, and a baby-blue golfer's visor meandered around the corner. In the grove beyond, a white-tailed deer watched with brown marble eyes, then bounded into the foliage.

Johnny Ray fed me more details as we circled the wooden structures.

Located north of the actual trace and reconstructed by the National Park Service, the rustic cabins are joined by a common breezeway. Robert and Priscilla Grinder had carved out a life for their sons here, operating the small inn for weary travelers. James Audubon traversed the trail in that period, painting his famed birds. Andrew Jackson, too, was a frequent passerby.

"You think they ever stopped in?" I peered through a dusty window.

"Wouldn't doubt it," Johnny said. "What we know for sure is on that night of October 10, 1809, Mr. Grinder and his boys were away on business. Governor Lewis and his servant paid Mrs. Grinder for a room, and by the next day Lewis was dead."

"Was she a suspect?"

"Well, local lore's always included the names of the Grinders. Mr. Grinder was arrested at one point, but they released him for lack of evidence. Wasn't till eighteen months after the incident that Mrs. Grinder gave a recorded interview. Her answers were contradictory."

"Maybe she was afraid of what her husband might do if she said anything."

"Maybe she was protecting him," Johnny noted, "or someone else."

He told me the rest of that night's account.

Before Lewis's demise, she heard him pacing and mumbling in the dark. Then a gunshot. A shout. And another shot. The governor crawled to her door, bleeding, and cried out, "Oh, madam. Give me some water! Heal my wounds."

At another point: "I'm no coward; but I am so strong, so hard to die."

He had knife lacerations. A slit throat.

In a downward trajectory, a bullet had carved through his chest and intestines. Had he been shot while on his knees? Forced into a position of submission?

"Can you imagine it, Aramis—an experienced soldier like him begging for his life? And if he did commit suicide, how did he botch it so badly? It just doesn't add up. I'm not the only one who's questioned it either. There was a legislative report in the mid-1800s that said something like, 'It seems more probable that he died by the hands of an assassin.'"

"That sounds pretty dramatic."

"It had to be one of Wilkinson's men," my brother said. "Wilkinson was on the Spanish payroll as a spy. They called him Number 13."

Johnny and I walked around the old buildings. My hand ran along the planks, extracting mental pictures from the rough wood: a miserable, insect-infested night…a slashing knife…a struggle in the dark and a gunshot…a man on his knees, dying.

"Okay. So Lewis knew some incriminating evidence, and Wilkinson had him murdered. How does any of that trickle down to the present—to Mom or to us?"

Johnny Ray shook his head. "I wish I knew." He stopped in the shade of an eave and gazed across the memorial site. "Somewhere out here there has to be a clue, some sort of relic that'll tie it all together."

"That's all you've got to go on?"

"Come on, kid. Help me start lookin'."

Johnny checked the speedometer, then glanced in the rearview mirror. We were headed back to Nashville empty-handed, despite a full two hours combing over the memorial marker, the rustic inn, and the surrounding grounds.

"Should've known."

"Known what?"

"You brought me on a wild-goose chase." I slapped the guidebook down on the seat. "You were always dragging me along as a kid, talking me into those crazy ideas of yours."

"That's not fair."

"Now look at you, acting paranoid, checking your mirrors over and over. What? You think we have nineteenth-century assassins on our trail?"

"Aramis—"

"Did they even know how to drive back then?"

"Laugh all you want, but tell me this." Johnny's eyes danced again to the mirror. "Have you even considered that the bullet yesterday could've been aimed at you?"

"Oh, you're good. I thought maybe you were onto something with all your conspiracy talk. Okay, say someone is following us. What could they possibly want?"

" 'You need the whip.' Isn't that what the Michaels kid said?"

"The whip. Like I have a stinkin' clue what that means. This is all so crazy, Johnny Ray. A big waste of my time."

"You're wrong. Secrets and lies will haunt you till you pay them their due."

"I like it. You've got a real hit on your hands."

"Do you really think you can joke your way around every pothole on life's road? You're steerin' for trouble. That's what you're doing."

"I kind of like trouble."

"And it obviously likes you too. Follows you everywhere you go."

"Yeah. We're buddies."

"Uh-huh, you and trouble go way back. You almost lost your life, had yourself some religious experience, and still nothing's changed."

"What do you mean, nothing's changed?"

"Don't get me wrong. You've polished up real nice, but inside you're still bitter as a cup of walnut juice. You've got to let things go."

"Let things go?" Fury welled in me, sudden and unchecked, and I threw my elbow against the seat between us. Johnny flinched. "Who do you think you are?" I yelled. "My judge and jury? For the past year I've worked my butt off to turn my life around and accomplish something worthwhile, something Mom would be proud of. You think you're better than me? Think you can tell me how to live, how to eat? Oh, yes. You're the smart one. The talented one. The firstborn son." I waved my hand in an exaggerated bow. "Oh, hail the mighty Johnny Ray Black!"

Fixated on the mirror, Johnny tugged on his Stetson.

"We're being followed," he said.

"Oh. My. Goodness. The man's finally lost it."

"That white Camry back there—it's been with us since we left the memorial."

I sneered. "And what was it they were after again?"

"Good question. Is our food all gone?"

"Our food? You think they're hungry?"

"No. We are. I'm gonna pull in at the Loveless Café, see what the Camry does."

The schizo aspects of his plan aside, I liked it. Food. Any excuse would do.

I pretended to hide my face as we made the turn onto Highway 100. Through dramatically splayed fingers, I glanced at the passing vehicle. There in the driver's seat sat the slumped man who had walked away from us at Grinder's Stand. Although his golfing visor shaded his eyes, I did sense an abnormal amount of interest burning my direction.

The man slowed the car, seeming unsure, then accelerated away.

Sitting in the Loveless Café, protected from the humidity, I couldn't help but chortle as I slathered homemade preserves onto scratch biscuits.

"Looks like we really gave him the slip."

"For now," Johnny said.

He was dead serious, so I tried not to burst out laughing.

The waitress approached, pleasant and middle-aged with a drawl thicker than the sorghum molasses on the table. I ordered country ham with red-eye gravy. Johnny mumbled his dietary concerns before selecting chicken salad and iced tea.

"Sweet or unsweet?" the waitress inquired.

"Unsweet."

I said, "A little sugar won't kill you, you know. What's gonna happen when you hit the big time? You'll go to one of those Country Music Association dinners and starve."

"That's the least of my concerns right now."

"My point exactly." When the waitress returned with his iced tea, I dumped a packet of sugar into his glass, counting on childhood tactics to bring him out of his funk. "Go wild with it."

He didn't laugh, didn't smile. Not even a crack.

# NINE

"Home, sweet home." Johnny pulled into the parking lot.

The evening sky was orange and pink, traced with the thin, white contrails that gather over Nashville International Airport. Our brownstone stood in the glow, two stories tall, partially shaded by oaks and a magnificent magnolia.

There are four residences in our building, all of them three-bedroom dwellings. Johnny Ray and I share the bottom floor unit. We each have our own room, and Johnny Ray claims the spare as a makeshift studio since his name is on the lease. He scrounged for months to line the walls with some sort of egg-carton material—"for acoustic integrity," he claims—but still he plays the guitar most often in the living room, in his boxers. Let the man do his thing, I say, even if he doesn't always make sense.

Creative types. Go figure.

"Aramis, take a look." My brother dropped the mail onto the dining table, then tapped the front page of the *Tennessean* newspaper.

The headline was cold: "Man Shot, Killed in West End Shop."

I turned the paper around, read the account. It was nothing new, but in black and white it was a jolt of reality. No suspects yet, no arrests. Nothing new on Darrell Michaels.

Black's was named as well. A favorable description followed—and

I felt like dirt. Lower than dirt. This is hard to admit, but the first thought through my mind was that this could be a blessing in disguise, a way of boosting business. I thought of the adage "There's no such thing as bad press."

I slapped the newspaper shut.

*Turn your eyes from greed…*

It was already happening. I was becoming a greedy, sick man. What sort of person would be thinking of financial gain at a time like this?

"Sorry, Darrell," I whispered. "I really am."

With newfound conviction, I decided that what had happened in my shop would not keep me from pressing forward. I'd put all I had into Black's—learning the art of coffee roasting, studying the demographics, decorating the place with Samantha's help—and I refused to let the shooting tarnish my mother's memory.

Black's is my ode to her. My mom deserves the best from me.

And my father?

He made his presence known when least expected, dropping words like grenades into my world. "If it doesn't kill you, it makes you stronger." That's the sort of thing he likes to say—as though he's doing you a favor, as though he's a real humanitarian, beating sense into you until he's beaten you senseless.

*Thank you, Papa Bear. Again. Hit me again. You're sure teaching me a lesson now. Oh yeah, it's really sinking in.*

I've been told he was a different person before Mom's death.

I try to believe it. And though some part of my brain rumbles with thoughts of a gentler man, his deep, droll tone brings the darkness back in a rush.

"Johnny Ray? Aramis?" Dad's voice boomed through the answering machine, rumbled down the hallway. "Pick up if you're there."

"Leave your message already," I said aloud.

I was in my bedroom at my computer, tapping away on the keyboard. My heavy-handed typing shook the Nashville Predators bobblehead atop the monitor, and the deformed shadow leaped all the way to the ten-foot ceiling.

"Johnny Ray, you listenin'? Son?"

I marched down the hallway. "No, Dad. Your firstborn isn't here right now." With one poke of a finger, I muted the machine. I'd listen to it later.

Johnny Ray had called some numbers stored in his Palm Pilot—"If you don't do your networking, you're lost in this town," he says—and had gotten a date. Another Friday night out.

Clubbing? Honky-tonking?

I didn't know, didn't care. I had the house to myself and a package of Oreos too.

I browsed eBay and found a vintage, autographed Kurt Cobain poster. I've always felt a kinship with this wild brother of the nineties, felt there were lessons to be learned from his misplaced idealism and resulting demise. He was haunted by doubt, yet refused to believe. In an act of desperation, the drugged-out grungemeister swallowed some of his own shotgun soup.

What a waste.

I split the last Oreo, ate it in sections, then placed a bid and hoped the poster would be in my hands by next week. Love-hate relationships—they define my generation.

I wandered to the fridge.

Blink-blink-blink… The answering machine beckoned. I guzzled milk from the container, stared at the machine, then caved. Hit the mute button again.

There was Dad's lazy drone—as if he wouldn't raise a finger, as if he wouldn't hurt a fly. "Seen all about the Elliston shooting on the TV. Sorry to hear it. Tied up with work, but I'll be down to visit when I get a chance."

Great. Just what I need.

"Johnny Ray, you keep playin' that guitar. You got what it takes, boy. Don't let no one tell you otherwise."

The room grew hot with my hatred of this man.

His closing words: "I want to talk with the two of you, but you in particular, Aramis. Regarding your mother. This whole shooting mess—well, it's got me thinking. You be careful now. Try not to go poking your nose into places it don't belong. You do that one too many times, and you'll get a snout full of buckshot."

Another sliver of sympathy from my father's rod of wisdom.

"Dad called. Left a message."

Johnny was humming when he got in at two in the morning. He propped his Stetson on the hall bookcase, beneath his shrine of framed country-star photos. Johnny Cash and Waylon Jennings peered down with troubled eyes.

"You listening? He's coming to Nashville."

Johnny waved me off. "Don't know what you're missin', kid. A beautiful night."

"What was her name? Wait, scratch that. I don't want to know, don't want to think about it. Did you hear what I said? About Dad?"

My brother nodded. "Go on, play it for me."

I braced myself and punched the button.

Johnny shooed away a fly, then reached for his Martin six-string and slung it over his shoulder. His fingers moved down the neck. His face split into a grin when our father's voice spilled from the speaker with words of encouragement: "You keep playin' that guitar… Don't let no one tell you otherwise."

"Wait," said Johnny. "That part about Mom—play it back for me."

"I'll have to start it all over again."

"And your point is?"

I hit Repeat, then watched for Johnny Ray's reaction. When Dad brought up the subject of our mother, Johnny's brow knotted, making it clear that I'm not the only one still toting family baggage. Through the years we've begged Dad for details of Mom's death and received sketchy answers at best. Now the crusty old scoundrel was volunteering information? I hated the way he thought he could waltz into our world and deliver the goods on his own terms.

"If he comes, he's not staying with us," I said.

"Of course he is."

"I pay half the rent. I don't want him here."

"Don't be juvenile."

"He can find a motel. There're plenty close by."

"Well, it's my name on the rental agreement." Johnny flipped his guitar around so that it hung on his back like a weapon of war. "And I say he's staying here. Is that clear?"

"Not in my room. Is *that* clear? He can have your precious studio."

"Give him a break. He's just a lonely old man with a lot of regrets."

"Poor old Dad."

# TEN

**E** lliston Place was quiet. Saturday morning in Music City.

I took my usual path through the park, past Rotier's Restaurant, to Black's. An officer handed over my keys, apologized for the trouble, and wished me the best. Metro would stay in contact, he assured me; they had some leads, and I might be called upon as a witness.

Alone on the curb, I eyed my shop. What a disaster.

I posted signs letting my regulars know we'd be open again on Monday. "Money to be made, and bills to be paid," I said under my breath. I filled a mop bucket with water and bleach.

This first day back was tough.

On Thursday, the police hubbub, the media frenzy, and the general sense of chaos had served to override my short-term memory; the flurry of news-in-the-making had kept me distracted. I'd given a statement, but I don't know what I said. A detective wrote it all down, then had me read it over before signing. Somehow my coffee-stained hand had remained steady.

I do remember being proud of that.

Now, back at the scene, I saw images in my head, heard words reverberate in my ears—my mother's words, but someone else's voice.

No wonder Johnny Ray was suspicious.

I thought of Darrell in his tattered sweater. In the grasp of methamphetamine, his mind had been tweaked beyond repair; he was on his way down before the pull of the trigger.

But I wasn't one to judge, not now. Some mercy was in order.

The same as I'd received in that Portland warehouse.

"Aramis?"

A hand touched my arm. The touch seemed familiar, comforting.

"Oh, hi, Brianne."

She grinned, freckles dusting the bridge of her nose. "So you remember me." She was tall and slender, with her blond hair pulled back in a clasp. She wore black sandals with a pair of beige shorts and a black blouse with netted sleeves. Downright dangerous for a guy committed to a new way of life.

"After what we went through together? Be hard to forget."

"I'm here to work, if that's still okay with you."

"Yeah. But I should have you fill out an application. Samantha likes things by the book."

"I can do things by the book."

"Gimme a few minutes. The paperwork's somewhere in this mess."

"I could start cleaning, unless you prefer that I wait for the official decision. You never know—I could be a hardened criminal."

"It's all good. There's a bucket over there, already filled. Mop's in the closet."

"Thank you, Mr. Black." She held out her hand. "I mean, Aramis."

I found my hand in hers, shaking it awkwardly. "Glad to have you on board, Brianne."

Brianne was industrious, handy with brooms, mops, cleaning rags, and industrial supplies. She was also sensitive to my moodiness.

"Been getting any sleep the past two nights?"

I wrung a cloth. "Hasn't been too bad. I keep thinking I'll be up all night, thoughts running wild and everything. But as soon as my head hits the pillow, I'm out."

"That's a good thing."

"It'll hit me later. Too many other things to think about right now."

"Emotions, Aramis. They can take a lot out of you."

"It's not that."

"Keep on bottling."

"Is that what you think I'm doing?"

"I'm an expert in these things."

"Of anyone, you would understand what it's been like. What about you?"

Brianne wiped an arm across her forehead, then set a hand on her hip. "Mostly hangin' in there." A wave of hair drooped in front of one eye. She separated a strand and set it between her lips, nibbling. "It's a cliché, but it's like I've got a movie playing over and over in my mind. I keep seeing him hit the floor. His eyes…that look before he…you know. Why would anyone do such a thing? There must've been a reason."

Gazing into the wood patterns in the counter, I relived my part on the macabre stage. My body twisting, dropping. The explosion of the gunshot.

"I should've tried to warn him," my mouth blurted out.

"The what-ifs," said Brianne.

"I might've saved his life."

"You can't let it torture you."

"Yeah, yeah, I know." I was lying, of course.

I removed flavoring bottles from the tiered plastic shelf and continued wiping them down one by one.

Tucked into the corner of the shop, the artist stage is covered in
maroon carpet, boasting hookups and wall jacks and rising a foot
above the tile floor. A velvet shroud drapes the back wall, with strings
of beads hanging over the upper left corner and a potted evergreen
standing by the lower right.

Poets gather on Tuesdays for open-mike sessions. We hear from
all types: jilted lovers, urban revolutionaries, postmodern thinkers
caught up in the zeitgeist, and shy geniuses who hang their heads as
they read, doubting their own heartbreaking magic. I love the gamut
of emotion. It's depressing and challenging, even inspiring.

On Thursdays, the stage belongs to local musicians.

Nashville's multitude of singers and songwriters have a hard time
booking a paying gig. Everyone plays guitar. Everyone's hoping for a
shot. Those who earned respect in their hometowns get lost in the
crowd here, and a musician's tip jar fills up slower than a Death Valley rain bucket. I've never told anyone this, but I always throw in
twenty percent of the night's earnings. Seems only right. It's my way
of giving back to those who lay their hearts and souls bare through
song.

This coming Thursday will belong to Johnny Ray Black. I've
already placed in strategic spots inside the shop and out the eleven-
by-seventeen-inch color posters he gave me to advertise the event.

I dream of Johnny being discovered in my shop. Someone's got
to take notice, right? He's already got the name. He's a country star
just waiting to happen.

Then there's me. Aramis.

The question begs to be asked: who would name their kid such a thing?

I never understood the rationale behind my brother and me getting such incongruous names. It's always nagged at me, like it deserved an explanation. I mean, my mother could've stuck with something simple like, oh, Jimmy Dean.

*Here they are, folks—Johnny Ray and Jimmy Dean!*

We could've formed a duo, gone on the road, made it big. Consider yourself lucky the world's been spared my singing voice.

But Aramis?

When I was nine or ten, I asked my father about it.

"It was your mother's fool choice for a name," he told me. "Who knows what went on inside that woman's head? Just one more secret she took to the grave."

I never asked again.

Brianne and I agreed to finish our work on Sunday.

"Are you a churchgoer?"

"Not much of one," I said. "I believe. I just don't fit in, I guess. One look at my tattoos, and most of that crowd turns away. I have to wear long sleeves, or I get the Not Welcome mat."

"I hear you."

"What about you?"

"I used to go. With an ex."

"Husband?"

"Boyfriend." She hesitated. "But he…"

"Go on."

"Well, he'd been in trouble in the past, and he was trying to 'get back into heaven.' He said he'd had a premonition—a vision, he called it—that he would die young. From then on, he toed the line as if he were being graded every moment."

"And that's what broke you up?"

"Not exactly. He became such a freak about it that he shoved away all his friends. At first it was his, well, his fervency that was so annoying. Like a guy who thinks he's in love and bows at the feet of his woman. It's cute and all, but it also gets kinda scary. Well, you can guess where it was headed, and it wasn't going to be pretty." She looked up through her blond bangs. "It was like that with him and the church, like this fanaticism."

I knew what she meant. I'd noted before the similarities between high-school romances and some of the born-again enthusiasts. In either group, the ones who impressed me most were those with the deeper, less splashy commitments.

"So what happened?"

"His old life wouldn't let him go. Started getting its hooks back in."

I nodded.

"He tried to keep up the church facade, but it wasn't working anymore, not around me. I saw right through him. He'd become such a little hypocrite."

"We all have our issues, Brianne."

"That's what I tried to tell him. He was so caught up in playing the game, though, that he just wouldn't fess up."

"That game can only last so long before somebody loses."

"Oh, he lost, all right. He's gone for good." When she looked away to hide the moisture in her eyes, an angry tone cut through her words. "That was one game nobody could win."

Afraid to delve further, I gave a noncommittal grunt.

"I shouldn't have dumped that on you, Aramis. Sorry."

"No problem."

"About tomorrow's schedule. How's nine o'clock?"

She was waiting at the front door when I arrived at Black's.

In my hand, I carried worthy compensation—a bag of Krispy Kreme doughnuts, fresh off the rollers, glazed and still warm. Fortified with sugar and coffee, we attacked the day's chores with vigor, and the place started shaping up.

Later in the evening I'd be dining with Samantha Rosewood—our usual business meal. Or supper, as Sammie called it.

I hoped to have a good report for her.

Time passed quickly. Brianne and I talked about family and friendship, favorite pets and first kisses, and the fact that neither of us had been to Disney World. She had a way of drawing things out of me, and it felt good to turn my thoughts from my worries.

So she was a few years younger than me. I liked her energy.

*Careful,* I told myself. *She's an employee.*

It was early afternoon when I opened the door to air out the place, and my friend Freddy C strolled in.

Freddy's a harmless old guy who sees himself as a crusader against urban sprawl. Maybe that's what the C stands for; I've never asked.

I can't help but like the old coot. His eyes are deep-set and watery. Close to his scalp, his hair is brushed back like dune grass flattened by an ocean breeze, and I swear you can almost smell the sea salt. Not an unpleasant odor—a mixture of sweat and bread and deep-fried hush puppies. Sounds strange, but there it is.

He knocked on the wall. "Anybody home?"

I turned from cleaning the ice machine. "Freddy C, my man."

"Artemis." That's how he pronounces my name, and after trying twice to correct him, I've let it slide. "That was some nasty business you ran into," he said.

"I'm hangin' in there."

"Knew you would be, knew you would."

When people repeat themselves, I wonder who they're trying to convince. I thanked him for thinking of me, asked how he was faring.

"Better than you," he said, "better than you."

"You wouldn't lie to me, would you? You can give it to me straight."

Freddy combed a hand down through his beard, a tapered curtain of gray. In different clothing and circumstances he could've been an executive pondering a pivotal decision, a man comfortable in his own skin despite the cutthroats lying in ambush.

"Got any cardboard?" he asked. "Any boxes I can take off your hands?"

"You know I do. Bagged some empties for you too."

I gathered a garbage sack from the storage area, and it clinked with cans. He took it with stoic approval, set it atop his cart.

"That should do it. You're a good man, Artemis."

With both hands gripping the cart handle, Freddy C let his gaze wander toward the pizza joint down the block. I knew he wasn't hinting at a donation for a meal—he'd never taken advantage of our camaraderie—but he did seem to be avoiding my eyes.

"S'up?" I asked. Barely interested—that was the way I knew I had to play it.

"You stay alert. You hear what I'm sayin'?"

"Alert. You bet."

"We got ourselves a problem."

Foreboding spread in a prickly rush through my shoulders. "Yeah? How so?"

He shuffled in his worn shoes, rolled his neck. "Later."

"Why not now? This sounds important, Freddy."

"Not very," he said. "Not very."

"I've got time. Try me."

"No one believes. Best if I stayed out of your hair." Large and wet, his eyes wobbled beneath sandy eyebrows. They roved down the street from one side to the other, then he turned and shoved off in the direction of Centennial Park, his cart rattling along. "Yep, that'd be best," he mumbled again. "Out of your hair."

For the second time in a week I knew I'd misread someone standing in front of me.

Freddy C hadn't been trying to avoid my eyes; he'd been watching someone or something down the block, and now he was hurrying away.

Which worried me.

I've seen Freddy stand his ground while another homeless man with an ice pick tried to snag his flattened boxes. I've seen him confront a businessman who'd tossed a Jack in the Box wrapper on the sidewalk. Word on the street says he was involved in government covert ops in the early eighties, though he's never confirmed it, and I suspect he started the rumor himself. Either way, the guy's no slouch.

Today, however, he was fleeing toward the green coolness of the park.

I ran my eyes back along Elliston, past popular music venues, a soda shop, and a bookstore. There, halfway down, was a white Camry.

It's a common car, sure. Still, I couldn't help but recall my brother's paranoia on Friday.

Could he have been right?

And Freddy C… What did he know that he wasn't telling me?

I took ten steps down the sidewalk, close enough to see the Tennessee license plate. Muttering the number, I went back into Black's and scrawled the info on one of my business cards: BHT 588.

# ELEVEN

Reserved, as always."

"Not trying to be, Sammie."

"When it comes to emotions, it's your modus operandi."

"Sometimes I also make jokes."

"Which," Samantha Rosewood said, "is simply another way of protecting yourself. By now, I should expect nothing more."

Under the guise of business, we "do supper" frequently. I'm the lucky benefactor of her culinary standards, and this night was a perfect example. Restaurante Zola offers great food with exemplary service, and critics from the East Coast and West have praised chef Debra Paquette's skills.

"Sorry." I set down my fork, heard it ping against the plate. The maître d' looked my way before realizing I was only clumsy, and diners turned back to their entrées. "My mind's sorting through a lot, I guess. The good thing is, Black's will be open again tomorrow, bright and early. Thanks to your generous help."

"We have insurance. I have no doubt they'll cover our losses."

"You're a rock, Sammie. I can always count on you."

"A rock. Am I safe to assume that was a compliment?"

"Of course."

As she watched me drink my third glass of Pinot Noir, her lips parted to reveal even, white teeth, feminine and alluring. In the candlelight, her hair came alive with honey-colored highlights. Her fingers ran over the tablecloth, then lowered to her lap as her eyes focused beyond my shoulder.

Thinking of better people to share dinner with, no doubt.

"You ready to go?" I asked, offering her an escape.

"Aramis. You still haven't answered my earlier question."

"About Brianne? Seems like she'll be a good worker."

"About you. You seem flighty."

"I do?"

Weighed down by recent events, I had hoped the wine would hide my concerns. Alcohol, in general, tends to be a risky pastime for me—particularly with the opposite sex within arm's reach—and I've been limiting my intake to two glasses. I'd already surpassed that.

"I'd like to think you can share anything with me," Sammie said.

"Nothing to share. I'm fine." Emboldened by the wine, I added, "If God had wanted you to read my thoughts, he would've installed a viewing plate on my forehead."

"Actually," Sammie said, "that's why you came with vocal cords."

"Okay…"

"I'm willing to venture that you're not okay."

I heard my voice momentarily falter as I leaned forward. "You know, it's been a rough couple of days, after what happened in my shop."

She tilted her head, let a strand of auburn hair unfurl along her collarbone.

"Our shop," I corrected.

"I like to think so."

"Things'll be back to normal in no time."

"I have faith in you. You've done a wonderful job of creating a loyal customer base." Her eyes moved to mine, then flitted away.

I found myself wanting to win her favor, prove myself worthy. I swirled my glass and finished it. Why not be playful? Flirty? I appreciated this woman and wanted her to know it.

"Samantha, you're a good partner."

Her shoulders stiffened. "Business partner, you mean."

"Uh. Yeah. You're the best."

"Right back atcha," she said.

Her response was so out of character, out of place, that I began to suspect she was surrendering to my suave ways. Johnny Ray was still having his way with women, but it had been a year since my last serious relationship. Felicia.

I missed the companionship.

I didn't care if the alcohol was loosening my tongue, didn't care who heard it. Not one bit. I felt more talkative, sure—and more confident. Ready to beat the daylights out of any man standing in my way and ready to sweep any woman off her feet.

Samantha was too good for me, too classy, but experience has taught me most women have a soft spot for the bad boy, even the bad boy under reform.

"You ever think about us, Sammie? On a romantic level?"

"Aramis, it's awfully late."

"That's my point." I drew an exclamation mark in the air and dotted it.

"You're on the verge of making a fool of yourself," she said.

"Southern belle's too good for a Northwest lumberjack?"

"I don't believe you've ever cut down a tree, have you?"

"Not exactly." I squirmed in my seat. "But, hey, have you ever worn a corset?"

"This is getting silly."

I grabbed at my chest in mock pain. "Only trying to have a little fun."

She flipped open her cell phone. "Tonight the fun will be on your own. I'm calling you a taxi."

"A cab? Samantha."

"Please, Aramis."

"Don't tell me you've never thought about us. You woman. Me man."

"You drunk."

"I resemble that statement." I laughed.

She set her napkin beside her dessert plate, then paused, her lips parting, her eyes softening. She drew a finger through the condensation on her water glass, then, in a decisive motion, she swiveled in her seat with the grace of a woman in petticoats dismounting a steed.

Before striding away, she said, "Good night, Mr. Black."

I felt like the proverbial horse's rear end.

In no mood for a sympathy taxi ride, I called Johnny Ray while downing another glass of the good stuff. He found me in the foyer—where I'd been directed by the maître d'—and carted me home without any questions asked.

As he helped me up the steps with his arm linked under mine, I felt like we were united in a family embrace, bonded by past and present. Despite sibling frictions and differences in our personalities, we're always there for one another. He's my blood. My brother.

I dropped onto my bed fully clothed, and in the dark a blanket settled over me.

"My alarm," I mumbled.

"Already taken care of, kid. Get some sleep."

In my dreams, my father usually appears in silhouette against a blazing sun. He stands stock-still. I want to reach out to him, because I sense a deep sadness. I'm convinced my face hovers in his sorrow, plaguing him somehow.

On this particular night, he turns. His hands hang at his sides, quivering.

"Come here, boy."

"No."

"Come here."

"No!" I take a step back.

He vanishes. The sun blinds me.

In the next instant, a gun presses against my forehead, cold and hard. Pungent smells assault my nose, and I realize I'm in Portland again, seconds from death.

The man with the Glock: *Not so tough* now, *are you?*

My eyes scan the strip of gloomy light at the crown of the warehouse, waiting for my angel of mercy. And here it comes…

Falling, looming large. An industrial light fixture.

The gunman cackles and steps back so that I alone remain in the path of impact. My head becomes a target of dark, matted hair and stubble. My dark green eyes grow wide. My mouth opens in a cry for help.

Propelled by the scream, I whip from the building.

The wind races by, whittling me into a streamlined projectile. I'm a bullet, rotating at impossible speed. Scorched by the friction. Hurtling toward a wounded man in a rustic cabin called Grinder's Stand.

He cries out: *Oh, madam… Heal my wounds.*

But it's too late for him. He is falling, falling…

Behind the cabin door, my mother covers her ears and shakes her head, torn with emotions too large for her frame to bear.

# TWELVE

Every Monday, rain or shine, I observe a ritual on my way to work. My mile walk winds through Centennial Park, and I pause there for ten minutes of silence.

A time of reflection.

In the center of the park, on a slight knoll overlooking a man-made duck pond, the world's only full-scale replica of the Greek Parthenon stands broad and proud. Up close, the structure seems massive, with monstrous rock slabs, tapered columns accentuating the height, and gargoyles leering down from the corners. Behind towering dark doors, a forty-two-foot statue of Athena stares with ominous eyes, and in her palm, Nike, the goddess of victory, stands six feet tall.

Constructed originally for Tennessee's centennial celebration in 1897, the Parthenon was meant to underline Nashville's claim as the Athens of the South, but the building fell into disuse. Years later the site was restored, and it's now a highlight on every tour guide's route.

There's nothing spiritual about the place for me. In fact, the edifice seems to stand in honor of humanity's accomplishments alone, a relic of those who diminished their gods by enshrining them in stone and myth.

I don't think we can hold God down like that.

I think it's more about humility. But I don't have it all figured out.

I opened Black's forty-five minutes later to a long line of supportive regulars. I could have hugged every one of them. Instead I poured their coffee and pulled their espresso shots with extra doses of goodwill.

Most of them rushed on into the day, but I'd like to think a few of them felt it.

Brianne showed up as scheduled. I hadn't trained her in the art of fine coffee, so I had her stock and clean and straighten.

In the late morning, I called Sammie to report our steady stream of business. Although the conversation was strained, purely professional, she seemed pleased. She did have things to do, she told me.

"One more thing, Sammie."

She waited. She wasn't going to make this easy for me.

"I'm sorry," I said. "For last night. I think I made a couple of lame comments and a general fool of myself."

"The wine was very good. You may have had a bit more than was prudent."

"That's putting it politely."

"I don't think either of us was in the place to continue a reasonable conversation."

"You're always so under control."

"Part of my upbringing. Did you make it home safely?"

"Johnny Ray picked me up."

"He's a thoughtful man, isn't he?"

"He is. There must've been some sort of genetic hiccup between the two of us."

"Aramis, you're forgiven, if that's what you're asking."

"Thank you."

She was classy about it, shaming me all the more—and I loved her for it.

As the day flew by, I began to believe that maybe, just maybe, routines and rituals would carry me through. No need to get involved. Move on.

"Seems to be a done deal," Johnny Ray told me later in the evening.

"What's that?"

"Dad's visit. He should be arriving any day now."

"I can't wait." I continued stuffing laundry into the washing machine.

"I know it's wrong the way he treated you, Aramis, but I think he wants to put things right. I think we ought to give the man a chance."

"Sure. Whatever."

"So you're okay with him coming?"

I grunted and started the cycle. "What can it hurt?"

Johnny and I eventually migrated to the couch to watch a *CSI* episode on DVD while drinking cans of Dr Pepper from the same six-pack. I hadn't seen my brother glug a soft drink in months, and this sharing of food and entertainment was our way of calling a truce, a moment of solidarity before our father's upcoming visit.

"He'll be sleeping in your studio. Right?"

My brother stood and cracked his knuckles. I thought for a moment we were going to have a good old sibling rumble—and we both knew who would win. Although he has the butt-kicking boots and the weight advantage, he can't compete with the fury our father instilled in me. Johnny hasn't beaten me in a fight since I grew my first mustache and got my first tattoo at fifteen.

"I was wrong, by the way. I've got to tell you that now, Aramis."

"Huh?"

"You *have* changed. I said otherwise in the truck on Friday, but I was trying to make a point. You have made a turn for the better. Still," he insisted, "you have to soften up a little."

"What are you really getting at? Just spit it out."

"Well, first there's Dad—that's obvious. And there's Uncle Wyatt."

The name was salt on my wounds.

"Until you wipe his slate clean, it's just words, is all. You won't really be changed, not deep down. Uncle Wyatt's a good man, and he deserves better than you've given him. Sooner or later you'll have to face it and make a choice."

"I'll keep that in mind, big brother."

"You do that. The choice might come sooner than you think."

My suspicions stirred at that point, but Johnny Ray's sudden grin diverted my attention.

"You should've seen them," he said. "They were eating out of my hand."

"What're you talking about?"

"Tonight at the Bluebird I performed my new song, and they loved it."

Located on Hillsboro Pike, the Bluebird Café is a staple of the Nashville music scene. A storefront establishment with a bar, a small kitchen, and no more than fifteen tables, the Bluebird hosts open-mike Mondays for those performing original tunes. No covers and nobody singing Toby Keith or Shania Twain. It's the real deal, and a number of bona fide stars have been discovered there—from Garth Brooks to Faith Hill.

Johnny Ray Black could be next.

I said, "We're still on for Thursday, right?"

"I'll blow the roof off, with the full band and everything."

"That's what I'm talking about." I slapped his arm. "We'll pack the place. I'll pull them in off the street at gunpoint, if necessary."

He lifted an eyebrow. "Let's not go that far."

"Bad choice of words. But you know what I'm saying."

"And I appreciate it. I really do."

In my bedroom, moonlight sliced through the venetian blinds. I inhaled and closed my eyes. This room was my haven. I reached for the box on the windowsill and traced the ebony surface with my fingers.

I often end my nights like this, holding the keepsake, thinking of Mom.

Her voice: *Hold on to this for me, okay?... Someday it'll show you the way.*

As I lifted the lid, the rich scent was a reminder of whispers and smiles and of Cracker Jack surprises she used to place in my stubby toddler hands. The recently returned handkerchief was the closest thing to having her with me.

A jolt shot through my fingers.

The handkerchief was gone.

Another object had taken its place. My fist closed around a clump of brunette hair—human hair.

In one motion, I let go, pushed at the box, and stumbled back.

# PART TWO

# WITH WHIP

*I fight only when forced....*
*But this time...a lady's honor has been compromised.*

—Alexandre Dumas, *The Three Musketeers*

# THIRTEEN

his is important," Detective Meade told me. "You do understand we're recording this conversation?"

Seated in an interview room, I nodded, and my chair squeaked under me.

"The tape cannot pick up a nod, Mr. Black."

"Yes," I said.

"That's better." Meade folded thin hands in his lap. His skin was coal black and smooth as motor oil, his head a patch of short, coarse hair. He seemed to have perfected an expression of bland disinterest. "We appreciate your time here. You may be instrumental in our investigation. Now, speaking clearly, tell me again where you found this hair specimen."

"On my windowsill. In a box."

"Did you bring the box?"

I shook my head. Catching the detective's eye, I said, "No sir."

"Okay then, would you please describe it."

"Let's see. It's made of ebony wood, with mother-of-pearl inlay and a velvet lining. My mom gave it to me when I was a kid. It's…it means the world to me."

"Can it be locked? Does it have a key?"

"No."

"And what prompted you to bring this…specimen to the station?"

My thoughts were going through the spin cycle. "Somebody robbed me—that's all I can figure. My mom's handkerchief was in there. Now it's gone. And that hair was in its place. It was creepy, the way that rubber-band thing was still attached."

"The pink scrunchy."

"Whatever it's called."

"So you know nothing about the hair? Is that what you're telling us?"

"How would I?"

"I'm not asking for conjecture, Mr. Black. Only for the reasons that prompted you to turn it in."

"Did I do something wrong?"

"Mr. Black, this is not an attempt to put you on the defensive."

"I'm not being defensive. I'm trying to understand your question."

"And we're only trying to understand your motive." Detective Meade's disinterested look was a tool, challenging me to impress him or convince him while giving no indication that either was possible. I wanted him to know that I was credible, that he needed to act on this.

"Why do I get the feeling I'm a suspect here?"

"Are you getting that feeling?"

"Look, it's not been an easy week."

"The Elliston shooting," he said. "I'm well aware."

"Anyway. I'm not really reporting the lock of hair. I'm reporting a burglary, I guess."

"You guess."

"Somebody must've broken in. We don't have an alarm."

"Was everything locked?"

"Far as I could tell. We keep things tight, deadbolts and all."

"Any windows left open?"

"There was one. In the bathroom. "

"Big enough for a person to crawl through?"

I nodded. "If they squeezed, I guess."

"Is there any evidence of an intrusion? Footprints? Things disturbed?"

"Besides the missing handkerchief? No sir. But I'm not the detective, am I?"

"Is it possible the handkerchief may have been misplaced?"

"No way."

Meade steepled his fingers, tapped them against his lower lip. My eyes wandered to a mole on his neck that was the color and size of a small raisin—something to remind me that he was human, that we were equals.

"Where does your brother work?"

"Ryder Transportation. He dispatches for them."

"Do either of you attend Vanderbilt University, Mr. Black?"

"No."

"Is either of you a student?"

"Johnny was in the summer music program at Belmont, and I've signed up for classes at Lipscomb University in the spring."

"When's the last time you were on the Vandy campus?"

I paused, not sure I liked this new direction of questioning. "A week ago last Friday. A friend invited us to a party."

"A student?"

"Think so. He's one of my customers at Black's. We went and had a few drinks. Danced. Mingled."

"We?"

"My brother and I. But I was out of there before eleven, Detective. Had to open shop in the morning."

"Did your brother return home with you?"

"No. He called me a boring old man."

Meade nodded as though familiar with such accusations.

"Listen," I said. "Why the twenty questions? This doesn't seem to be getting me any closer to finding my mom's handkerchief or the person who stole it."

"Jessica Tyner."

"Excuse me?"

"Name mean anything to you?"

"Not offhand."

"We'll have to run some tests for verification, but we have reason to believe, Mr. Black, that this hair belonged to her. Ms. Tyner was assaulted on the Vanderbilt campus ten days ago. On a Friday night."

I could feel the intensity of his eyes watching, assessing. He'd planted his feet on the linoleum with his knees pointed at me.

"Yeah, I did see something about it on the news."

"She was at a party, Mr. Black, right before the assault."

I measured my words. "With all due respect, Detective, it doesn't make sense. How would... I mean, why would someone stash her hair in my mom's keepsake?"

"Here." Meade opened a file on the table and produced a case-numbered Polaroid. The victim's face was turned, her eyes closed, her straight, brunette hair gouged. "Take a look, then tell me if we don't have a potential match."

In the photograph, the remaining pigtail was intact and neat, gathered in a matching hot pink scrunchy.

And I remembered Jessica Tyner. We had, in fact, been at the same party.

*That girl, the brunette with the belly ring—she was into you, and you blew it.*

"One last question."

I shifted in my chair, sat up straight. "Yes?"

"By chance, you haven't come across any other specimens, have you?"

"Others? I don't understand."

"Little trophies, Mr. Black. Evidence to help us establish a criminal pattern."

A cold sensation curled around my ribs. "No," I said. "Definitely not."

Vanderbilt University's police department can't monitor all activities that occur in what amounts to a small city. I understand that.

A girl sexually assaulted on campus, though? Wasn't anyone watching?

As the largest private employer in Middle Tennessee, the school is a monument to Cornelius Vanderbilt's original million-dollar vision. In 1873, he may never have imagined that thousands of students from around the globe would converge on this site for a first-class education—at a first-class price, it's pertinent to note. Undoubtedly, his dream has been surpassed.

Situated not far from Black's on the other side of West End Avenue, the university comprises ten schools, ranging from arts and science to engineering, law, and divinity. The on-campus population hovers around twenty-five thousand.

Crime on campus? Don't get me wrong. I know that no school's immune.

It sickened me, nonetheless. The thought of Jessica Tyner's helplessness. Her disgrace. It's true, the Vanderbilt police provide a shuttle service for safe escort, but she never called the Vandy Vans. Who knows why.

I remembered the story from the news. A lively sophomore with lots of friends, Jessica Tyner left a Kappa Sigma party and told her best friend she'd be back soon. When she failed to return, a search party was organized.

They found her hours later in the bushes near the Alumni Lawn, raped and unconscious, partially clothed.

Chief Serpas gave assurances about Metro's commitment to solving this heartless act. He asked for calls from anyone with potentially helpful information.

I hadn't called. I hadn't known her, not by name.

Detective Meade promised to check around, find out if anyone suspicious had entered our brownstone, but he seemed unsure of my story. I didn't blame him. I'd never imagined my life would be intertwined with Jessica Tyner's, never realized I might offer a clue.

The discovery of her bunched, brown hair in the ebony box changed all that.

Why hadn't the authorities continued splashing details of Jessica's assault across the headlines? Were they withholding information to use later as leverage in their pursuit of the rapist? Perhaps they wanted to curtail any panic on campus.

I thought again about the lackluster security that had failed her—then remembered my own inability to protect a customer. Transferring guilt did little to make me feel better.

*They're coming for you next…* That's what Darrell Michaels had told me.

Was his warning connected to the disappearance of my mother's handkerchief?

It was time to reconsider the Elliston shooting and its connections to my family's past. This wasn't just going to go away.

In the back of my shop, I roasted coffee into the early morning. I scooped the beans, pale green and raw, into the rotating drum, and set the time and temperature for my house blend, a mix of Guatemalan, Colombian, and Kenyan coffees.

I call it the Back-in-Black Blend.

The routine was good. Work. And caffeine. Worthy antidotes for the darkness swirling through my head.

I called Johnny early to remind him to secure all windows and doors before he left for work. I didn't want anyone browsing through our things again.

Once hostility enters your world, it hangs stubbornly in the neighborhood. Some friends of mine don't understand. Their fathers' hands were instruments of compassion and love. I listen to their stories and wonder what it's like to have a soul still soft in all the right places.

Why couldn't my father have kept his mouth shut while he slugged me in the nose and let me bleed? On the bad nights, he'd beat me with a piano-moving strap that produced welts as thick as slugs.

That much I learned to handle.

It's the words that still ring in my ears. The verbal blows. Long after the visible evidence fades, you still hear the rage in a parent's voice; you still see the loathing that lurks behind the eyes.

I tugged at my shirt sleeves and brought my tattoos into full view.

*Bring it,* I thought. *Let me know who I'm fighting, and let's do this!*

# FOURTEEN

H ere they come," said Mrs. Thompson. She was in her usual seat near the window, a romance novel spread open next to her caramel latte.

"Who, Mrs. Thompson?"

Her eyes ran along the sidewalk, beyond my line of vision. "A camera crew, I think. Yes, they're aiming for your front door."

"Just what I need."

The morning rush was over, Brianne was in the back prepping soups and salads, and the lunch crowd was a good hour away. I swiped a paper towel over a coffee ring on the mahogany. I flashed to the Polaroid of Jessica Tyner and wondered if the police had released information regarding the clump of hair.

"My, you've had *your* share of trouble recently, haven't you?"

"It's gotta stop soon." I lowered my voice. "Or I'll make it stop."

"Oh, look." Mrs. Thompson leaned closer to the glass. "Isn't *he* a handsome one in his suit and tie? He's carrying a clipboard. And here comes a redhead in heels. Honey, how're you *ever* going to walk in a skirt that tight?"

I had to see this for myself.

Drying my hands, I went around the bar. The sun's heat met me there, oozing and thick against the windowpane. To her credit, the lady in the skirt was balanced quite nicely, approaching in a fluid motion that swept her hair about her shoulders. Its color was subdued, a richer version of the fiery leaves in the trees that served as her backdrop.

An unmarked white van gave no clues about this group's intentions.

The door chimed as the cluster of five entered: two smooth-faced guys bearing television cameras on their shoulders, another dude corralling cords and a battery pack, a man holding a clipboard, and the lady in her dark blue blouse with matching heels, a cream jacket and skirt, and nylons.

"Good morning," I said.

The lady's smile came on like an electronic device. "Hello."

Normally I stay behind the bar so as not to intimidate. No upselling. No pressure. Customers appreciate this casual approach, and they come back.

With hands on hips, I stepped forward. "Looking for anything in particular?"

"Mmm," the lady purred. "Nothing like the aroma of fresh coffee."

One cameraman said to the other, "I'd rather have Starbucks any day."

I'd have to fight this battle with the weapons at hand. I tightened my green apron strings and circled back to my glistening espresso machine. Started the grinder. Dispensed the coffee into the porta-filter. Tamped down and twisted.

"What can I make for you?"

The three crew members settled down in a corner booth while

Mr. Clipboard and Ms. Watch-Me-Walk-in-Heels nudged toward the counter.

"A tall, nonfat latte, please," the lady said. "Extra hot, no foam."

"Whipped cream?"

"No thank you." She smiled again, full voltage. "We'll have three SoBes for the crew—any flavor's fine. And Greg here, he's the show-off. He'll take a venti house coffee, black."

"For here or to go?"

"For here," Greg said. "Thank you so much. Speaking of which, we're looking for a Mr. Aramis Black. Is that you? You're shorter than I expected, but I must say the photograph did no justice to your eyes." He touched the lady's wrist. "See, Carla. Aren't they much greener than you thought they'd be?"

Carla's bold stare was meant to stroke my ego. A year ago it might've worked; now I simply turned my focus to the milk frothing in the metal pitcher.

"Yes," she said.

"So you're Mr. Black?" Greg tapped a finger on his trimmed goatee.

"In the flesh."

Carla said, "If you haven't noticed, Greg, this man's not on your playing field."

"You don't know that." He glanced at me.

"She's right." I handed him a mug of Back-in-Black Blend. "Sorry."

"*C'est la vie.* We're here on business anyway."

"Please," I said, "don't tell me this has to do with last week."

"Last week?"

"Never mind."

"You'll have to pardon our intrusion. We're talking network television."

"Ahh. That clears things up."

Carla dismissed my comment with a wave of her arm. "We've come to offer you an opportunity. It was your brother's idea, actually. Tell him, Greg."

"Prime time, Mr. Black. Can you say 'reality TV'?"

I finished preparing the lady's latte and set it on the bar along with the SoBes. A few taps at the register gave me a total for the drinks. No matter where this was leading, they would pay for their order. Show business, shmow business—I wasn't going to start handing out freebies just to get my name in lights.

"That'll be thirteen twenty-six. With tax." I smiled. "Welcome to Nashville."

There was a dose of reality for you.

They weren't kidding. Joined by the camera crew, coproducers Greg Simone and Carla Fleischmann had flown in from Los Angeles on a red-eye, rented a van, and checked in at Loews Vanderbilt Hotel. Mere hours after their arrival, they'd pushed through the door of Black's. They were here for me, at Johnny Ray's request.

"My brother? I don't get it."

"See for yourself, Mr. Black."

I reached into the envelope on the table, found a paper clip holding photographs to an application. My brother's writing, no doubt about it.

A customer entered the shop. Brianne heard the chime, winked my direction, then stepped to the counter to take the order. I nodded in thanks.

"We represent a reality TV show," Carla was saying. "Slated for next season."

"Like we don't have enough already?"

"Our job as producers," Greg said, "is to find fresh ideas." He slipped a packet of guidelines, waivers, and forms into my hands. "And this idea—if I may say so—is wickedly wonderful, appealing to the best and worst in us all."

"Surprise, surprise."

"It does have its redeeming qualities."

"This I've gotta hear."

"The show's called *The Best of Evil*."

"Ooh, sounds scary."

"The premise... Do you mind, Carla?"

"Carry on." She took a sip of her latte, licked her lips.

"The premise is that we've all been wronged at some time, in some way, by someone. What if you could go back to such a person? What if you could pay them back for what they did?" Greg paused. "You with me so far, Mr. Black?"

I shrugged.

"The catch is—and it's always good to have one—you don't pay them back in a vengeful way, an eye for an eye, a tooth for a tooth. That'd be too easy, too predictable."

"I don't know. I think justice has a purpose."

"Oh, absolutely, absolutely. The beauty here is that we provide viewers and participants with a transcendent justice, based on something much stronger than revenge. Instead of getting even with the perpetrators, we give the show's participants the chance to"—Greg inserted quotes here with his fingers—"get the best of evil by doing good."

"For example," I offered, "Hollywood types descend on your store, and you agree to help them out at no charge."

Carla looked up from her drink. "You know, Greg, I like this guy."

"Let me give you a scenario, Mr. Black. Say there's a mother who'd been verbally abusive throughout her daughter's childhood. The daughter gets a chance to meet her mother face to face, to confront this issue and work through some of the emotions. The show, of course, will seesaw between their two viewpoints leading up to a climax. Beforehand, we will have obtained permission from both parties, and we'll have heard one of the mother's long-unfulfilled desires. All part of the interview process. She won't have any idea where this is heading."

"Sounds manipulative."

"It's television," Carla said.

"But these are real people."

"The payoff is worth it."

"In the ratings, you mean."

"You're missing the purpose," Greg said.

"The purpose?"

"Reconciliation, Mr. Black. Forgiveness. The wronged party takes this chance to bless the perpetrator in a totally unexpected and undeserved way, making a dream come true. It's beautiful—estranged loved ones coming to terms with the past so that relationships can be restored."

"Come on," I said. "That's just the emotional hook."

"And a superbly noble one, at that."

"Isn't it really about weepy-eyed viewers tuning in weekly?"

"No no no."

"Maybe just a little bit," Carla said with a grin.

"You…you two are incorrigible!" Greg crossed his hands over his chest. "This is a theme dear to my heart. Can't you see that?"

I could see it. And in that moment, I began to like the guy—not in the way he might desire, but as a fellow human being. Greg Simone had genuine passion for the project. He was wearing his heart on his sleeve, fully aware of the ridicule that might be flung his way.

"Where do I fit in? And what's my brother have to do with this?"

"He submitted your name, along with a brief biography," said Carla. She gestured toward one of the cameramen, and he lifted the lens in my direction. "We'll be shooting the show's pilot at the beginning of next month, and we're in the process now of narrowing down our selections."

"So," I joked, "who'd you round up? Who's mad at me now?"

"Your story's a compelling one," Carla continued. The camera light was on.

"What'd Johnny Ray tell you?" I demanded.

"You can read it there on the form."

"Who gave him permission? Did he tell you where to find me?"

"Anger's also normal."

"He wrote down the name of someone for me to forgive. I bet that's it, isn't it?" I turned my palms up and beckoned. "Let's hear it. Tell me who it is."

Carla dangled the application like a red flag. "Wyatt Tremaine."

Uncle Wyatt? Two decades after the fact? Never.

"Okay." I stood and turned to face the table. "You're starting to make me angry. Marching in here, throwing this in my face. Please— shut off the camera."

Greg's eyes locked on to me, practically pleading.

"And you." I pointed at him, feeling like a bully on a playground. "Take your soft-hearted, bleary-eyed fluff and get outta here. You hear me? I don't need sympathy."

He never blinked. He said, "You're wrong. Everyone does."

"Yeah, you're the expert."

"Your Uncle Wyatt needs it too."

"And you've spoken with him? He told you that?"

"As a matter of fact, yes."

"Whatever."

"It's the truth." The words came from behind me.

Sonorous and warm, the voice rolled over me. It stirred a volatile mix in my head, releasing emotional odors and toxins that seemed almost palpable. As I turned, my mouth went dry. The roots of my hair tingled. My heart came to a brief standstill before slamming into my rib cage.

"Uncle Wyatt?"

"Aramis." He extended his hand.

# FIFTEEN

**E**ven after all this time the sound of my uncle's voice was a wrecking ball.

There I was. Six years old.

He was giving me orders in a low growl.

"Get your head down, boy."

Fingers grimy and strong enforced the demands of his gruff whisper. Already on my belly, spying through stalks of wheat at my captive mother on the riverbank, I felt my chin grind into the mud. A cloth circled my head and cinched between my lips.

"Keep still, and not a peep outta you. It's for your own good, Aramis."

A knee was in my back. A belt was strapped around my wrists. I was one of those insects I used to catch and pin to cardboard. Helpless. Confused.

Pinned down by Uncle Wyatt. Why was he doing this?

He left me there with rain drumming on my head, splatting my eyes with mud. I craned my neck so I could see where he was going. I knew he was heading toward Mom. Did he realize the other man had a gun? I tried to warn him. The downpour drowned out my mumbling. Uncle Wyatt stood tall and walked straight for the riverbank.

I hoped he knew what he was doing.

The morning had started like any other, with me stuck at home. Even though I wanted to be big like my brother, I couldn't go to school till next fall.

After breakfast Mom had set down her coffee and smiled at me. One of her sad smiles.

"Come here."

I crawled onto her lap, and she hugged me. It was almost scary how tight she held me, like she was afraid I'd dissolve into thin air. She handed me a shiny black box with velvet lining. I'd never seen it before. Inside, folded up nice and neat, was the handkerchief she'd been embroidering the night before.

"Hold on to this for me, okay, Aramis? I have secrets wrapped in here. Someday it'll show you the way."

"It's soft."

"Take special care of it, you understand?"

"Okay, Mom. But you're squeezing me. I can't breathe."

"I love you," she said.

"Love you too."

She let go. "Don't forget. That's just for you. Why don't you go hide your new treasure in your tree fort?"

"What about Johnny?"

"You're getting to be a big kid. I think you can make it on your own."

Looking back, I recognize that she was talking about more than tree climbing. She was preparing me; she knew what was coming.

I bounded outside and clawed my way up into the fort Dad had built with me and Johnny Ray. I tucked the box into a hollow in the oak, where puckered wood led to a dark space. A gentle rain began tapping on the leaves, but there was another sound too.

An engine was rumbling, getting louder and closer.

I peered from my leafy refuge and saw a black Trans Am slide into our driveway. A darkly tanned man with bleached blond hair jumped out, holding a gun.

Mom stepped on the front porch, twisting her silky hair in her hand.

The man was yelling, cursing like she was nothing more than some stupid dog. From where I was, I couldn't catch it all, but he was angry. That was for certain. Angry enough to shoot her. She held up her hand, ushering him inside.

What was she thinking, letting a strange man in our house?

I was shimmying down the rope ladder when I heard the front door open again. I dropped into the rain-dappled dirt, ran, and ducked behind a tractor.

More yelling. A slap. Footsteps scuffling over stone.

"Tell me where it is!"

"It's gone. I threw it in the river."

"You wouldn't be that stupid. Where? Tell me where."

"It's wrong. I know what you'll do with it."

"You have no idea what I'll do! Go! Get moving—that way."

I trailed them through the wheat field. My mind was packed full of questions and fear, but I prayed the Lord would send someone to stop this madman from doing bad things to my mother.

Yelling threats, waving the pistol, the man made Mom stand at the river's edge. The drop to the water was a good eight or nine feet; I'd made the jump before on a dare and had gotten the breath knocked out of me. From my belly now, hoping to remain unseen, I could tell that Mom had clammed up—same way she did with Dad some nights.

I felt helpless, terrified. Where was everyone? When did Dad get off work? Shouldn't Johnny Ray be outta school by now?

These thoughts were running through my mind that moment in the field when Uncle Wyatt arrived and shoved me down. At the sound of his voice, I thought help had come.

I was wrong.

"You?" The gunman pointed at my uncle. "Shoulda known you'd show your face. Well, thanks for joining us. Your sister's not talking, so maybe you can tell me."

"Nothing to tell."

"Don't give me that! Somebody knows."

"All right. Okay, I'll tell you. Just let Dianne go."

"You think I'm stupid, Wyatt? Do I look like I flunked kinder-garten?"

"No sir. But I think you're desperate enough to get yourself killed. I made a call. The cops're on the way, and they don't take kindly to men pointing guns."

"What've they got in this hellhole? One cop car? A horse and buggy?"

"Take your chances. It's up to you," Uncle Wyatt reasoned. "But let her be. She's no good to you."

The gunman guffawed. "Now that's the first honest thing you've said."

"So don't do anything stupid. C'mon, put the gun to my head and let her walk."

"Might as well drop you both where you stand. I finally track you down after all these years, and you're still useless as dirt. Shoulda known." The bleached-blond man pulled back the hammer on the gun. My mom didn't flinch. "Maybe this'll loosen your tongue."

He fired into my mom's thigh, and she dropped to her knees with a scream.

Uncle Wyatt yelled at the man and rushed forward, but the gun barrel angled his way and froze him in place.

I was bawling. The belt was biting into my wrists, the cloth in my mouth muffling my cries. I managed to get up on one knee, and then I stood. My uncle caught the movement in his peripheral vision. Raindrops were spilling down his nose, and terror contorted his face.

"Hey!" He took a step toward the assailant.

The blond man gestured. "Stay back. Come any closer, and she gets it through the head."

I was drenched and shivering. Mom was shaking with quiet whimpers.

Maybe the man would have sympathy if he realized my mother had a child. He wouldn't shoot a kid, would he? Fear coursed through my body, but I couldn't watch my mom die. With my shoulder, I scraped at the cloth in my mouth, pulling, tugging, working it free. I filled my lungs with fresh air.

"Mom!"

"Get outta here!" Uncle Wyatt yelled at me.

The gunman turned toward my voice.

"Don't shoot her again! Please." I scooted forward, ignoring the slap of soggy wheat on my cheeks. "That's my mom."

"This woman is your mother?"

"Please." I stumbled, landed in the mud.

"Keep quiet," Uncle Wyatt insisted.

The blond man waved the weapon at my uncle. "You stay out of it."

"The kid's lying," Uncle Wyatt continued. "I don't know where he came from."

"I'm not lying."

The blond man's voice softened, and he put one hand on his heart in a show of concern. "I didn't realize you had a younger son, Dianne. If only you'd told me."

"It's true," I said. "Please, mister. Don't hurt her anymore."

"You're a good kid. I can see that."

"Please believe me."

"I do." He lowered the gun. Crouched down to look me in the eye.

It was a turning point. Why didn't Uncle Wyatt see that? The attacker might back down in the presence of a begging six-year-old. No. Uncle Wyatt launched forward. Maybe he thought he was doing the right thing. Figured he could be the hero. The mighty rescuer coming to his sister's and nephew's aid.

But this mistake changed everything.

I saw him coming. So did the blond man.

A coil of anger knotted the assailant's mouth and corkscrewed through his eyes, turning his face from a mask of sympathy into one of unrestricted evil. The transformation was instantaneous. The man's arm jerked forward, jabbing the pistol into the black strands of my mom's hair.

Uncle Wyatt was still charging when the man pulled the trigger.

Now, in my own espresso shop, I was facing my uncle for the first time in decades. I thought I'd started a new chapter, but my credo was still etched on my arms, on my heart.

One look at Uncle Wyatt's sun-weathered face, and I exploded.

He stood before me, nearly half a century of life under his silver belt buckle. His jeans were faded, and his cowboy shirt bore visible stitching and pearl buttons. He was crusty and raw, yet there in the solid line of his jaw, the prominent cheekbones, and wide, dark eyes, I caught a glimpse of his sister's genes.

My mother. Dianne Lewis Black.

In two seconds flat, the negative energy I'd been trying to contain here in Music City came unleashed, like a rubber band stretched to its limit before snapping back with stinging force.

My fingers rolled and clenched. A stone hammer.

In a practiced motion, swift and sudden, my fist catapulted into his mouth. A tooth caught on my knuckle and broke away.

I stood over the fallen man, my mind caught in a sea of red and rage. My breathing was deep and steady, the way I'd learned in my years on the streets. My uncle's idiocy had moved from my mom to my father to me in a torturous trickle of consequences. He'd never tried to reconcile with me; he'd watched his own sister die, then disappeared from my life.

Would've been better if he'd stayed gone.

Stepping into my shop? He had it coming.

And who did Johnny Ray think he was, setting this ambush? Did he think such a confrontation would erase the past and put everything right?

I pointed to Uncle Wyatt. "Get him outta here! All of you. You've got sixty seconds to pack up your stuff and get off my property. *Out!*"

Greg Simone and one of the cameramen reached for the bloodied man.

Carla Fleischmann stood in front of the other camera. I thought I saw its light still glowing, but when she stepped away, it was dark. She wore a slight smile, and I could just imagine her pleasure. This was what *The Best of Evil* was all about, the real struggle of real people with the illogical concept of grace.

My little outburst? By her measure, she probably thought it was good television.

"I haven't signed any releases. Air this, and I'll see you in court."

"Don't flatter yourself, Mr. Black."

She turned in her cream skirt and led the way out, leaving the packet of papers on the table.

In Rome, baristas call it "the tail of the tiger."

I placed a demitasse cup beneath the Italian machine's porta-filters and pulled myself an espresso shot. The crema thickened atop the liquid. Near the end of the shot, a lighter trail of coffee trickled through, indicating the flavor had been extracted and only acidity remained.

In Nashville, I call it "your past will come back to bite you."

I wrapped a wet towel around my hand. My knuckle was throbbing, and the skin was ripped. Old inclinations boiled in my belly— testosterone and hatred. In the alleys and storefronts off Portland's Burnside Avenue, I'd taught others a lesson or two, mirroring my father's actions toward me.

But no. I was not like my father.

Unlike Kenny Black, I've never struck a woman. Women play by rules that require mental and verbal acumen. Men? We can't keep up, not in that game. Size, attitude, intimidation—these are the coins men pay to get what they want.

Today I'd found I still had a few coins left. One bought me a solid right hook. What of it? I wanted nothing to do with Wyatt Tremaine.

I tossed back the espresso shot in a gulp, felt it burn a hot trail down my throat.

Yeah, my uncle deserved what he'd got.

# SIXTEEN

Windows rattled as I slammed through the front door of our brownstone. The place was empty. Tuesday. One of Johnny's tanning-booth days.

I had to get out. Get away.

I snatched the car keys from my coat hanging by the door.

Stuffed into the small cockpit of my Honda Civic, I made a sweeping reverse maneuver out onto the street, slipped into first, and peeled across the pavement. I drove toward no destination, taking side streets I'd never traveled in an attempt to lose myself. Not hard to do in Nashville. A spider web of thoroughfares radiates from downtown—Nolensville, Gallatin, and Lebanon pikes and West End Avenue. Circling the city, Old Hickory Boulevard, Harding Place, and Briley Parkway connect these threads.

Caught up in the web, I was a bug of no consequence. Racked with poison, I knew the numbness was on its way.

＊

I know of only one way to combat this poison.

When the venom of regret seeps into your veins, when the paralysis of depression holds you in its icy grip, you need to turn your mind from your own struggles to another's. This is no easy thing to do. Self-preservation mode is strong. Darwin recognized its power and integrated it into his theory of our species' origins.

If good and evil do exist, we are caught in a war. Comcast Cable, the Cheesecake Factory, and MySpace.com will insulate you from it only so long. The larger struggles—conflicts in the Middle East, the fight against racism, corruption in the legal system—are reflections of the internal wrestlings of each human heart.

Murder, hate, envy, and greed.

Theft, lies, lust, and adultery.

No wonder some turn to the power of confession. Others find solace in pleasure. Even the very act of philosophizing can be an escape.

And they all work—for a while. I've tried them.

But there's one thing that works more powerfully than any other—an act of selflessness. Maybe that's because selflessness connects us with God. Didn't he give up his rights as Creator to walk this earth, to face the same temptations, and to surrender his body in payment for our sins? At least that's how the story reads.

He was a redeemer. A remedy. And an example to follow.

No easy thing, that. All the baggage that's been added to the story makes me doubt. Makes me wonder what's really true. I want to believe. I want to follow the example. But the war in my heart still rages.

To talk about it and turn away is to lose another battle. I owed a grieving woman a visit. I looked up her address.

Neely's Bend.

Laid out between two ridges on the northeastern perimeter of Nashville, the valley is quiet, with farmland still stretching between homes and encroaching developments. The road turned darker the farther I went. Angling my car to catch the numbers on the mailboxes, I was able to locate the correct address.

"Who is it?"

In the dark, on her uneven doorstep, I swallowed hard. "My name's Aramis Black. Is this the Michaels residence?"

The house gave a weary groan. A porch light came on.

A voice said, "You wantin' to sell us somethin'? We don't talk to no *sales*man."

"Nothing like that, ma'am."

"Speak your business then. Ain't got all night."

"Uh. I'm Aramis Black."

"Done told me that already. You slow or just plain stupid?"

I recalled Mrs. Michaels's face from the newscast a few nights ago, her sorrowful eyes. I couldn't turn back now.

"I'm the owner of Black's," I said. "The place where your son was killed."

Silence.

Drawn by the bare light bulb over the porch, a huge moth fluttered along the door, changed direction, and bumped into my neck.

"Mrs. Michaels, I was there when it happened, and I can't stop thinking about it, so I can only imagine the hell you've been going through. I thought maybe you'd like someone to talk to about it. Or maybe I need to talk. I don't know. I want to understand why. I wanna know who would do such a thing."

A whisper. "You don't even know."

I gave her a moment to continue, but no words came. "Know what?"

Along the street, piles of leaves were coming to life, crawling along the lawn, leaping and spinning into ghostly shapes. A storm was approaching, a sorcerer using the wind to recruit dead things for the evening's show.

"Know what?" I said again. "I want to understand."

"You can't…can't even *begin* to know the way it rips out a mama's heart. Mr. Black, you have no right. No right at all. You wander onto my property thinkin' that's gonna give you some insight? Only a mother can know what I'm talkin' about, and I don't need you or those tele*vision* folk pokin' them fat noses into my life. I done the best I could—that's the Lord's honest truth. Now. Get yourself *down* off my front step. And don't you come back. Y'all took my son from me. Ain't that enough?"

Her last words were provoked by anguish, but they were unfair. I didn't take her son from her. I kicked at her doormat, watched dust swirl and whip away in the breeze.

"You're right, ma'am," I said. "I don't know what it's like for a mother."

She was waiting—I could feel it.

"But you don't know what it's like either," I added.

"How's that?"

"You don't know what it's like to be a son and lose a mother. That's something you'll never go through. I watched my mom die. Shot just like your son, like Darrell. You're not the only one feeling mad and lonely, and you're not doing me—or yourself, for that matter—any favors by keeping the door closed." I made a quarter turn, still hoping. "Just thought you needed to know that."

"Now I know."

"Can we talk? Please."

"Get yourself gone, Mr. Black, before I give a call to the *police*."

"I just wanna—"

"Good-bye."

The porch light winked off, and I heard the retreat of scuffling feet.

As I trudged to my Honda, dead leaves swirled in my path, crisp and brittle. The same wind that weeks before had enhanced their fiery glory with waving gold and red now beat them down, demanding obedience to the wishes of the night.

# SEVENTEEN

One by one, the mysteries of the past few days riffled through my mind. Driving often frees me in this way. Maybe it's because my hands and feet are occupied, leaving my gray matter to wander at will.

Darrell Michaels. Shot before my eyes. *Spare your soul…and turn your eyes from greed.*

Jessica Tyner. A clump of her hair left in my bedroom, in a box.

Dianne Lewis Black. Her handkerchief, returned and then stolen again.

Freddy C. His warning. *Stay alert… We got ourselves a problem.*

Zigzagging through the streets of Nashville, lost in thought, I was slow to notice I was being followed. Considering the erratic route I'd taken, this had to be intentional.

A white Camry. Shimmering in my side-view mirror.

How long had it been back there? Had it tailed me to Neely's Bend?

We were now traveling down Chickasaw Avenue. I recalled the excursion with my brother along the Natchez Trace Parkway and the enigma of Meriwether Lewis's demise. I'd mocked Johnny's suspicions then, yet here I was, cruising the late-night streets of Music City with this Camry sucking my exhaust.

The dude in the golfing visor?

Watching my mirrors, I made a few turns, sped up, slowed down.

Still there. If he wanted something, why didn't he just come after it?

I crushed the brakes. My Honda swerved, caught, and came to a halt. In the mirror, I watched as the Camry lurched forward, the driver's forehead nearly striking the windshield. It was the same mousy-faced, slump-shouldered man from Grinder's Stand. If not for his antilock brakes, he might've been harder to recognize.

I was out of my car. Slamming my door to make a point.

"You got a problem? We gonna do this?" I marched straight for him, armed with the tire iron I keep under my driver's seat. "Get outta that car, and tell me what you're after!"

His eyes showed me all I needed to know. The heat behind my own eyes is a tangible thing, able to burn through the bravado of most men, and when that fire comes from long-burning embers, it's not easy to douse. Some guys try to keep up the front longer than others, but I always know. I just *know*.

This dude didn't have a chance.

He marked that fact and wasted no time with pretenses. In a flash, he accelerated in reverse, showing admirable skill as he kept it straight as an arrow. He was nearly a block away when he backed the Camry into a driveway—no bumped curbs or tire marks on the lawn—then shifted into first and squealed away in a haze of burnt rubber.

I thought I caught a glimpse of the letters on his license plate. BHT.

My car was no match for the chase. I made my way back onto Dickerson Pike, determined that I would find out who had killed Darrell Michaels and who'd attacked Jessica Tyner.

I was parched. Dog-tired. Ready for a dreamless sleep.

I angled home, driving west over the Woodland Street Bridge, immune to the magic of the lights shimmering on the Cumberland River. Farther south, in the Cool Springs area, stars blinked like warning lights against the bad weather's dark edge.

I pulled into the parking lot next to Johnny Ray's Ford Ranger. He owed me an explanation. An apology at least.

"Uncle Wyatt told me what you did."

"I walk through the door, and that's the first thing you have to say?"

"Hi, Aramis."

"Is he here?"

" 'Course not," Johnny said. "He's no glutton for punishment."

I kicked off my shoes. "I hope he leaves town as quickly as he came." I dropped onto the couch.

"They've put him up in a motel out by the airport."

"They? Meaning the TV show?"

"Uh-huh." My brother tossed me a can of soda and took the armchair.

"Johnny, you had no right."

"Just tryin' to help, kid."

"Thanks, but no thanks."

"Where ya been anyway? I was gettin' worried."

"Out. Driving."

"So why not do the show? What could it hurt?"

"I never asked for your help."

"You wouldn't recognize help if it hit you in the face."

"Ask Uncle Wyatt about that."

"Clocked him pretty good, from what I hear."

"Yeah."

"Feel better now you got the poison outta your system? Ready to let bygones be bygones?"

"Listen. I don't wanna fight with you too, Johnny. Not now. But you set me up."

"You never woulda agreed to it, and you know that's the truth."

"Not. Right. Now."

Johnny Ray wouldn't stop. "I talked with Ms. Fleischmann, and she tells me their crew won't be leaving till tomorrow. She's still inter-ested in talking with you, thinks your story's one that could touch viewers' hearts."

*The Best of Evil.* A nice idea. Too bad it doesn't work like that in the real world.

"It can."

I shook my head. "Shut up already. I'm going to bed."

"Get some sleep, kid. You've had your plate full these past few days."

"Good night."

"And don't forget," he called after me down the hall. "Loews Van-derbilt. Checkout's at eleven. Ms. Fleischmann said she can wait till then but not a minute longer."

"Great. I'll keep that in mind."

"I'm just sayin', is all."

That would've been that. End of story.

One little problem. Detective Meade knocked on the door before I'd finished brushing my teeth.

My previous encounter with the detective had been perfunctory. This time I sensed a shift in attitude.

"May I come in?"

"S'up, Detective? Something wrong?"

"I'd rather talk about it inside, if you don't mind. The storm out here's kicking up something fierce." As if to verify his words, a crack of thunder shook the ground and filled the air with electricity.

"Sure. Okay."

I pulled on a bathrobe and ushered Meade into our dining area. I cleared the table of Johnny's papers, pencils, and granola crumbs. He'd written some lyrics and made chicken scratches, which I identified as the Nashville Number System—a means of writing music or chords or something.

"Water?"

"Please."

I filled two glasses from the Brita pitcher in the fridge, then joined Detective Meade at the table. He was glancing around the room. He was a pro. Nothing obvious. Real casual.

"I like the calendar," he said.

"Yeah? Lotsa great lighthouses in Oregon."

"Never been. It's God's country, from what I hear."

"It's beautiful, if that's what you mean."

"Sorry to disturb you, Aramis. Don't mind if I use your first name, do you?"

I shrugged.

"You're tired," he said. "Long day, I take it?"

"Listen. I'll level with you. I've had some scrapes with the law— not recently, of course—but this isn't real comfortable for me. If

you've got something to tell me, let's get to it. I have to open my shop in the morning."

"Black's?"

"In honor of the family name."

"A noble thing. Family comes first."

"Gets complicated, if you ask me."

"That's why I'm here."

My eyes snapped up. "What now? What's going on?"

Leaning back, glass of water in hand, Detective Meade evaluated me with what seemed to be genuine concern. His gaze was steady. Raindrops looked like glass beads in his short hair. His black leather jacket gave off an earthy scent. Underneath, he wore a T-shirt from an impressionism exhibit at the local Frist Center for the Visual Arts.

I'd been to that one. Spent hours basking in the vibes of artistic genius.

He said, "I caught wind of your encounter with a television crew."

"Word gets around. What'd you hear?"

"That you weren't too thrilled to have a camera in your face."

"That wasn't it. Least not all of it. Who told you?"

"Well, the story was corroborated by Brianne. Real vivacious girl you've got behind the counter there."

"She's new."

"Seems to be a bright girl."

"Good to hear. I felt guilty."

"Guilty?"

"Leaving the way I did. In a hurry."

"She was holding her own. Why did you leave? Because of the television crew?"

"Because of my uncle," I said.

The facts spilled out. Against my better judgment, I found myself starting from the beginning—bits and pieces, weighing the detective's reactions. Then details. Of course he knew about my mother's handkerchief, but now he got the background details. Felt good to let it out, and I actually welcomed the detective's apparent concern.

On some level, I was establishing my innocence. I wanted to build trust, earn his respect. My word is important, and even in Portland during the days of using and dealing, I stood by it.

On the streets, those without integrity are the scary ones.

But the scariest ones? The ones *with* integrity. When they talk, people listen.

"I think you should reconsider," Meade told me.

"Reconsider?"

"Meeting with your uncle. I think he's another piece in this puzzle."

# EIGHTEEN

isten, Detective. I'm not planning to go on that show."

"*The Best of Evil.* It's an intriguing premise."

"It's manipulative."

"It's television," Meade said.

I set down my glass. "She's brainwashed you, hasn't she?"

"Who?"

"Carla. Ms. Fleischmann. Did she put you up to this?"

"Not at all."

"Or that guy. Greg Simone."

"I assure you I stumbled upon something all by myself. It's part of my job."

"Sorry. Didn't mean it that way."

"Apology accepted."

"But I still don't see the connection. Please. Fill me in."

"It has to do with your mother's handkerchief."

"What has to do with it?"

Detective Meade moved forward on the seat, his leather jacket creaking beneath his arms. "Everything," he said. "Or nothing at all. If you've got a little time, I'd like to take you back to the office and show you what I found. Then you can decide for yourself."

Each summer the *Nashville Scene* holds a contest called "You Are So Nashville If…" Johnny Ray and I always pick up a copy when they post the winners, along with honorable mentions and chuckle-worthy submissions.

Some entries reveal political and religious issues: "…your church congregation is referred to as 'the studio audience.'"

Others rib those who move here with dreams of making it on Music Row: "…you slip your demo tape into the bags of trick-or-treaters."

I followed Detective Meade into the West Precinct building on Charlotte Pike and down a long hall to his windowless office. File organizers held his paperwork in neat stacks; pens stood at attention in an insulated, plastic Titans mug; behind his economy desk chair, a framed eight-by-ten photo showed him at Centennial Park, in front of the Parthenon, with his arm around a woman who was holding a baby wrapped in pink.

Under the photo, he'd tacked up a past *Scene* winner: "You Are So Nashville If…you think our Parthenon is better because the other one fell apart."

I pointed. Gave an obligatory laugh. "That's one of my favorites."

"Mine too."

"Is that your wife?"

"Of seven years. Our daughter's five now, full of smiles, and a budding artist. She just started first grade."

"I don't think I'm ready for the married life."

"You're never ready. It's all about choosing the one you love, then loving the one you choose."

I nodded as though such sage advice was commonplace in my circles.

"Take a seat." He slid a business card my way, which read Detective Reginald Meade, Investigations Unit. "Speaking of home, I'm looking forward to seeing my baby soon."

Did he mean his wife? His daughter? His private life was none of my business.

"Am I keeping you?" I asked. "We can do this tomorrow."

"Not at all. I'm working third shift, and it's because of people like you that I'm here."

"So." I shifted in the seat, crossing one leg over the other and rubbing the back of my neck. "Let's hear it, Detective. What've you got?"

"We're still waiting on reports from the scene in Black's. We'll be getting ballistics info within a day or two. The lab's doing tests—spectrographic, chemical, radiographic, all that good stuff. We're cataloging latent prints, and the coroner's office will be submitting a medicolegal autopsy for our investigation."

"Real-life CSI."

"Nothing that dramatic, and it takes a lot longer than an hour."

"What about the guy in the Old Navy shirt? Any word on him?"

"A few of your customers remember seeing him, but no one's identified him."

"I'd never seen him before Thursday."

"And he was there only five minutes?"

"At the most."

"In all my interviews, no one actually saw him fire the gun."

"It was under his coat."

"Yes, you mentioned that in your statement."

"At first it was just a flash of metal. When I realized he had a revolver, that's when I hit the deck. Instinct more than anything."

"Might've saved your life."

"What about Darrell Michaels? I could've dived forward and pulled him down too."

"Never works that way, Aramis. Only in the movies."

"I should've tried."

"Don't beat yourself up over it."

"I feel…"

"Responsible? That's a normal reaction."

"Guilty."

"Because you didn't smell the evil in the air? Because you didn't react with superhuman powers? Because you failed to recognize a killer?"

"Yes."

Detective Meade reached into his bottom drawer. "Let me introduce you to others just like you." He hefted the Nashville white pages onto the desk, where it landed with a thud. "They're called human beings."

"Thanks. I appreciate what you're trying to say."

"Believe me, our unit's not done with this case."

"I hope you catch the guy." For Mrs. Michaels's peace of mind if nothing else.

"We're doing our best to apprehend the responsible party. We subpoenaed the security cameras from adjoining establishments in case there was footage capturing sidewalk activity. Unfortunately, we found nothing helpful."

"Something'll turn up."

"We're counting on it." Meade thumbed through the files on his desk, pulled one loose. "As for the residential burglary you reported, well, I did some investigating. Initially I ran a background check on you to determine your character and credibility, not to mention your potential for a crime like the one perpetrated on the Vandy campus."

"The assault on Jessica Tyner."

"Exactly. And in all honesty, after pulling up your list of priors, I decided to have her come in and look through some photos. I added yours to the mix."

"You what?"

"She said she saw you at the party—"

"Great."

"She cleared you, though. Like the assailant's other victims, she only saw him for a split second, but she says he was shorter and older."

"Good. I mean, I'm relieved."

"We have to consider every angle, every possibility. You've never been charged with a crime of that nature, of course, but it's not unusual to see cross-contamination between drug dealers and sex offenders."

"I've been clean over a year."

"That's to be commended." He lowered his chin. "And I say that with the utmost sincerity and respect, Aramis. Couldn't have been an easy thing to do."

"Still not easy."

"One day at a time. You're on the right track." He spread the file open. "I'm sure you've heard of the Neighborhood Watch program. Directors and block captains funnel information our way, keeping us posted on suspicious activity in specific areas. Nationwide, we're finding community participation to be a vital link in crime prevention."

I could vouch for its effectiveness. In the past I'd dreaded those pesky neighbors who felt obligated to inform the authorities of every shady transaction.

Funny the way things turn around. Now I was hoping for such a report.

The detective said, "I paid a visit to the director in your complex."

I sat up. "We have a narc in our building?"

"A caring neighbor, Aramis, not a narc. It's all a matter of perspective, isn't it?"

"Who is it?"

"Her name's in the public record."

"Mrs. Vaughn?"

"She did have something to report."

"Should've known. She's always walking her dog, working in the gardens—"

"Sounds mighty dangerous."

I laughed at that. "Okay. What'd she say?"

"She'd already documented some of Monday's nonresident activity in and around your building. That evening, while out with her dog—"

"A bulldog. The thing scares me."

"Apparently it scared a middle-aged male exiting your building. He looked down and tried to hurry past Mrs. Vaughn. She caught him coming from your entryway and shoving something into his coat pocket. She marked the time as 5:18 p.m."

"Before Johnny or I get home from work."

"Hence her concern."

"Could she identify the guy?"

"She described him in detail. She's been very accurate in the past." Meade ran a grooved fingernail down the report. "In her words, he had 'an angular face, crow's-feet around dark eyes, and black hair with spots of gray near the temples.' "

"That could be a lot of people."

"He wore 'peglegged blue jeans and a cowboy shirt with pearl buttons and white stitching, and his boots were scuffed at the toes.' "

"Sounds like Uncle Wyatt."

"Wyatt Tremaine. Yes, I'd have to agree."

"How do *you* know him?"

Detective Meade leveled his gaze, tapping a finger on the phone book. "He was here earlier, filing charges of a physical assault. Somebody punched him. He brought witnesses, as well as photographic evidence."

I jolted to my feet. "Did he tell you *his* part in the deal?"

"So you admit to it?"

"Is that what this is all about?"

Meade held up pale palms to settle me down. "Please take your seat, Aramis."

I ran through my options. Paced. Then eased myself back into the chair.

"Don't misunderstand my intentions," the detective said. "Family comes first. I believe you and your uncle have some grief between you, and it may be a good time to air it out. Face it, deal with it, and put it to rest."

"Am I free to go, Detective?"

"You are. But I should mention that Mr. Tremaine's willing to drop the charges."

"If?"

"If you agree to face him on the television show."

"Blackmail. I'd expect nothing less from the man."

"Well, it's also an opportunity, the way I see it. There must be a reason he wants that handkerchief. This might be your one chance to put all the pieces together. Not to mention, Aramis, that years of unforgiveness get old—for you and for everyone else. It really is a matter of maturity, isn't it, when all is said and done?"

# NINETEEN

Forgiveness? Maybe it comes easy to some people. Not to me.

So why, standing in Black's this morning, did I dial Loews Vanderbilt Hotel?

Aside from my desire to avoid assault charges, I hoped to corner Uncle Wyatt and get some answers.

"Carla Fleischmann's room, please."

"Fleischmann? Thank you, sir. I'll put you through."

A short pause, two rings, and there she was. Even at six o'clock, she sounded composed and professional. When I explained the purpose of my call, she expressed cautious optimism. "Really? So you're interested in doing the show."

"Yeah."

"Glad to hear it, Mr. Black. I'm sorry if you feel coerced in any way."

"Oh, that? A little blackmail never hurt anyone. No worries."

"For the record, it was Greg's idea. He's well intentioned, in a subversive way. He believes in the passion of your story—really owns it on a heart level."

"I'm touched. Now do you need me to sign those papers you left?"

"Yes. If we can go over them together, that'd be optimal."

"I can't guarantee my response on the show."

"Any more violent outbursts, Mr. Black, and you *will* face criminal charges."

"Of course. What I meant was, I don't know if I can forgive my uncle. Don't know if I can actually say the words. Is that a problem?"

"All the better, actually. Good editing can streamline or sanitize the show, but it all comes down to human drama. It's the bread and butter of reality television. Oftentimes the unpredictable episodes are the most effective."

"And they get the highest ratings?"

"That too."

"When do we—what's the terminology—shoot the segment?"

"The actual filming will take place next month. If you're selected, we'll fly you to an undisclosed location and lead you through the process. Expenses will be covered as well as a per diem for meals. First things first, though," said Carla. "We'll want to do a recorded interview and go over the eligibility requirements. You'll fill out a nine-page questionnaire—"

"Nine pages?"

"There's also an authorization and release form as well as certification of veracity. If any provisions of the certification are breached, you agree to pay the network one hundred thousand dollars per breach, plus disgorgement of any money or valuables received in connection with the breach."

"You're scaring me now, Ms. Fleischmann."

"We'll also have complete access to your public records, credit reports, and such. It's legal protection for both parties."

"Uh. What about minor blemishes?"

"Meaning?"

"My record. It's not squeaky clean. Got a few drug-related issues, but that's not who I am. Not anymore."

"There's actually nothing to fear so long as you're honest and uphold your end of the agreement. It's all in print, in black and white for you to see, and you'll receive a copy for your own peace of mind."

"Well, in *that* case...," I said with exaggerated enthusiasm.

"Still want to proceed?"

"If I didn't know better, I'd think you were trying to talk me out of it."

"On the contrary," Carla said, "I'm setting the hook. Once you take the bait, we don't want to lose you."

Brianne was punctual and cheery, a real angel. Although five years separated us, twenty-two didn't seem too young to me. Not when we were together. She carried herself with confidence that conveyed she knew what she wanted and wouldn't let obstacles stand in her way.

I like that in a woman. Particularly if I'm what she wants.

Brianne's desires, so far, remained unclear.

Bottom line? She was good with customers, satisfactory with espresso drinks, and a reliable employee. Brianne Douglas: better-than-expected employee. Aramis Black: better-be-careful bossman.

"Here you go, sir." She handed a blended coffee drink to the last person in line. "Thank you, and have a great day."

"You too. Don't lose that smile."

On his way out, the man nearly bumped into my packaged whole-bean display.

"Brianne." I nudged her hip with mine. "He was into you."

"He was just being nice."

"Right."

"It's the way guys are, you know? Flirty and charming as long as they're waiting to get what they want."

"Like girls are any different?"

Brianne shook her head. "They're totally different."

"Says who?"

"Once a guy gets what he wants, he's bored. Challenge over, ready to move on to the next thing." She was wiping down the espresso machine. "Girls, on the other hand, are harder to read."

"No kidding."

"It's true." Brianne twisted the knob so that steam hissed and curled. "Once girls set their eyes on something, they'll do just about anything to keep someone else from cutting in."

"I've seen guys like that."

"No you haven't. Not to the same degree."

"You lost me."

"Guys," she clarified, "can usually let go and let a relationship slowly die. Girls will almost die before letting the relationship go."

"Okay, okay. I'm convinced you know exactly what *you* mean."

"Aramis, you are a hopeless cause."

"Is that any way to speak to your employer?"

"Ahh, he's playing the boss card."

"Get to work," I said. "I've got errands to run."

"Ha ha."

"No. Seriously. I'll be back in a while, so feel free to make yourself a sandwich and a drink. I'll have my cell. I won't be far away."

"Where're you going this time? Aren't you going to tell me what all this hush-hush stuff's about? It's driving me crazy."

"Sorry, Brianne. All top secret."

"You're determined to keep me in the dark, aren't you?"

"I'll tell you all about it when I return. Let me just say this." I placed a hand on my chest. "Brianne Douglas, you may be in the presence of a future star."

"Hey, not fair." She stomped one foot in mock petulance as I moved away. "Aramis, come back."

I threw my sweatshirt over my head, winked, then headed out the back door.

Carla Fleischmann and I agreed to meet for an early lunch at the hotel restaurant. I headed to Loews on foot after a detour into FedEx Kinko's for the required copies of my driver's license as well as digital photos of family, friends, and yours truly. I pulled a travel-size cologne from my pocket and slapped some on my face, under my sleeves.

Carla met me in the lobby—in a charcoal gray slit skirt with black nylons.

"Quick question, Mr. Black, before we get started."

"Sure."

"Have you or any of your immediate family ever been a member of SAG?"

"Excuse me?"

She tossed her red hair to the side. "The Screen Actors Guild."

"Uh. No. Doesn't seem to run in our genes."

"Wonderful. We can't allow any conflicts of interest. How about civil-action suits? Any filed by you or anyone related to you?"

"Off the top of my head, the answer's no."

"Good."

Greg Simone joined us for the meal, clipboard in hand. He was all business. Before I'd finished my first bite, he was guiding me through the paperwork trail, verifying that I would subject myself to all network obligations, stipulations, and heretofore undisclosed gyrations.

After the forms were explained and completed, signed and sealed, he and Carla led me to a private meeting room where we rendez-voused with the camera crew. They'd arranged some of those shiny, silvery panels to help with the lighting and set up two plush armchairs at an angle to each other to give the interview a cozy, we're-here-in-so-and-so's-living-room feel.

"Will I have to face my uncle again?"

"We have an interview with him later today. But you? No. Not until the filming next month, assuming you are selected."

"Okay."

"We prefer to capture that first encounter with no script, no coaching." Greg leaned closer, as though divulging a trade secret. "We can always go back and make changes."

I curled my lip. "I'd say Uncle Wyatt and I already had our first encounter."

"Yes, well. We got that on tape, didn't we, Roger?"

One of the cameramen answered Greg Simone with a nod.

"And the charges? They've been dropped as part of our agreement, right?"

"Absolutely," Greg assured me.

I played it cool. Eased into an armchair while staring at the cameraman. Wedged my sleeves up onto my elbows, displaying my tats for all to see. Over the years I'd figured out how to spend my coins of attitude and intimidation, and it felt good—downright intoxicating—to know they still bought me instant respect.

Every man yearns for and needs respect in the same way that women need love. But just like love, respect can come in guises so tainted and deformed that we risk damage by embracing it.

For example, some might think fear's the same thing as respect. It's not.

I learned that from my father.

# TWENTY

Sitting on our couch that evening, feet propped on the coffee table, my father didn't have the courtesy to get up or the thoughtfulness to offer sentiments about how long it'd been and how he'd missed me and that he hoped my shop was faring well after the Elliston shooting.

"'Bout time you dragged yourself in. I been waitin' here since the beginning of *Star Search*."

"You watch those old reruns?"

"And I been thinkin' of your brother every minute it's been on."

"Yeah. He's gonna be a star."

"Got that right. Just a matter of time."

"Is Johnny here?" Hoping for a buffer.

"Stepped out. He'll be back with some sorta ethnic food—Thai, Vietnamese, or what have you. Told him to pick us up a case of beer so we can celebrate."

"What're we celebrating?"

"His gig tomorrow."

My dad lives in the suburbs of Bowling Green, Kentucky. Since my move to Nashville, he's visited twice, and on both occasions he failed to set foot into Black's. However, now that the favored son was performing, it'd be different. Good to know where things stood.

"Well, Dad, I'm gonna go change."

"Do whatchu gotta. Don't worry about your old man."

"Okay. Just, uh…make yourself at home."

He folded his arms behind his head and sank another inch lower on the cushions. "Already taken care of."

"I can see that."

On my way down the hall, I inched open the studio door and sighed with relief when I spotted Dad's stuff sack. He'd be in here, as agreed.

"Yeah. The spare floor space will suit you just fine," I whispered.

They carried on deep into the night, Dad and Johnny Ray.

Dad had said he needed to talk with me—something about my mother—so I pried him for answers. As usual, he was more interested in talking about himself.

After two beers I bowed out of the conversation. From experience I know the third beer is where discretion begins to dissolve. I just wasn't ready for the easy banter that passes between Johnny Ray and Kenny Black. I don't hold it against my brother. It's just a melancholy thing that twines around my chest and throat and leaves me incapable of decent conversation.

Except that being out of sight but within earshot is almost always worse.

I threw aside my covers and stomped along the floorboards.

"Does anyone in this house, anyone at all"—I pierced each man with a glare—"give a rat's tail that I have to be up at five o'clock?"

"Sorry, kid." My brother's face was a picture of contrition. "We'll keep it down."

"You go back to bed, Aramis, and show some respect for your old man. We'll behave ourselves. Ain't that right?" My father bumped Johnny's knee with his own. "Just sittin' here with a few long-necked friends. No harm in that."

"This, Johnny—this is what I warned you about."

Johnny Ray wobbled forward. "Here on out we're quiet as church mice. Promise. Scout's honor and hope to die."

"You swear?"

"Swear?" Dad's voice had gone raspy. "Johnny, did the boy say 'swear'?"

Before my brother could respond, Dad burst out with laughter and slurred through a stream of epithets and curse words that nearly exhausted my own hefty list. Johnny acted horrified, before collapsing over his knees in a fit of giggles. My father, offering up the *pièce de résistance,* slapped his left hand down over his right elbow and lifted a single-fingered salute to the only man in the room who had dared to interrupt the party.

I'd like to say I was the better man.

I wasn't.

Dad and Johnny watched my tantrum, amused as I swept their bottles from the table in a spray of beer and foam. Shiny caps spun through the air. One bottle hit the wall, shattering. I kept the focus of my wrath on things inanimate and nonhuman—rising above the standards set by my father.

Or so I told myself.

Their giggles turned into wonder and then indignation.

"Hey, boy, what's your problem?"

Johnny put out an arm. "Lemme talk to him, Dad."

My father started to rise, then fell back. "He ain't changed a bit. Same whiny little runt!" His eyes were bleary, but deep at their core an old fire burned.

I was shaking. Ready to establish a new pecking order.

Before I could give his drunken carcass a beating, I swiped my keys and headed out the door.

Tranquilized by the sound of tires on wet pavement and the warmth coming through the Honda's vents, I drove. And drove.

My soul called out for a listening ear, for assistance.

When dawn peeled back the first strips of Thursday morning, revealing pink-tinged grays and ruffled clouds of orange, I sensed a shift inside. More than anything I suppose it was a weariness. A surrender.

Same whiny little runt?

There was a truth here I'd have to face. I couldn't run forever.

The needle on the Honda's gauge was nearing E, so I headed down Eighth Avenue to a favorite economy gas station. While the tank filled, I ate a chocolate cream-filled doughnut and guzzled a Purity orange juice.

From there, I followed Eighth until it became Franklin Pike. I knew now where I was headed. A few minutes later I turned onto Tyne Boulevard. The road here dips and curves, hugging the hills between beautiful homes set far back among the trees. It was only the fifth time I'd been here, only the second time uninvited.

But I knew Sammie wouldn't mind.

Pillars of mortar and brick, topped by lead-paned lanterns, stand on both sides of the driveway. Set into the stonework, a mailbox bears the name *Rosewood* in simple black letters. Samantha's parents passed away a few years ago, and she lives here with Miss Eloise, keeping her grandmother company in her final days.

There is no gate. The property is off the main thoroughfares, and Samantha claims the horses' movements in the stable and the bark of her trusty golden retriever are security enough.

Her claims were substantiated by throaty howls as I edged up the drive, but I knew the dog to be old and harmless.

"Hi, Digger." I stepped out and let him sniff my hand. His tail started wagging, and he lifted a paw. "There you go," I said. "Good manners, just like your mama."

"Aramis."

I looked up, flashed a sheepish smile. "Am I too early for breakfast?"

From the wraparound porch, Sammie returned the smile. "I suppose not. I've been up for bit, reading to Miss Eloise. She couldn't sleep. What about the shop?"

"I have twenty minutes. Maybe twenty-five before I need to head over there."

"We'll work with the time available."

"I needed to see you."

"Good to see you too."

"No. I mean… Never mind." I climbed wide steps to the porch.

"Hmm. Tell me, Aramis, do you think a cheese omelet, grits, and hickory-smoked bacon will suffice?"

"Sounds great," I said. "But what about my coffee?"

Sammie laughed. "You'll have to see to it yourself."

# TWENTY-ONE

Mystery built upon mystery that morning, from an unexpected source. Life—you gotta love it. Always keeping us on our toes.

"Aramis, we made it through our first week together."

"Huh? What're you talking about?"

"Since the Elliston shooting." Brianne brushed back her blond hair. "You and I, we put things back in order and cranked this place back into action."

"Didn't lose too many customers, that's true."

"Most are more loyal than ever, I'd say. Plus the tips've been great." She grabbed a bag of whole-bean coffee and weighed it in her palm. "Think about it. You could've given up, but, no, you rose to the challenge. You're Back-in-Black."

She nailed me in the chest with the bag.

"Hey." I looked into the dining area. "We have customers."

She glanced up from beneath dark eyelashes and put her finger to her lips in feigned remorse. "Sorry, boss."

"What's got into you this morning?"

"Well, you have been leaving me on my own quite a bit, so—"

"Done a great job, by the way. Thanks."

"It's just nice to have you around."

"Now you're buttering me up. What do you want, Brianne?"

"Can't a girl have a little fun?"

"Without trying to get something? No. Not from my experience."

"You're a bitter old man."

"Twenty-seven is not old."

A smile played along her lips. The sun was shining through the front window, cocooning us in the morning's warmth. Standing there in our ridiculous aprons amid the heat and the aroma of coffee, I felt a rush of attraction. Her gray blue eyes locked on to mine, holding me in place.

"We should have dinner together," she suggested.

"Not a good idea."

"How about tonight?"

"Can't."

"Give me one good reason."

"We've got Johnny Ray packin' the house at seven thirty."

"Tomorrow night then. I'll cook calzone, my specialty."

"No, Brianne."

"You're avoiding it, aren't you?"

"Avoiding? No, listen. We're in a working relationship."

"So let's work at it."

"I'm your boss. It's not right."

"And I'm your only employee, so what's it matter?"

"What is with you college girls? What happened to subtlety? Used to be that the guys made the first move."

She arched an eyebrow. "All I did was mention dinner."

I retied my apron, turning toward the mahogany counter.

"Anyway," she added, "you *are* interested."

"Get to work. Make sandwiches for lunch. Clean the sinks. *Anything.*"

"Your tattoos don't fool me, Aramis. You're afraid of your own emotions."

I looked back at her. "Listen. We shouldn't be mixing our work and our private lives. I doubt Sammie would approve."

"Now I see." Brianne blinked once. "It's okay if it's you and *your* boss."

"Hey. Wait."

She moved into the kitchen and started cutting ham into thin, precise slices.

The chiming of the door pulled me away to meet the next customer. This tug and pull, this hesitation on my part—these are the reasons workplace relationships are unwise. I couldn't even focus on my job.

All that was forgotten when I saw the heavyset woman at my counter, her fleshy face recognizable from the Channel Two broadcast a week earlier. She wore a loose floral blouse over her wide frame, pleated slacks, and white nurse's shoes.

"Aramis Black. You know who I am, don't you? Reckon we can talk?"

"If that's what you want."

"Didn't make the drive down here for *nothin'*, now did I? Been a week today."

"Today," I echoed.

Mrs. Michaels let her violet eyes run over the counter, the tiled floor where her son had died, then back to my face. She teared up, raised a hand to her mouth, and nodded toward the entry.

"Yes," I said. "Let's take a walk."

⚊⊏⊐⚊

After tossing aside the green apron and informing Brianne that I was stepping out, I joined Mrs. Michaels on the sidewalk. Don't ask how it happened. Within ten strides along Elliston Place, I'd taken the woman's hand in mine.

It felt natural. Necessary.

We walked like that for the next five or ten minutes. A mother. A son. Cut through with grief, she clung to my hand so tightly I thought my bones would break. Her hips and tummy quivered with each step, and I watched approaching pedestrians move aside in veiled disgust.

I thought she was beautiful.

A woman without much education who'd raised seven children. She was someone to be honored and appreciated. She would not walk this earth forever, as I'd been reminded by Miss Eloise's feeble form at the Rosewood table a few hours earlier.

"I don't hold nothin' against you," Mrs. Michaels told me. "I didn't mean what I said. Weren't the fault of you or no one else, what happened to my boy."

"I should've done something…"

"Darrell, he just got hisself mixed up with the wrong sort. Can't punish yourself over that, Mr. Black. He's in the good Lord's hands now."

"The killer should be brought to justice."

"Let's keep walkin'," Mrs. Michaels said. "Got some things I'd like to tell ya."

The cool shadows of Centennial Park's magnolia trees welcomed us. The day was warm. I spotted ducks bobbing on the pond's wind-feathered waters. Magnolias and dogwoods extended over the serpentine path where a pack of college students jogged, some old men played chess, and a bag lady inched along with a wooden cart and a dog on a rope.

The dog strained to reach me as we passed, yipping, wiggling its body.

"She's just the cutest, ain't she?" said Mrs. Michaels.

"She knows me. We visit almost every morning on my way to work." I freed my hand and waved. "Hey, Tina. Seen Freddy C?"

Tina barely lifted her chin. Between her mumblings, she said, "Hard to find, by daylight's glow. An owl flying at night, so low."

"Tell Freddy hi for me if you see him. Tell him to swing by."

"Walking in alleys, rarely dallies."

"See you later."

As we continued on, Mrs. Michaels gave me a questioning look. "Not to be rude, but that woman don't seem *right*. You say she lives in the park?"

"Something like that. Rhymes are Tina's thing, her trademark."

"Is she able to feed herself?" Spoken with concern.

I nodded.

"And that dog?"

"They get by. I've brought stuff from home a time or two, but Tina prefers to scratch out a living on her own. She makes crafts, wall hangings, centerpieces from twigs and flowers. All sortsa stuff. Sells them when she can."

"Mighty respectable."

"And she always feeds her dog first."

"A good woman." Mrs. Michaels looked back over her shoulder.

"So." I stopped to scoop up a stone. "You told me you wanted to talk."

"Mr. Black, I just plain don't know how to start this off."

"Look, I'm skipping rocks. Just say what comes to mind."

"An awful lot on my mind these days, and that's the Lord's honest truth. But he don't give us more than we can bear. Ain't that so? He won't allow it."

"Seems like he allows a lot of things. I don't claim to understand."

She sighed. "My boy. Darrell."

I threw another stone, counted eight skips.

"Darrell was trouble right from the get-go. My third child. A preemie. Not quite four pounds and able to fit right here in my hand. Like a little bird. We was livin' in Memphis then, didn't have no insurance, and that put us in a spot. His daddy started workin' overtime, two jobs and some mechanical repairs on the side. Anything to get by—that's what he done. We had two children already. The twins and the rest came later." She watched my next throw. "Wasn't no one's fault, not really. But when his daddy started sellin' dope, with his buddies at work and all, we thought we *finally* had ourselves a way out. Just long enough to get our heads above—that was the plan."

Five large skips. And a frightened duck. I looked up at Mrs. Michaels.

"Darrell seen his daddy go to jail the first time when he was eight or nine. The second time, his daddy got eighteen years. Still there. Well, he was Darrell's hero, and my boy weren't *never* the same after that." Mrs. Michaels shook her head and brought both hands to her neck so that bags of flesh wobbled on her arms' undersides. "Yessir, he was his daddy's shadow. That's how it was from day one. He did just like him, followin' his footsteps. The drugs. The jail time. All along, even when the judge was pointin' that finger, I knowed he was a good kid. Heart big enough to go 'round."

"He was cleaning up, wasn't he?"

"Hard to say. I moved here in ninety-eight, that house on Neely's Bend. Old place, run-down, but a fenced yard for the young uns to play. Told Darrell he weren't welcome bringin' his *crack* hoes into *my* home. He was a charmer. Always had hisself a girl. Well, he comes knockin' on my door one night, all the ways from Memphis. He's in real trouble. Done got a man ready to kill him."

"Let me guess. A jealous husband."

"Coulda been. Didn't ask, didn't wanna know. I told him if he wants my help, he first needs to take hisself straight to the *po*lice and tell them what he done. Drugs and all. Get it off his chest and stop runnin'."

"I like your style."

"Helpin' my boy—that's all I had in mind."

"So he did it? Went to the cops?"

"And he was sittin' at my side come Sunday. A good kid, like I told you."

"Okay. He did time, got out, did the church thing, and straightened around."

"His PO was keepin' an eye on him, said he been testin' clean."

"Leroy Parker, right?"

She huffed in agreement.

"They said on the news that Parker suspected drug dealers in Darrell's death. Do you think that's true?"

"Could be. Darrell had been tryin' to keep clean. He was supposed to meet up that mornin' with his PO. They'd been worryin' themselves over some deal, some money-makin' scheme. Darrell and Mr. Parker, they found somethin', they said, a gift from above." She noticed my expression. "'Tween you and me, Mr. Parker ain't the *shiniest* penny in the jar. But he's smart, yessir. He was keepin' my boy occupied. Fact is, I think he made it up, the whole entire thing."

"You lost me, Mrs. Michaels. Made what up?"

"Oh, this nonsense about gold bullion and Meriwether Lewis."

"As in Lewis and Clark?"

"All a big secret, accordin' to Mr. Parker. Don't tell no one, he says. Well, plain as the nose on my face, it was hogwash. A lie to keep Darrell's mind off them drugs and all. Seemed like a good thing. Until it went belly up on 'em."

"You don't think he was telling the truth?"

"Mr. Leroy Parker may be many things, but an honest man? No sir."

"So it was all a joke."

"A joke?" She cupped her hands over her belly and peered across the water. "Not now that my boy's dead, it ain't."

"Maybe there's something to it, though."

"Not by my reckonin'. That Mr. Lewis, he's been dead and buried two hundred years. The man took secrets to the grave, and all y'all would be better off not knowin' what they were. Darrell ought never to have listened to Mr. Parker. I see that now. They was just *askin'* for trouble when they started diggin' up them ghosts."

"Ghosts," I repeated.

"That's right."

"Can I ask a silly question?"

"Don't see hows it can hurt."

"Leroy Parker. Does he, by any chance, wear golfing visors?"

She turned and gave me a curious stare. "Seen him wear orange for the Tennessee Vols, but come basketball season he's a Tar Heels fan through and through. He puts on North Carolina blue."

# TWENTY-TWO

On stage Johnny Ray Black becomes a different person. He pulls down the brim of his Stetson, corralling that hair, shading his eyes above a glistening smile. He prowls—I swear that's the best description—like a caged cat. Oh sure, he's aware of crowd perception, but there's no gimmick to it. No pretense. It's still my brother up there—in amplified form.

He's the bigger, better, badder Johnny Ray. The man every woman wants to be with and every man wants to be.

Black's had never seen so many customers. Advertisements in the *Scene* and *All the Rage* had paid off, and fliers distributed by a dedicated street team added numbers to our gathering.

Sammie was here, radiant in a fitted, white, sleeveless dress. Her auburn hair brushed against her smooth back as she allowed me to give her a gentlemanly hug.

"She likes you," Brianne said.

"No. That's Sammie's style, just being polite."

"What about you?"

"Huh?"

"Would you be so polite as to join me for calzone tomorrow night?"

"Didn't we settle this already? Get another pot brewing, please."

The first set kicked off at seven thirty. All original tunes.

Freddy C ambled in midway but disappeared before I could speak with him. He still owed me an explanation for his concern.

Johnny Ray started strong. The audience latched on and stayed with him. By the third song, he was singing with his heart on his sleeve, his mouth brushing the microphone as he held a fist to his chest.

"Where'd I go so wrong…in tryin' to do things right?

"I'm winnin' the war, that may be true…but still I'm losin' this fight."

The crowd followed him, note for note.

"When I'm comin' through the back door…why does a cold front chill my bones?

"Our love was a thing of beauty…but our house, it ain't a home.

"So I'm askin'…"

He held out the microphone, and the crowd repeated his cry: "I'm asking…"

"Where'd I go so wrong…in tryin' to do things right?"

Nashville music fans are jaded and educated. They dip their toes into the waters of blues and rock, punk and reggae, country and hip-hop. On any given night, you'll find live music in this town; oftentimes, accomplished musicians play for a pittance, just to sharpen their chops.

It's a running joke that there are no real Nashvillians in Music City. To find a true born-and-bred is to rub shoulders with nostalgia. This place has seen it all. And yet, beneath the surface, there remains a little-brother stigma—always one step behind LA and New York City. Always trying to catch up, to earn respect.

Maybe that's why I feel comfortable here.

There I stood, the little brother—and hugely proud—taking orders, making drinks, cleaning tables, directing the man at the mixing board to add more bass. As if I had the slightest inkling about sound dynamics.

I just knew I wanted to feel it in my bones.

Although cutting edge and heartfelt, Johnny Ray's songs pay homage to the Nashville sound, with mandolins and fiddles and an upright bass providing texture. I saw a couple of my older patrons tapping toes and nodding heads. Dad was clapping his hands in rapt approval.

Twenty-somethings made up the majority of the crowd. They were less demonstrative, more interested in each other. But they were here. That said a lot.

Johnny Ray: "So I'm askin'…"

Audience: "I'm askin'…"

I joined in: "Where'd I go so wrong…in tryin' to do things right?"

Johnny Ray never discusses his lyrics, convinced that each listener should enjoy the songs on a personal level. He says if he tells where the lyrics come from, he'll jinx it. Suck out all the magic.

Maybe he's right.

Tonight I didn't want the song's inspiration interfering with my interpretation. I could feel those words down in my bones.

*Where'd I go so wrong…in tryin' to do things right?*

Watching him perform, I was happier than ever to have joined him in Nashville. The changes I'd made here were worth the effort, and yet my previous lifestyle seemed determined to tag along. Darrell Michaels's murder had ushered it all back. But after my stroll with Mrs. Michaels, I was starting to make some sense of it.

Darrell believed there was a cache of gold to be found. He went looking for it, came up empty-handed, then turned back to old habits in disappointment. It seemed logical.

Last week, in desperation, he came to me. I could still feel Darrell's fingers locked on my wrist.

Seconds later he was dead.

Then there was Parker. Following Johnny Ray and me. Tracking me the other night when I was alone. Did he hope to be led to some treasure? Did he actually believe it existed?

Perhaps Johnny Ray was right. Maybe we were descendants of Meriwether Lewis. Could that be why Mom died—trying to protect hidden gold?

"What're you doing, Brianne?"

She had tied off a garbage sack and was half dragging it toward the alleyway door. The floors and walls throbbed as the band started the next song.

"I'll get that."

"I'm a big girl, Aramis."

"Not that big."

She smiled and let the bag rest. "It's not heavy, but it sure smells." She wrinkled her nose. "Thank you, Aramis. I'll make sure the counter's covered."

I lifted the bag and pushed through the reinforced metal door.

Humidity had settled in the alley, trapping odors, muffling sound. An SUV turned past the alley's mouth, its lights splashing the brick wall before slicing around the corner.

Key in hand, I reached the Dumpster and worked the padlock loose. I'd tossed in the bag and reset the lock when a jolt exploded in my lower back. The impact waved a black curtain over my eyes, and I almost buckled. I was back in Portland. In the alleys.

Survival mode.

Instincts slammed into gear; in counterattack, I thrust back my right elbow as I dipped and swung around my right leg like a wooden plank.

Before I connected, another blow bounced off my shoulder.

I stumbled. Tried to regain control.

A third blow caught me in the side.

Reeling, spinning...

Dropping.

My forehead bounced against the dark green Dumpster, the impact wringing out consciousness like dirty laundry water.

I willed myself to hang on. Pain swarmed through me.

"Aramis Black. You lackin' in smarts there?"

My face was down. A knee in my back.

"Why don't we just make this clean and simple," the voice continued as a zip tie was yanked tight around my wrists. "You help me out, gimme the 411 on this Lewis deal, and I let you go. Done and over. Nothin' personal."

I groaned.

"Here's the other option, in case you got fool-crazy ideas in that head of yours. You don't help me out. You decide to get smart with me… Well then, me and that cute little blonde in there get to be friends. Brianne Douglas? I say that right? Yeah, I take her hair and throw her down. Show her what she's been missin'."

I could see the man's shadow on the pavement. I could smell his sweat and the stink of stale cigarettes. Something about his tone… I knew this guy.

I took deep breaths—regaining clarity, gathering strength.

"Tellin' ya, Aramis. All you got to do is answer one question."

"What do you want?"

"One tiny little question, and then I drop outta sight. Deal?"

The hollow thwump-bumpa-thwump of the bass was audible in the alley. My brother was rockin' the place, and my father was proud as could be. Brianne was responsible for the bar and the customers. There was no one to worry about me, no one coming to my rescue.

"Okay."

Smoker's breath feathered through my hair. "Where is the whip?"

"The what?"

"The whip."

"Parker," I said. "Leroy Parker sent you, didn't he?"

"The man's pathetic, so forget about him. The guy I work for, he's in a whole other league." The breath got thicker, hotter. Closer. "I'm not messin' around."

Arching my spine, I thrust my head back into the man's face, felt my skull slam into the ridge of his nose. He growled and cursed. I tried to roll, but his fingers twined through my hair and yanked back.

"The whip! Where is it?"

"I don't stinkin' know about any whip."

"Last chance. Where is it?"

"I. Don't. Know."

He released my hair, directed a hard kick into my thigh. "If I was you, lover boy, I'd be keepin' an eye out for Brianne. What happened to poor Darrell—that oughta be a warning to you. *In cauda venenum.*"

ICV—my old anarchist pals from Portland, Oregon. Why were they here now? Had Darrell been involved with ICV? Had the anarchists moved beyond Oregon's and Washington's borders?

*They're comin' for you next...* Darrell had tried to warn me.

In the stink of the alleyway, I willed myself into a sitting position. My attacker had vanished, giving me no clues to his identity except a rear glimpse of his hooded sweatshirt, jeans, and black high tops.

I found my keys in a pool of sludge and worked the edge of one against the zip tie till it popped free. Rubbing my wrists, I entered the shop and went to the back washroom to clean the blood and straighten my clothes.

"Aramis." Brianne watched me take my place at the espresso machine. "You okay there? You're limping."

"Slipped. Out by the Dumpster."

"No wonder you're all dirty. Maybe you should sit down."

"I'm fine."

"You're sure?"

"I'm sure."

"Well, anyway, clumsy," she called over the music, "we're falling behind. Can you help with these drinks while I clear tables?"

I reached for the order in her hand.

# TWENTY-THREE

Unbelievable, Johnny Ray. You knocked 'em dead! If those Music Row executives don't sit up now and pay attention, then I say they got their heads up—"

"Dad, I get the point."

"It's the truth, Son. You had 'em eatin' outta your palm."

"I still gotta pay my dues. Show some respect. They don't take too kindly to outsiders throwing their weight around."

"Outsider? You been at this for a couple of years now."

"I'm just sayin', is all."

"Well, you done good, mister. Made your old man proud."

Johnny tilted his hat back, ran a hand through his hair. He was basking in the afterglow.

I set a plate in front of him—a dill pickle beside a whole-wheat sandwich packed with lean turkey, lettuce, tomatoes, and sprouts. He didn't even ask about the condiments, so I knew he must be famished. He took a bite and closed his eyes as he chewed. A woman slipped into the seat beside him and dabbed at his mouth with a napkin.

"Thanks, Sarah."

"Sure thing, sugar."

I rolled my eyes. "That was our best turnout ever, Johnny."

"Thanks, kid." He poked my side. "I did have inside connections."

I grunted. Tried to mask my dull aches and pains.

Dad jabbed me in the other side. "Aramis, whatchu think about this brother of yours? Wasn't he amazing? Keep bookin' him, charge a cover fee, and you might just get this place up and off the ground."

"Yeah, Dad? Great advice. I agree Johnny's ready for the spotlight."

"That he is. On his way to the top."

"First," Johnny Ray noted, "I need to get a record label."

Elegant, yet unimposing, Samantha Rosewood joined us in her glimmering dress. Her arms were slim, her hands laced around a small clutch purse. "Your songs are beautiful," she told Johnny Ray.

"I was shooting for manly."

"That's precisely what makes them beautiful. A rare combination, actually."

He tipped his hat. "Appreciate you sayin' so, Sammie."

Dad nudged my ribs. Again. "Even the fine Ms. Rosewood's smitten with your brother."

"With a voice like that," Sammie said, "he could make any woman melt."

Her face flushed then. Flat-out, no-mistake-about-it flushed. Having never witnessed such a reaction from her, I found my mind racing with sullen remarks.

"Well, he's all mine," Sarah cooed. "Aren't you, sugar?"

"He's *my* brother," I cut in, "so you can all *back* off."

Everyone laughed as if I'd discovered my calling on the comic stage.

I held my side, winced, then turned back toward the kitchen

where Brianne—a woman threatened, a woman scorned—mopped
the floor without complaint. Taking hold of her arm, I led her around
the corner from the view of the dining area, pulled her close, and
looked into her startled eyes.

The mop handle banged against the upright freezer.

"Aramis?"

"I love calzone," I said. Then kissed her fiercely and walked away.

Before leaving Black's, I placed a call to Detective Meade.

Everyone else was gone. Brianne helped me clean up, then caught
a ride home with a girlfriend. My impulsive agreement to dinner
with Brianne turned me into a bundle of nerves, stirring thoughts of
boundaries, workplace ethics, and a young woman's tenuous future.

I couldn't ignore ICV's threats, not in light of all that had gone
on the past week. The anarchist's words, his hot breath, still buzzed in
my head: *I take her hair and throw her down... What happened to poor
Darrell—that oughta be a warning to you.*

Memories straddled my daily activities, and a conspiracy pulsed
around the secrets of Meriwether Lewis.

Ghosts. That's what Mrs. Michaels called it.

*Diggin' up them ghosts...*

First priority: Brianne's safety.

"Would you like to come down and report the incident?" Meade
asked.

"Fill out paperwork? Not really. Would it help anything?"

"It would lend credence to later criminal charges, should they be
filed. It also starts a paper trail on this ICV group since I'm not aware

of them being previously active in this state. It's routine. And it's always wise."

"I'm tired. Right now I'm more worried about Brianne."

Meade cleared his throat. "You think it's the Rasputin Rapist?"

"The who?"

"The guy who assaulted Jessica Tyner."

I swallowed a lump of anger that tasted a bit like fear. "Could be. Rasputin?"

"That's his moniker within our precinct," Meade explained. "Based on rumors—surely spurious—that Rasputin had a habit of deflowering virgins and then burying patches of their hair in his garden in glass jars."

"You're kidding."

"It's in several accounts. Who's to say?"

"That's wrong and twisted."

"And sick too. If you would though, please keep it to yourself, Aramis. We've held back that bit of information from the press. They'd have a field day with it."

"No kidding."

"We don't want to stir panic. By taking you into my confidence, I trust you'll be able to help us."

"Jessica Tyner wasn't the first, was she?"

"The fifth in six months. Snips of hair seem to be his trophies."

"One minute with the guy and I'd find out how *he* liked being snipped."

"It's neither your place nor mine to take the law into our own hands."

"Not that I'd really do it, but…"

"Off the record, Aramis? I'd be right there with you."

"Nothing better happen to Brianne."

"I'll have an undercover officer sent over to her place right away."

"That'd make me feel a lot better. Oh, one other thing." I thumbed through my wallet, found a card. "Might sound schizo, but I've had this car on my tail the past few days. Think you could run the plates, see what comes up? Is that allowed?"

"Why not? Have the number with you?" After he'd taken it down, Meade said he had another issue to discuss. "I met today with the Neighborhood Watch director."

"That's still creepy to me—Mrs. Vaughn watching our every move."

"In light of what you've recently endured, I'd say you have better things to worry about."

"Or worse."

"Exactly." Not an ounce of humor in his voice. "She gave a positive ID of your uncle. Wyatt Tremaine was there near your front door on Monday, the day of the break-in. Considering the hair specimen left behind, that qualifies him as a suspect in the sexual assault cases."

"Uncle Wyatt? That doesn't make sense. Not that I'm defending the guy—believe me—but I don't see how he could be connected to the dude in the alley."

"We have to keep an open mind in these cases. Look at it from all angles."

"Wait… Uncle Wyatt just flew into town a few days ago."

"A few days ago? What makes you say that?"

"Uh. Well." My head was a flurry of thoughts. "After we had our confrontation, the television people put him up at an airport motel. Footing his bill, I'm sure."

"You are correct that he stayed at a local motel." Detective Meade's hesitation set me on edge.

"But what?"

"Wyatt Tremaine never flew into, or out of, Nashville. Not recently anyway."

"They made him ride Greyhound?" I grinned. "He deserves it."

"Actually, he lives just over an hour away. Being his nephew, you shouldn't be surprised."

The words were like fists slammed into my gut. "We haven't talked in years. Where did you hear this?"

"When he filed charges against you a few days back. He's a resident of Lewis County."

Lewis County has no large cities. With a short list of options, the answer to my next question was obvious.

"In Hohenwald?"

"I thought you knew that."

"Seems there's a lot I don't know."

I arrived home around midnight, exhausted and sore. In the dark entryway, a postmarked mailing tube bore my name. I peeled it open and found the Kurt Cobain poster I'd ordered off eBay.

I rolled it under my arm and peeked through the studio door. Dad was passed out, drunk, basking in the glory of his older son's performance.

In the next room, with light oozing beneath the closed door onto the hall's hardwood floor, my brother was performing an encore for an audience of one. Most certainly the girl named Sarah, whom he would set aside within a week. I'd seen the pattern. Lost in the revelry of fresh pheromones, he's affectionate and cuddly, but he runs from deeper intimacy and commitment.

Embarrassing stuff.

I used to be the same.

After tacking up the poster by my computer, I dropped into bed. I thought about the fallout of Cobain's existence. He changed the landscape of modern rock, and yet his personal life was a shambles.

I used to idolize the man. I embraced his despair.

And look where it got him. Six feet under.

I knew it wasn't right, the bitterness between my father and me. I'd fed it long enough, with no benefit to either of us. But how to cross that barrier?

My eyelids grew heavy. Still clothed, I pulled a blanket over myself.

I can see my father's silhouette. He's reaching for me, calling for me, then he morphs into a hollow-cheeked creature with bony fingers.

The fingers clamp onto me. I pry at them, and they snap off. Shattering.

"I'm sorry," I tell him.

When I look up, I'm staring at Brianne Douglas. I hear distant screams, but my focus is on her shoulder where a creature rests, translucent red, its tail dripping poison. Brianne has tears in her eyes. She's shaking her head.

"Hold still." I flex my fingers. "I'll try to knock it away."

"No," she begs. "Just leave it alone." In her hand, she's clutching my mother's handkerchief. "Please, Aramis. If you act like it's not there, it won't hurt anything."

The tapered tail whips around.

"Brianne!"

But it's too late. She disintegrates into a swirl of brittle leaves, floating down, covered by a square of white silk.

# TWENTY-FOUR

There are some secrets better left buried, Aramis."

"You sound like you know something I don't."

In his Tabasco boxers, Johnny Ray stretched, scratched, then lumbered into the bathroom. I was hurrying through my second Pop-Tart to avoid his disapproving look.

When he wandered back into view, I hid it under the table.

He picked up his six-string and found his cross-legged position on the hardwood floor.

"By the way," I said, "you did great last night."

"Thanks for settin' it up. Had myself a heckuva time."

"During? Or after?"

He waved his hand in a downward motion. "Shh. Sarah's still sleeping."

I could feel Pop-Tart crumbs landing on my toes. I was hungry, and I needed to leave for work in a few minutes. "It's not right, Johnny. Taking advantage of her like that."

"She's knows it's nothin' permanent. That was clear from the get-go."

"Oh, well, in *that* case…"

"You missed out. She woulda brought her friend for you, Aramis, but I told her you were in trainin' for the priesthood."

"You're joking."

He shrugged as he brought his guitar into his lap.

"Well. You might like to know I'm having dinner with Brianne tonight."

"That girl who's workin' for you?" It was his turn to shake his head.

"Friends. Nothing more."

"Mmm, I'll take your word. I wouldn't trust her though. She's got her eye on you."

"Can you blame her?"

He sneered at me. "Back to your other question, about Uncle Wyatt."

"Yeah. He's lived here all this time, and you didn't think to tell me?"

"Only found out myself a few weeks ago."

"Oh, really?"

"He disappeared after Mom's funeral, so how was I to know where he'd gone? The thing with you and Mom at the river—I don't think he ever got over that."

"How'd you find out that he was in Hohenwald?"

"He called me."

"What? Just for fun?"

"Outta the blue. I picked up, and there he was, introducin' himself and askin' to speak with you."

"With me?"

"You'd never let that happen, so I met with the man myself. Had lunch."

"You met with him?"

"He said he wanted to spill some family secrets. Time to rattle the ol' skeletons in the closet, he told me."

"And you had to keep it all to yourself."

"Who drove you to the Lewis monument a week ago?"

"You did—"

"And who's kept tellin' ya about the connections to our own history?"

"You have. But—"

"Hold on now." He held up a hand and bowed his head. "Tell me, please, who set you up to go on national TV and put this thing to rest? Your big chance to get *The Best of Evil*?"

"You did, oh wise and wonderful big brother."

"Now that's what I'm talkin' about."

"But you tricked me. Suckered me into it."

"'Cause you won't listen." He tapped the latest issue of the *Scene*. "Can't even spare a minute of your time. Just bound and determined to fix it all on your own. Been that way since you were six. You're the strong one, isn't that how it goes?"

"If you say so."

"You're not so doggone complicated as you make yourself out to be."

"Okay. You have me all figured out. Tell me, Johnny, what do you see?"

"It's all written there on your tattoos."

"Life on the edge," I said. "Nothing wrong with that."

"You've watched *Gladiator* one too many times, kid."

"Seriously. What're you keepin' from me?"

"Like I been tellin' you, it's high time you faced the stuff in the past and moved on. But I can't make it happen. You gotta let go. Till you do that, you won't be ready to face the rest of these ghosts."

"What ghosts? What secrets?"

"You listenin' to a thing I've said?"

"I've gotta let go first. Okay. I get it."

"If you don't, they'll haunt you till the day you die."

"Am I the only one in the dark here?"

"We all are, Aramis. Each one of us, just tryin' to find our way."

"Whatever."

I brought my Pop-Tart from under the table and nibbled around the edges. Licked my lips. Savored each warm and gooey bite.

"All that sugar in your system?" he said. "It's no wonder you're so cranky."

Sarah's breathy voice floated into the kitchen. "Johnny Ray Black? Did I hear you say 'sugar'?"

I was outta there. I hurried toward the park still fumbling with the buttons on my shirt.

Centennial Park was quieter than usual this Friday morning, so it was no surprise to hear Tina shuffling along with her dog.

"Hi, Tina."

"Walking and talking, an old crone, alone." The mist thinned her voice.

"Stop by if you need a hot cup of joe," I said. "I'll be open at six."

"A matter of time, to find the dark grind."

A layer of fog hovered over the wide lawn, giving shrubbery and stonework the illusion of poking through wisps of battlefield smoke. I could almost smell the gunpowder as I thought about Civil War conflicts where blood was spilled and history etched into the landscape and disposition of the South.

The past fifty years in Music City have echoed those racial struggles.

In 1960, hundreds of African Americans staged nonviolent protests, taking seats at lunch counters in downtown Nashville. Had Detective Meade's parents been here then? Watching the world change before their eyes?

After numerous beatings and arrests of unresisting young black men, the general population's sympathies swung to the protesters' side. On April 19, when a councilman who had spoken up for the cause had his house bombed, nearly four thousand marched in silence on city hall. Addressing the issue without compromise, the mayor stated that discrimination based on color was morally wrong.

The next day Martin Luther King Jr. spoke at local Fisk University, declaring, "I did not come to Nashville to bring inspiration, but to gain inspiration…"

Within weeks, lunch counters began opening to diners of all races, all colors.

In some ways we've come so far. In others, we're just scratching the surface.

Through the fog, I spotted Freddy C curled on cardboard beneath a tree.

"Freddy C." I nudged his shoulder and caught that salty hush-puppy scent.

One eye crept open. Watery. Slowly focusing. "Artemis?"

"I'm on my way to the shop. Where've you been?"

"Nowhere special." He sat up, pulled a hand through his graying beard.

"You hungry? I'm running over to Krispy Kreme if you wanna

join me." I'd had breakfast already, but I knew he would never let me watch him eat. "I can't do a whole box by myself."

"Shouldn't show my face. Shouldn't do it, not today."

"You okay?"

"Thanks for wakin' me. Gotta get movin'." He folded the cardboard beneath his arm while his wary eyes surveyed the park.

"Is this about that warning the other day?"

His neck stiffened, and his eyes rolled my way. "Could be."

"You said something, Freddy. Said I had trouble."

"*We* got trouble."

"Okay. We."

"A man's been watchin'," he said. "Hangin' around. He's not a good man."

"Who is he? Does he have a hooded sweatshirt and black high tops?" It was worth a shot.

Freddy C shook his head, his reedy hair shifting on his scalp. "He's not really a man. Not a man at all."

"A ghost?"

Freddy stood upright. "You think I'm crazy? Think I have a few screws loose?"

"Not at all. What do you mean then, he's not a man?"

Freddy buttoned his coat, tucked in his scarf, and withdrew his grocery cart from its hiding place in the bushes. "Stay outta my hair, you hear."

"I didn't mean to offend you."

"And if you're smart"—he tapped his finger against my temple—"you'll get him. You'll get into his hair. He'll no longer take what doesn't belong to him."

"Is it my Uncle Wyatt? Do you know him?"

"Gotta go." Freddy C pushed past me. "He's here somewhere."

I glanced around. "We're fine. I think we're alone."

"I'm not safe to be around. I'm tellin' you now, I'm no longer safe."

# TWENTY-FIVE

How could a place change so drastically in the span of a few hours? Last night's performance had jolted Black's with electricity. This morning's gloom washed surfaces in cheerless hues.

The Purity delivery driver arrived with my milk order. He, too, seemed morose. In silence we unloaded gallon containers—whole, two percent, and skim—into my upright fridge, then quarts of half-and-half into the undercounter unit.

"We billing you?"

"Yeah," I said, "I normally just sign."

He extended his clipboard. I scrawled my signature and then locked the door again as he left. Extra security measures seemed like a good idea.

I was ready for opening. And glad to know an officer had been assigned to Brianne's place. She would be here soon.

Between the silence and the thought of seeing Brianne, my thoughts seemed to come together.

Had I washed my hair? Brushed my teeth? Scrubbed both armpits? A clean bill of inspection.

Checked zipper? Done.

With my mind rattling over these adolescent anxieties, I found a zone. Maybe I'd been trying too hard previously, shoving puzzle pieces against one another in hopes of finding a match, but in that moment I saw something. So what if Johnny Ray and Uncle Wyatt wanted to keep secrets from me? I'd piece this together on my own.

I bumped into a table and sat in the empty dining area with my first cup of morning joe, a special concoction of my own. I blew and sipped. Blew and sipped. I looked back at the mahogany bar and thought of Darrell Michaels standing there, his back turned as he faced the counter. An easy target for the guy in the Old Navy shirt and painter jeans. No more than twelve feet away.

*You need the whip...*

What whip?

I theorized out loud, "Lewis had a whip of some sort...and ICV wants it because it leads to the gold...if such a treasure exists. Maybe a Spanish payment in gold Lewis intercepted on its way to Wilkinson."

It all made sense.

But a few questions remained. Where was the whip? How had these secrets been passed down through the centuries? Who'd sent the handkerchief to me? And who had planted the lock of brunette hair in my bedroom?

"Got a minute?" Ignoring appalled stares, Detective Meade stepped to the front of the espresso line. "I need to speak with you about last night."

"What happened?"

His gaze went from Brianne's position at the espresso machine to a padded leather booth. "Let's take it over there."

"Now?" I jerked my chin at the line of patrons.

"Aramis," he said softly, "someone was outside her place."

Brianne looked up at the next customer and smiled. I didn't think she'd heard.

"Be right back," I said.

Her mouth turned down, and she continued steaming an ordered triple breve.

"We've stood here patiently, and now you're leaving?" a woman called to me.

"It'll be quick."

"The past few times I've been in here, this poor girl's been left to shoulder the majority of the work. As the owner, you owe it to your—"

"Folks." Meade stepped in, holding up his identification. "I'm Detective Meade, Metro Police. If you'll be so kind as to let me pull Mr. Black from his duties for just a few moments, I'll be better able to do my job of protecting you and your loved ones." He was circumspect enough to avoid mentioning last week's murder on this spot. I appreciated that about the man. The less said, the better.

Grudging nods and furtive whispers released us to our corner.

"Who?" I asked again.

"Forgive me. I didn't mean to disrupt your flow," the detective said.

"Who was it? Tell me what happened."

"The same man we spotted on security footage at your parking lot."

"What camera? At Johnny's and my place?"

"Your brownstone. We obtained the tape last evening, the one from the day your mother's handkerchief disappeared."

I hadn't even known the parking lot had a security camera. But I was suddenly thankful it did. "So, Detective, who is this guy? What's he look like?"

Meade's face adopted that disinterested look again, his eyes dark and dull against his coal black skin. "I need you to look at the video. See if you can provide a positive ID."

"You can't tell me what he looks like? Did he have one of those hooded sweatshirts? That's what the mugger was wearing. Jeans and high tops."

"A fairly generic description, I hate to say."

"Or maybe a golfing visor?"

"That's an odd thing to ask, isn't it?"

The beauty of the detective's method struck me. By leading and hinting, he had me throwing out suggestions, popping off theories. He wasn't trying to tie me up in my own words, though he seemed capable of it. Rather, he was priming the pump of information. Perhaps my subconscious had a few facts still down there.

"Leroy Parker," I said.

"What about him?"

"He's a parole officer."

"I know who he is. We've been in contact with him regarding the death of young Mr. Michaels. He'd been overseeing the kid's progress."

"Did he tell you about the Spanish gold?"

Meade's eyebrows rose, slow and purposeful, bulldozers shoving furrows into the dark earth of his forehead. He folded his arms across his chest. "Gold, Mr. Black?"

"Uh. Yeah."

"Spanish?"

"That's what he told Darrell."

"And why would Mr. Parker say such a thing? He's been silent on the subject in our interviews, not a word in his reports. Perhaps you can enlighten me."

"Never mind."

"Please continue now that it's out on the table."

Customers were checking their watches and looking at me. I was losing my grip on reality, and soon I'd be losing business as well.

"The line," I said. "I need to help Brianne. When I come in to look at the footage, we can talk about Parker."

Detective Meade nodded. "We'll do that."

"Can we jump to the description? Real quick?"

"Sure. The man on the film is middle-aged, graying hair and long beard, squat build, dressed in layers of sweaters and coats. He looks like a homeless gentleman."

"Freddy C." I thought it out loud.

"That's right. He's never been fond of police officers, or any authority, for that matter. With things recently uncovered in his record, he's become a person of interest in our"—Meade let his eyes slide across the room as he lowered his voice—"ongoing investigation of the sexual assault cases."

"That's hard for me to believe."

"He's from Chicago. Did you know that? He was a janitor at an elementary school, indicted on molestation charges eight years ago. Went to trial, but they failed to get a conviction. The defense argued that the victim's testimony had been coached by the prosecuting attorney."

I shook my head. "Freddy's my friend."

"Regardless."

"I wanna see the footage."

"The sooner the better. Meanwhile, we can't ignore threats such as the one you received in the alley. Last night the officer was unsure of Freddy's mental state and called for backup before approaching him, but Freddy vanished. We'll be sweeping the park, bringing him in to answer a few questions. I'd like to put this case to rest."

*Stay outta my hair, you hear... I'm no longer safe.*

I suspected that Freddy would be nowhere to be found.

"I'm authorizing round-the-clock surveillance on Ms. Douglas," Meade added. "No need for her to know for the time being. But it might put your mind at ease to know she's being watched."

"Thanks. I appreciate it, Detective."

"I'll let you get back to your customers."

I sat up. "Wait. Will they be watching tonight?"

"Undercover officers? Yes."

"Oh. That's a good thing, I guess."

"Aramis, is there something you're not telling me?"

The idea of a date under the eyes of armed officers seemed disturbing and a bit creepy. If we shared a good-night kiss on the porch, would it be recorded in some report? "Thing is," I said, "we're having dinner. Me and Brianne."

"Together?"

"You're sharp, Detective. Nothing gets by you."

"You just behave yourself, and there'll be no problems."

"It's not like that."

"I believe you." Meade cocked his head toward me and wagged a long finger as the hint of a bemused smile touched his cheeks. "Remember, we'll be watching your every move."

# TWENTY-SIX

Office space is hard to come by. Mine is a converted broom closet. Tucked into the corner of Black's, behind the kitchen and wash area, it has two cinder-block walls, and it's not a place I choose to spend my afternoons. Hot or cold, the space smells like the inside of an old balloon.

Not pleasant.

My files and receipts are stored there, and a safe crouches beneath the gray metal desk. Photos and permits hang on the walls, and a dinky computer monitor sits atop a stack of Jack London hardbacks, which I bought on eBay months ago but have yet to read.

Who has the time? Plus, they're collectibles, and I'm afraid to crack the spines.

Next to the mouse sits my pocket-size, gold-leaf New Testament. A modern translation, thank goodness. The way I see it, Jesus never spoke English—King James or otherwise—so I'm sticking with what I can understand.

My mom read the Bible once in a while. Never said much about it, just read.

I do the same, to make her proud. To be reminded I'm not alone.

Today I went online with hopes of cracking open the secrets of Meriwether Lewis. Rumors of riches had trickled down to the present, and—just my luck—these weren't warm, friendly rumors. They'd left me with a knot on my forehead, a bruise on my thigh, and piercing pain in my side. They'd cost my mother's life. A young man's as well. And now they threatened Brianne's safety.

"Twenty minutes left," Brianne called to me from the counter.

"I know."

"I didn't get a lunch break yesterday. I really need it."

"I know." I went to the Google search engine.

"Not that I'm complaining, Aramis."

"Yeah, I know."

"Why do you keep saying that? If you know, you'd let me go. The truth is, Mr. Smarty-Pants, I need to do some shopping for our meal tonight, get some fresh veggies from Farmers' Market."

Tonight. Me and her and the calzone. I could just picture it. Me dancing through a minefield of romance while undercover officers watched my progress through binoculars.

"We're still doing that?" I said.

"Doing what?" she purred.

"Well. Dinner, of course."

"How can you ask that? Tell me you're kidding."

I poked my head through the office door. "Are there customers out there?"

"What do you care? If I didn't know better, I'd say I'm running this place. 'Make the sandwiches. Heat the soup. Mop the floors. Take care of the drink orders.' I've really tried to keep a good attitude, considering I'm new to the job and still learning the ropes. But honestly, Aramis, it's starting to get to me. We were here until what time last night? After ten thirty?"

Her tirade was slowly building steam, and more troublesome, it was fueled by truth. The hours had been long, and she'd borne the brunt of it.

"Hold on," I said, trying to do damage control.

"Hold on?"

"Please. Just gimme a couple more minutes. Can we talk about it then?"

Silence.

Golden and beautiful at first, the silence started to worry me a bit. Had I pushed too far? Then, with the sound of water running in the sink and dishes clanking, I was reassured of Brianne's presence. She was pouting. I made a mental note to pick up something special on the way to her place tonight.

Into the search box, I typed the words: "Meriwether Lewis. Whip. Riding Crop. Spanish Gold."

Although the combination of terms brought up interesting results, one particular item stood out. Might seem like a small thing, but in light of everything else, it was significant.

In St. Louis, the Jefferson Memorial's collection displays a number of Lewis's belongings, including a watch that was discovered in a New Orleans pawnshop. The watch, as well as a diary, a revolver, and a compass, were donated to the memorial by one of Lewis's relatives— the great-great-grandson of Lewis's sister, Jane Lewis Anderson.

Jane Lewis Anderson…Dianne Lewis Black.

Could it be true? Mom's name was more than a coincidence?

I became a man convinced. From childhood horror to recent robbery and murder, the weight was too much to carry. I took a breath, set down this pack of denial, and allowed myself to look over the items inside. No matter how much the truth hurt, I needed to understand; I couldn't keep tying up these issues and throwing them over my shoulder.

*Let's see where this leads.*

I scrolled further down the page of search results. There was more, of course. Much more. With time running short, however, I highlighted the sections of interest and sent them to my printer. The ancient machine shook to life and started spitting out sheets of information.

"Almost done, Brianne. One more minute."

"Fine. No big rush."

Her calm tone reassured me that things would be okay.

"Be right there." I gathered the papers, folded them in half, and slipped them into my apron's front pouch. Rounding the kitchen corner, I found her with her back turned. "Brianne, you're an angel. Okay. Your turn off the clock."

"If you say so."

"I thought you were anxious to go. Farmers' Market, all that."

"You said you love calzone." She faced me.

"Yeah. Sounds great."

"You also kissed me."

I squared my shoulders. "Yeah?"

"You shouldn't have done that."

I shifted my weight. My gaze brushed over her lips, then I looked past her into the dining area, where Mrs. Thompson was at her regular seat and a student was bobbing his head to iPod tunes.

"Uh. You're right, Brianne. That was a mistake."

She mouthed the words "a mistake," then pinched the bridge of her nose and closed her eyes.

Relieved to see we were on the same page, I said, "So are we still on? We can be mature adults, right? Have dinner. Keep it platonic. Enjoy getting to know each other better as friends. If, of course, you can forgive me."

"Forgive you?"

"For a stupid kiss."

Her voice rose in volume and pitch, and she paid no attention to my gestures to keep it down. "Aramis, how can you be so blind? You already seem to have a habit of leaving me behind. Every day it's the same. Obviously your own company is so engaging that I would only be in the way at dinner, no matter how platonic you think it could be. What was I thinking? Yes, you're cute. I even thought you were nice and"—she barked out a laugh—"sensitive."

"I've been called worse."

"You want calzone, Aramis?" She threw down a wet rag, and a loud splaattt sounded throughout the shop. "Make it yourself."

"I can't cook."

"Then I guess you'll starve, leaving me with one less thing to worry about."

"Which one? Me or the calzone?"

As usual, it was an ill-timed attempt to get a laugh.

Brianne tore the hair tie from her blond locks, then turned and marched out the front door.

Before it swung closed, Samantha Rosewood stepped through. She looked professional in a tailored burgundy suit with an ivory silk blouse underneath. The place responded to her presence. Heads turned. The polished wood and brass seemed to gleam a bit brighter.

"Is everything under control?"

"Sure."

"Wasn't that Brianne? She seemed upset."

"Personal issues. Sammie, I'm glad to see you. You look... fantabulous. What're you up to? Here to check on my questionable operation?"

"Actually," she said with a twinkle in her eye, "I don't come often enough to enjoy this fine establishment. I've made arrangements to meet someone here for lunch."

"You and who?"

"Johnny Ray."

"Oh."

On the scale of gleaming good cheer, the mahogany and brass dropped back down a notch.

# TWENTY-SEVEN

Pushing seven o'clock, I ran through the closing procedures. Some say the shop should stay open later on Fridays, but in Nashville's West End the options for weekend entertainment exceed the draw of a modest espresso shop.

Plus, I have a life. Or so I like to believe.

"Sir? We're closing the doors in one minute. Can I take that mug for you?"

"Do you always rush your customers like this?" The man looked up from his notebook computer, his face made bitter by the screen's pale glow. "This is the second or third time in the last five minutes that you've made an issue of this."

"I apologize, but—"

"I'm the customer. You can't tell me to leave."

I hooked the mug with a finger. "I'm the manager. It's time to lock my doors. I still have things to do, especially since my employee never returned from her lunch break."

"Lunch? That was hours ago."

"Exactly."

"Hmm. Hardly surprising." The man clicked his computer shut and strolled out slowly enough to prove he was doing so on his own terms.

I try not to stereotype. Honestly. Yet with hospitals and medical clinics throughout this district, I could guarantee the guy was a pharmaceutical rep. A very well-paid drug dealer with a big expense account. Nice clothes and car to go with it.

What a day.

Breakfast kicked it off with Johnny's and Uncle Wyatt's family secrets. Lunch consisted of me staying as busy as possible, trying to ignore the banter between my brother and Ms. Rosewood. Dinner...

Well, there was no dinner. I'd smacked those plans down hard.

At least the undercover boys would be in for a long, dull night.

With the shop door locked and the lights turned low, I sat on a stool and perused the pages I'd printed earlier. I was surprised by the number of sites dedicated to the life of unfortunate Governor Lewis. Most of them documented his accomplishments on the Lewis and Clark expedition; others detailed the events surrounding his untimely and mysterious death; conspiracy theories ranged from "worth consideration" to "who thinks up this nonsense?"

I made a list.

*General James Wilkinson...*

It's well-documented that Wilkinson received from the king of Spain tens of thousands of dollars for his betrayals—often in gold. Andrew Jackson was so incensed by these shenanigans that he challenged Wilkinson to a duel and called him a "double traitor." With sly ease, Wilkinson avoided such confrontations.

*Governor Meriwether Lewis...*

Lewis kept record of Wilkinson's suspicious activities and even brought them to the president's attention as early as 1804. With new gossip circulating, Lewis headed from his outpost in St. Louis to the halls of power, carrying two trunks of personal belongings and documents. A man with a mission.

*Agent James Neelly…*

Less understood—but certainly conspicuous in retrospect—was Neelly's entrance on the scene in late September of 1809. He was a personal appointee of General Wilkinson.

Was he sent to keep an eye on Lewis? To steal his papers? Or to end his life?

At Chickasaw Bluffs near Memphis, where the Wolf River runs into the mighty Mississippi, Neelly joined Lewis and his servant. He acted as their escort from Fort Pickering to the perilous Natchez Trace. The morning after they crossed the Tennessee River, Neelly told them to go ahead to Grinder's Stand while he went after two packhorses that he claimed had been spooked during the previous night's thunderstorm.

The horses were carrying some of Meriwether Lewis's sealed pouches.

The next day Lewis was dead, but it wasn't until the following week that Agent Neelly reported it, calling it a suicide.

*Lewis's artifacts…*

There are quite a few still floating around.

Transcripts from the PBS show *History Detectives* include an episode with a Minnesota man who stumbled upon an exquisitely crafted cane, which he believed to be a Lewis family heirloom.

The Oregon Historical Society's site mentions a collection of artifacts that belonged to Lewis, including a branding iron with *U.S. Capt. M. Lewis* engraved on it. The brand was found among rocks on the north shore of the Columbia River.

I could find no site, however, documenting a whip—bullwhip, horsewhip, or otherwise—though Lewis's journals did mention an Indian giving a horse "the whip." Lewis, being an accomplished horseman, was known to use riding crops.

Maybe Lewis owned a riding crop with markings that indicated the location of buried riches.

The more I mulled it over, the more plausible the idea seemed.

A quarter after eight. Would the detective be at the West Precinct? I found his card and dialed. He answered on the second ring.

"Investigations Unit, Detective Reginald Meade."

"Reginald? As in Reggie?"

"Reginald. As in Detective. Who am I speaking with?"

"This is Aramis. Dude, you work some long hours, don't you?"

"I was packing up and heading home just as you called."

"To see your wife and kid…"

"They're the reason I do this job." His voice was stern. "That's what it's all about for me, trying to make this world a safer place."

"I admire that, Detective. You're certainly the best cop I know."

"Until this Rasputin Rapist is behind bars, that's a matter of debate. But we may have our man. We had an incident at Brianne Douglas's place not too long ago. Guess you hadn't made it over for dinner yet."

"Is she okay?"

"Everything's fine. We took your homeless friend into custody."

"Freddy C? Tell me you're joking."

"An undercover officer caught him moving toward the back corner of Brianne's building, confronted him, and took him down with a Taser."

"He's a harmless old guy!"

"He was armed. It was fully within the officer's rights."

"Armed with what? A recycled Pepsi can?"

"You're not being objective. The truth requires us to lay aside assumptions and prejudices. You're a case in point."

"Huh?"

"You realize, Aramis, that you've been a suspect—considering your presence at the party with Jessica Tyner and the hair specimen found on your property."

Yes, all along I'd guessed this. But to hear it said aloud? Considering my past troubles with the law, it made me a bit jumpy.

"Do I believe you're guilty?" Meade continued. "Down in my gut? No. It does create a measure of caution on my part, however. You know the license plate you had me run? Guess whose name came up. Parole Officer Leroy Parker."

"As I suspected."

"I spoke with him and found out he's been investigating you on his own, concerned that you had something to do with Darrell Michaels's murder."

"That's crazy."

"But it's one of the options I need to consider."

Were my suspicions of Parker misplaced?

"Considering Freddy C," Detective Meade said, "he's on camera, caught in your parking lot the day you discovered the handkerchief was missing. Did he plant the hair, trying to set you up? Was he trying to scare you so you'd take future threats against Ms. Douglas seriously? I'm still chewing on these questions."

I was doing the same. This could explain Freddy's nervous

behavior in the past week. Was he a man with a guilty conscience, bearing secrets from Chicago? I thought again about his name.

C for Chicago. C for Custodian. What about…C for Child Molester?

Was he a predator hoping to get caught? To be saved from himself?

"Would you like me to tell you what he was carrying, Aramis?"

"I'm all ears."

"A pair of scissors. Inevitably, they get nicked and dulled by use, and they're often stained by adhesive and other residues. Within forty-eight hours, the lab should be able to determine if the blades match the incision patterns on Ms. Tyner's hair."

"Brianne? Are you alone?"

She hesitated.

"It's me," I said into the phone. "Aramis."

"I know who it is, but I… Will you forgive me for walking out on you?"

"I deserved it."

"You did. It was still wrong of me, considering it's my job. Or *was* my job."

"It's a new day tomorrow," I said. "A clean slate."

"You were right about not mixing work and relationships."

"It makes things tough."

"It's been tough enough running the shop on my own," she said.

"Ouch." I laughed out loud. "Seriously, Brianne, you've been great. I want you to stay, as long as you promise not to run out again."

"Wait a second. You *need* me to stay, don't you?"

"That's why I hire employees."

"What is it this time? Where're you going tomorrow?"

"Listen. There's always stuff to get done."

"Are you meeting that detective?"

"Detective Meade."

"I knew it."

The tone of her voice planted a small doubt that rolled through my head and got stuck, like a pebble in the grooved tread of a shoe. Why should she care about my dealings with the police? Bringing her back might not be such a good idea after all. I could see us repeating the pattern—her age and our chemistry.

What had come over me anyway? I'd planted a hard kiss on her lips, in my shop.

Samantha Rosewood, investor and dining partner, would object on all sorts of levels—and she would be justified on every one of them.

Unless, of course, the objection involved Sammie's personal feelings for me. In that case, Sammie could forget about it. She'd sacrificed her classy facade the moment I saw her getting all giggly around my brother.

Talented and nice? I'd give Johnny that much.

Good-looking? Say it with me: "fake tan."

"Aramis," Brianne said, "I'm worried. You know they found a guy outside my apartment. I think it was that homeless guy who comes into Black's sometimes. I've got undercover cops sitting outside as we speak. Detective Meade knows you were coming for dinner and said they'll stay until you get here."

"But I thought...the way I acted..."

"Let's just forget what happened this afternoon and start fresh.

Like you said, a clean slate. But no need to wait until tomorrow. You and me, with food and candlelight. Friends, keeping each other company on a Friday night."

"Friends," I said. "I'll be over in a few."

Bad idea? Probably. When it comes to women, I don't always row my boat with both oars.

# TWENTY-EIGHT

**E**nter," said Brianne, "if you dare."

"Funny."

"Turn and wave good-bye to the gentleman in the unmarked car."

"Which one?"

"The one that's unmarked."

She giggled at her own joke, but as soon as she said it, I knew which one she meant. It was parked beneath a streetlight, the cabin in shadow.

I waved. Brianne laughed.

As the car pulled out, the window lowered, and the driver gave us a sly salute.

"Nice," I said.

"Okay," Brianne urged. "Let's get to the calzone. It's already nine thirty."

"It's Friday. The night is young."

"Please tell me you won't be making comments like that the whole time you're here. Just friends—that was our agreement."

"Of course."

"Are you hungry?"

"You know it."

"Then you've come to the right place."

The condominium was spacious, efficient, and orderly. The living room and dining room joined somewhere in the middle, with a long marble bar separating them from the kitchen. The cabinets were teak, with spring hinges on the doors and gliding drawers. The appliances gleamed black and silver, with a hanging rack for pots and pans.

"Beautiful place."

"Glad you noticed."

"All this on an espresso-shop paycheck?"

Her face darkened. "I didn't have a lot growing up. I swore never to live that way again, so I started pinching pennies, saving up till I could buy the best or nothing at all."

I looked around. "I can see what you mean. Very stylish."

"Thanks." She handed me a lighter. "Can you get the candles?"

While I circled the table, Brianne hit a button on a remote, and Andrea Bocelli's rich voice seeped into the air. White plates sat sparkling on black cotton place mats. Stemware reflected the flames as each candle leaped to life. Brianne moved around the bar and slipped on oven mitts, so I dropped the lighter into my pocket. I'd hand it back when she was finished.

I inhaled. Ah. From the oven, the food sent heavenly aromas my direction. Garlic and prosciutto ham. Oregano, mushrooms, and olives. And was that Gouda cheese?

Yeah, this was gonna be good.

"Are you a wine drinker, Aramis?"

I grimaced. "Last time I had some, I made a fool of myself."

"From what I've seen, you're capable of that without wine."

"Oooh. I'll let that slide."

She handed me a corkscrew and a bottle of Riesling. "You mind doing the honors while I change?"

I filled each glass halfway, waited for her return.

When she entered from the hallway, she looked stunning. Her hair was pulled up, with thin tendrils brushing the pearls on her neck. Although her sleeveless top was casual, the aquamarine material brought her eyes to life. Dark slacks and pumps accentuated the length of her legs.

"A girl likes to feel good about herself. What do you think?"

"Amazing."

She was still beaming as she carried in a stoneware platter bearing toasted calzones sprinkled with herbs and grated cheese.

"Dinner is served."

"Now that's what I'm talkin' about."

I'll admit I have a pesky desire to settle down someday with a wife and kids. Sure, I used to brag about being able to make lots of women happy—a different one every night. I swear, though, I haven't got a clue how the married men do it. Keeping the same woman happy for years on end? In my book, that's a miracle with a capital *M*.

After the meal we moved to the black leather sofa. Brianne snuggled in the corner, her shoes off and her legs folded beside her. With her head cocked, her hair dangled along her bare arm.

Friends, I reminded myself.

Yet when our fingers started touching on the cushion, they soon found a way to link our hands and draw us closer. The music played on, soaring to cover the night's noises, lulling us from the concerns of the day. I slipped my arm around her, and Brianne laid her head on my shoulder. I caught the scent of her hair, light and herbal.

"Are you really going to be on that reality show?" she asked.

"It's looking like a good possibility."

"So tell me, Mr. TV Star, what's been going on? You've been acting strange."

"Strange*ly*," I corrected.

Brianne poked my side. "You think you're so smart."

I winced.

"You all right?"

"Sore. A little bruised, that's all."

"Is there something you're not telling me?"

"Those cops." I jerked my head toward the curtained window. "They were there because of me."

She gave a false gasp. "Why? What're you going to do to me? I do know how to protect myself, so no funny business, mister."

"I'm serious."

"What happened?"

"You remember last night when I took out the garbage?"

"During Johnny Ray's gig."

"While I was out there in the alley, a guy attacked me. He told me he would hurt you if I didn't help him find something."

"Oh, Aramis. What'd he do to you?"

"A couple of body blows. Some bruises. No big deal."

"What'd he want? How'd he even know me?"

"I'm still trying to piece it together myself. Has nothing to do with you. It has to do with my mother and"—I knew this would be hard to swallow—"Meriwether Lewis."

"Meriwether Lewis? Okay, now I'm really confused."

"Believe me, so am I."

"Help me out here. Tell me what you know."

For the next half hour I shared all the details. She was a good listener, asking just enough questions to keep me talking.

"It's so horrible," she said. "I can still see Darrell's body lying there
on the floor. You think he was trying to warn you? Why didn't he
cooperate with Parker if they were in on it together?"

"I don't know. I'm not sure about Parker's motives."

"So are we talking about a good chunk of money?"

"Gold. Worth a lot more now, two hundred years after the fact."

"A hundred thousand dollars?"

"Who knows? Maybe a half million."

Her eyes grew big, blue irises capturing the candlelight and dif-
fusing it through gray specks.

I kissed her.

She responded with surprising tenderness, then pulled away.

"So why don't we find this treasure, you and me? Can you imagine, Aramis?"

"It's not ours. If it exists at all."

"But what if? Honestly, wouldn't that be incredible? You could
sell the shop and live on a yacht. Or go skiing in the Alps and drink
Swiss hot chocolate every evening. You could take me along, your
own little snow bunny."

"Tempting. All sounds fun."

"But?"

"I live here in Nashville. Johnny Ray's my family."

"What about a family of your own? Doesn't that interest you?"

"Maybe someday."

"What about 'I do' and 'till death do us part'?" She fixed me with
earnest eyes. "Don't you believe in all that? Behind your big tough act,
I know there's a romantic hiding out."

"You caught me."

"So let's do it."

"Uh. I was just hoping for another kiss."

She giggled. "No, I mean, let's find the gold and run away."

"But I have no idea where the whip is or if it even exists. I don't even know why they've targeted me, except that my mother may have been a Lewis herself, a direct descendant. They think I know something, but I don't."

"What about that handkerchief? Your mom said it was special."

"It was a gift. Yeah, she told me it would show the way."

Even as the sentence spilled out, it took on meaning and weight. I'd always thought of it as an abstract sentiment, Mom's thoughts and love guiding me along. What if she'd been trying to guide me to a specific location? Beyond sentimental value, I'd never seen the memento as anything more than a piece of material with initials and some patterned embroidery. Now it was gone.

Mom's statement: *I have secrets wrapped in here…*

"You could be onto something."

"So we get the handkerchief and go from there."

"Detective Meade thinks Freddy C has it. Or maybe my Uncle Wyatt."

"Does Freddy know about the gold?"

"I doubt it."

"What about your uncle?"

"If he took the handkerchief, I'd have to assume so. I just don't know."

"But at least we have a plan. That's a good thing, right? We'll find the handkerchief and see where it leads." She brushed her hair back with one hand and held it there while she gazed at me. "And a plan is worth celebrating, don't you think?"

She brushed her lips against mine. My throat tightened.

"I'll be right back." She rose from the cushions. "Sit tight."

My discomfort had everything to do with squandering the peace I'd found during the past year in Music City. ICV was here, nearby and watching, waiting for me to lead them to a cache of gold. And Uncle Wyatt had experienced firsthand the bitterness still flowing through my fists.

Now an assault on a different level. Temptation…in the form of a single woman.

It took me a few seconds to register the scuffling. Gasps were coming from the bathroom. I bolted upright.

These sounds didn't fit the picture. Something was wrong.

As a six-year-old, face planted in the mud, I had responded to my mother's desperation, rising to my feet and working at the cloth between my lips until I was free to call out her name. I was small. Weak. Yet I believed there was a chance I could save her.

In that split second on the couch, I had no time to reason it out.

Had to do something, had to help. No weakness. No fear.

By the time Brianne's first stifled cry reached me, I was charging—and ready to kill.

# PART THREE

# TALL SKINNY

*The most important thing we have
to decide is…which of them loves money most.*

—Alexandre Dumas, *The Three Musketeers*

# TWENTY-NINE

Nothing prepares you for it.

I rounded the corner, spotted Brianne crouched in the bathroom and struggling against the hairy arms of a man standing behind her. All at once a constellation of stars shot through my head. Electricity radiated through my chest and extremities. My tongue swelled and retracted, making me gag.

Without realizing it, I'd fallen to the hall floor in a fetal position, shaking in a prolonged spasm.

Had to get up. Help Brianne.

With the current lingering in my curled torso, my body refused to respond. As the tension receded, I started to breathe again.

"Don't move," Brianne pleaded.

Was she talking to me?

I could see her, still slouched in the bathroom doorway, squirming, trying to get free. She needed my help. The man's head was down as he struggled with her.

In the hall's darkness, facing me and holding a futuristic-looking weapon, stood a second man. He seemed familiar in a disturbing way.

I'd let my guard down, caught up in the moment with Brianne and deaf to the little creaks and groans that are typical in any residence.

Except these hadn't been typical. Someone had trespassed on her property.

I pushed myself up for a better look.

"Don't hurt him again!" Brianne wailed. But it was too late.

This time I landed hard on the carpet as my body convulsed, rigid and out of my control. A few seconds shook hours out of me. When it was finally over, the ebbing energy felt like physical fluid draining from my fingertips and toes.

"This, my friend, is a Taser."

I knew what it was. As if the jolt hadn't convinced me.

My eyes jerked in increments toward the calm voice. I followed twin silvery lines to the rectangular contraption in his hand, where his finger wrapped around a trigger. I'd read about these, particularly since Nashville's police force had adopted them, leading to a number of questionable deaths.

"See those two electrodes stuck to your sweatshirt? They don't have to penetrate your skin, as you've discovered. They use a shaped pulse to deliver fifty thousand volts, which results in neuromuscular disruption—a fancy description for that bacon impersonation you just did. And all perfectly legal. No special permit required."

I grunted. "Can I sit up?"

"Can you?" He took a step closer and chuckled at my flinch. "Don't worry. Move slowly, with your back against the wall and hands in your lap. That's right."

My assailant's face was in the light now, revealing a slightly crooked nose and wavy dark hair. I recognized my enemy. It was my customer from last week, the one who'd hidden the revolver under his coat.

"You're the one."

He peered down at me. "What?"

"You killed Darrell Michaels."

He let out a mocking laugh that mingled with Brianne's scream from the bathroom. She was throwing her body against her captor, trying to break free.

When she failed to do so, she fell silent and still.

The man with the Taser turned toward her. "I hope you're listening, cutie. If Aramis does his part, he doesn't get any more zaps. If you keep trying to fight or escape, he gets every last bit of juice from these batteries."

I leaned against the wall, exhausted and still pulsing with a dull ache. From what I could remember, most deaths linked to Taser usage involve multiple firings on those with existing heart problems or with a large amount of drugs in their systems. I was healthy, and I'd been drug free for more than a year.

Of course, a couple more rounds, and I might prefer death. No more pain.

"He doesn't know anything," Brianne insisted.

"We've asked before, haven't we, Aramis? Where is the whip?"

"You're with ICV."

"*In cauda venenum,*" he said. "Yes, you used to be one of us."

"What're you doing in Tennessee? I don't have any whip or know about any whip or wanna know about any whip. I think someone's making a mistake. Wasting your time."

"It's no mistake. You are a Lewis, after all, a couple of generations removed."

"Don't tell them anything," Brianne said.

"Aramis, you're the next in line. The next descendant."

"This is all wrong."

"Not according to your father. He insisted your mom gave it to you."

*My father?* What hadn't Dad told me? Had he been attacked as well? I hadn't seen him since the night before, passed out in the studio.

Brianne's voice was strident. "Take your hands off me! Leave us alone." She fought the man behind her. In their skirmish, his face lifted, and I caught a glimpse of his hooded eyes. It was a man I recognized: Parole Officer Leroy Parker. I should've known.

I started to move.

My body went into another teeth-grinding convulsion.

My muscles thickened into steel cords, snapping taut and beating me against the floor. The contractions wrung the strength from me, subsiding at last with a chalky taste on my tongue. The stink of my sweat hovered in the air.

"I'm sorry. Please, don't hurt him any more. Please..."

Her voice. Hollow and far away.

The ICV man stepped closer—the tiger tamer, punishing me into submission to make me jump through his rings of fire. His finger was on that trigger, and I was still linked by insulated wires to the despicable toy.

"Aramis, you won't be much use to me if I have to keep this up. Of course, if you want to die, that's up to you. For me, it just makes for a long evening."

I was quivering, fearful of another hit.

Darrell Michaels's murderer was standing here before me. And Leroy Parker was holding on to Brianne. Parker was involved all right—a crooked, lying weasel of a man. I'd seen his type before. Pathetic wannabes. Those who get into law enforcement for all the wrong reasons, seeking the power and control they know they lack.

"Okay." I gave a raspy cough. "I'll tell you."

"That's the sort of compliance I'm looking for. Thank you, my friend."

My body was cringing and subservient; my will, however, was far from surrendering. A plan was forming. From my brief reading about Tasers, I knew they could be volatile around flammable items. The hall was empty, though. Nothing in reach.

I coughed again, exaggerating just a bit. "Listen. I swear I don't know about the whip. But I think my mom's memento holds a clue."

Brianne was crying, balled forward.

Parker shoved her a step into the hall and addressed me. "It's a map, isn't it?"

"I think it could be."

"Yes!" Parker told the other man. "I told you those papers were the real deal. But we don't need them now, just the map. We're going to be rich."

"All well and good," said the tiger tamer. "I'm interested in the documents."

Parker smirked. "Have at 'em, pal."

"More proof of this government's corruption, right back to its inception."

If not for the tension stretching every muscle tight, I might've laughed at the absurdity of the scenario—lost gold and subversive papers and an incapacitated man on the hallway floor. If this had been a movie, I'd have been wearing a bulletproof vest while sporting an M-16.

No such luck.

I coughed again, bent over in pain. And slipped my hand along my leg.

"Yeah, yeah," Leroy said. "*In cauda venenum* and all that anarchist mumbo jumbo. You just help me get to the gold, then you do your thing, and I do mine."

"So tell us," the man with the Taser said to me. "Where is this handkerchief?"

"I...don't know."

"Think carefully. We hold on to your girlfriend here until we confirm the location, and then you're both free to go back to life and love and making little Lewis offspring."

"Parker's a crook." I pointed a finger at the slump-shouldered man.

"What?"

I let my free hand fall back toward my chest. "Ask him. He already has the papers, and he's just using you."

"Parker?" The man with the Taser shifted his attention. "You said that Michaels kid took the papers."

"He did. He swiped 'em from me. I swear it."

As the ICV man paused, I gripped my sweatshirt with my left hand and tore it over my head. In the same motion, with my right I lifted the lighter—the one I'd used to light our dinner candles—and flicked the flint wheel with my thumb.

The man whipped back toward me.

A half second later, the Taser's pulse stretched forth. Carving through the material, it snapped with hungry electricity and bit down on the fumes of the lighter's flame.

I tossed the sweatshirt away from me, but the explosion was immediate.

I yelled as the heat stripped off the hair and first layer of skin along my fingers and wrist. In the dark hall, the yellow orange burst of the sweatshirt was sudden and blinding. I clawed forward in a low crouch, drove my head into the man's gut, and rammed him into the wall. I heard Brianne scream, followed by a deeper yell, as picture frames crashed to the floor.

My opponent tried to counter my attack, stabbing joined elbows down onto my back, sharp and desperate.

I found strength in his frenzied motion.

*Live by the Sword...*

I wrapped up his legs, lifted, and twisted him around.

*Die by the Sword...*

I snapped my upper body, hammering him down onto the floor where ribs and spine made contact with a sickening thud. His legs still in my grip, I pistoned him down the hall, shoving him before me until a closed door ended the forward progress of his skull.

Brianne?

I dropped the unconscious man's legs and swung around to see the corridor on fire, the blaze already licking at the baseboards and the lower walls. At the other end of the hall, Brianne had scrambled free from Parker's grasp. She kicked back at him, then tumbled through a door. Behind her, a bed and nightstand offered meager hope for protection.

"Get back here!" Parker shrieked. "You can't tease me like that! Live up to your part of the deal."

He was holding a pair of scissors as he crashed after her.

# THIRTY

Scissors.

I jumped past the blackened sweatshirt, the disabled Taser, the growing stalks of jagged flame, and ran toward the bedroom.

Parker turned and sneered. Threw the door shut.

Still two strides away, I had no time to stop; I careened into the wood, the impact jarring my depleted frame.

A loud crack rang through the condominium.

"Brianne!" I yelled.

I lifted a leg and thrust my heel against the handle. Another crack rang out, then screws popped loose, the strike plate peeled back like a half-opened tin can, and the door panel sprang free. Before me was a room with glowing sconce lamps and plush curtains that matched tan and cinnamon patterns on the king-size bedspread.

Brianne, on her knees, had both hands joined around the butt of a gun. The drawer of one nightstand was open and dangling, about to fall.

On the carpet, Leroy Parker was dying.

Curled on his side, he had blood throbbing from the holes in his back and chest. I could see she'd nailed him as he'd turned and shut the door, then again after he'd fallen.

The scissors were open on the floor beside the fallen parole officer. In his hand, he held blond strands matching the bare patch above Brianne's right ear. He must've cut them during their struggle in the bathroom.

"Why did he make me shoot him?" Brianne was shivering. "Why didn't he stop? Why?"

With tears spilling over soft freckles, she clicked the safety on the gun, ejected the clip into her palm, and set it on the bed.

Activated by the gathering flames, sprinklers kicked on. Brianne was motionless. She stared at the man on the carpet, letting the water soak her from above, as though it were a healing shower capable of cleansing her stain.

Leroy Parker's blood had spread into the tan carpet, and he was dead.

Brianne continued to stare.

There was something surreal about the moment. We were together again, facing the horror of humanity gone bad. A part of me shut down, refusing to process the obvious.

"The fire," I blurted out.

I grabbed a towel hanging from the bathroom shower rod, ran it under the tap—gritting my teeth as water hit my burns—then helped the sprinklers by beating out the blaze in the hall. The smoke was noxious, scratching at my throat. I crouched beneath its deadly haze and moved toward the ICV man at the far end.

He was still out, stone cold. His chest was moving up and down.

I stood guard and called to Brianne to pick up the phone and dial 911. Guilt was her enemy now, able to paralyze. I knew all about that.

When the sprinklers turned off, I flicked on the lights.

No doubt about it. It was the same man who'd been in my shop. He'd acted so casual, complimenting me on the drink and dropping change into the tip mug before killing Mr. Michaels to keep him from passing on secrets to me.

I shook my head. At least Mrs. Michaels might find bittersweet justice for her son's death.

Brianne nudged up behind me.

"Make sure he doesn't move," I said.

"Where're you going?"

"My hand."

She recoiled at the sight of blistered skin that was elastic and angry red. "There's gauze and ointment under the sink. Let me help you."

"I'm fine. Keep an eye on him."

After running the wound under cold water, I wrapped it gently. My fingers throbbed, and a flash of dizziness swept over me. I gripped the sink with my good hand and looked into the mirror, willing myself to deal with the pain.

Two men had crept into the condo and ambushed us soon after the cops' departure. Was there anyone else? How had they gotten in? What about the anarchist dude who'd jumped me in the alleyway? Where was he? I made a sweep of the condominium, checking every closet and dark space. In Brianne's bedroom, I stepped around the dead man on the floor—*focus on your objective, Aramis*—and noticed her window cracked open with dirty footprints as evidence on the carpet.

"Brianne, has he moved at all?"

"Nope."

I checked under her bed, peered into the walk-in closet. Talk about a penchant for footwear. Brianne's collection was impressive. What is it with women and shoes? I swept my arm along dresses, skirts, and jackets, all hung in immaculate rows.

Nothing to worry about. No one hiding behind the hosiery.

"Everything all right?" Brianne asked upon my return.

I nodded.

She pointed at the unconscious man. "You must've got him good."

"It's the man from the shop. The one who shot Darrell Michaels."

"Then he deserves whatever you did to him."

Her words were bitter. I put my arm around her shoulder, comforting her in the way she had done for me in Black's. She seemed smaller now, shrinking inward. She was gonna have a rough next few days, facing her own demons.

"Brianne."

She tucked her head against my chest.

"You did what had to be done," I said. "You'll be okay."

She glanced toward the bedroom, where Parker's feet were visible in the doorway.

I asked, "What did he mean, about you living up to your end of the deal?"

"I told him that I…" She hung her head. "That I'd let him have his way if they'd just let you go. I was so scared. I thought they might kill you."

"Don't ever let a guy like that touch you. He was scum."

"And I killed him."

"He was armed and threatening you."

"Will I go to jail?"

"No."

"What'll happen to me?"

"You had every right, Brianne. I mean, the guy was coming at you with a pair of scissors." I ran my good hand over the thin spot above her ear. "Maybe we should've let him finish the haircut. Kinda cute."

"Aramis." She screwed her eyes shut as sirens wailed in the distance. "That's not *even* funny."

"Sorry." I took her hand in mine. "Listen, we'll get through this."

"We?"

The sirens were close now. Staring into her emotion-wracked face, I saw a fair maiden waiting for the knight to raise his standard and declare his love. After years of reckless decisions, I wanted to prove I could be honorable, could be that hero every boy dreams of being.

"You and me," I said.

She wrapped herself in the words. "You and me."

Was it brash and illogical? Why do men turn goofy and goggle-eyed in the presence of beautiful young women? Was I setting up Brianne—and myself—for a crushing fall?

I'd only known her for eight days. Criminal psychologists can give you case after case in which life-threatening situations have created inexplicable bonds between people. Fellow victims call each other years later to rehash jarring moments no one else understands. Romantic inclinations flourish. Of course, this link can become a sick thing too. Hostages and kidnappers have formed symbiotic and emotional relationships, now recognized as the Stockholm syndrome.

I guess I realized it was unwise, ill-advised.

And I just didn't care.

She felt warm and comforting, and she needed me. Sometimes that's enough.

"Aramis?"

"Yeah. Just me, Johnny."

I closed the front door of the brownstone and paused in the entryway. Did I really wanna talk to my brother?

"How'd dinner go?" Johnny inquired. "One in the morning? Does this mean my little brother's back in the saddle and done moping around?"

"Give it a rest."

"That bad? Well, just keep swingin'. You got a message today from Los Angeles, so that's a good thing. Carla Fleischmann says you and Uncle Wyatt, you got the green light."

"Great." I kicked off my shoes.

"They'll be flyin' you outta here on the eighth of November."

"Together?"

"Separately."

"Smart thinking."

I braced myself in the kitchen doorway and watched him dice carrots, his version of a midnight snack. The man's not right in the head. He turned to see my disheveled appearance and knew instantly to drop his line of questioning.

"The cops got him," I said. "The dude who murdered the Michaels kid."

"That's a good thing, isn't it?"

"He broke into Brianne's place. Ambushed us."

"Are you kiddin'? You've had one heckuva week, kid. How's she doin'?"

"She's in a hotel for now. Shaken up a bit."

"If I know my brother, the man didn't last long."

"Yeah? Well, after he Tasered me a couple of times, I busted his head open."

"Tasered? Is that what happened to your hand?"

I looked down at the gauze and grunted. "Let's drop it. I'm dog-tired."

"In the morning I'll expect details, the whole shootin' match."

"Deal."

"Glad to see you alive."

I stopped. "I need to talk to Dad."

"Out like a light on the couch. The man likes his booze, but he's pretty harmless. Not as torn up as he used to be, if you know what I'm sayin'."

"Not really."

"Sorry about the other night. Guess we were pretty rough on you."

"I wasn't exactly on my best behavior either. "

"Dad's been wrestlin' with a lotta things, and I think it's done him some good. Cut the ol' man some slack, Aramis. All this trouble you've been facin'? I'm figurin' it's all tied together."

"He's got some stuff to explain."

I stalked to the sink, filled a glass of water, and marched toward the living room. Johnny Ray followed, picking up the intensity in my stride. He set a hand on my forearm and asked where I was going.

I stiffened and stared down. "Let go, Johnny Ray."

"You've had a long night. Why don'tcha take a minute to calm down?"

"Let. Go."

He let go.

I spun toward the slumbering figure on the couch. In a movement that barely scratched the surface of the aggression racing through my mind, I flung the water flush into the face of my prostrate father.

# THIRTY-ONE

**A**rms flailing, he came up from the cushions. He was spluttering and disoriented. His foot slipped on the spilled water and careened into the coffee table, causing him to dance on his other leg. He cursed at the air, then at me, as his senses reminded him where he was.

"Aramis?"

"We need to talk. Now."

"Don't see no call for throwin' water in the face of your old man."

"A lot softer than a fist."

"What? Why, you little runt!"

"Come on, show me what you got. You were more than willing to dish it out when I was a kid. Come on!"

My father glanced toward the kitchen. Still groggy and without any alcohol to fortify him, he seemed unsure what to do. I'd never challenged him like this.

"Get away from me. You're just a know-it-all punk."

"What do you know that you're not telling me? Need me to spark your memory? Tell me about Meriwether Lewis and the whip. Why would you say Mom gave it to me?"

"You lost me, boy."

"What do you know about ICV?"

"Icy what? What's gotten into you?"

"Someone broke in tonight and attacked us—me and this girl I'm seeing—and there was a fire. Another man's been shot dead. All because they want this thing, this whip. I don't know where it is, not even sure what it is. But they're convinced I have it. Why would you tell them that?"

"I ain't told no one nothin'."

"So they were lying?"

"I don't got any idea who *they* are, and I don't take kindly to you throwin' accusations at your old man. What I see here is a snot-nosed little tyke havin' hisself a tantrum. But then again, I've been wrong before."

"There's a news flash," I said.

I set both palms on his chest and shoved him back onto the cushions. The flare of heat in my right hand ignited a deeper explosion of anger, and I felt its power curling through my belly, up into my lungs. My shoulders flexed.

Dad looked toward my brother. "You gonna tell me what's the trouble here?"

Johnny Ray shrugged. "That's between *y'all*." And then he headed outside, closing the door behind him.

How many times had Johnny rushed to my aid? How many nights had he sat next to me on the bed after Dad's drunken outbursts had run their course? How many mornings had he walked with me to the bus, side by side, as brothers, as equals?

For all those things, I loved the man. I'd fight for him. Heck, one day I hoped to be a part of his big break.

But it was for this moment that I loved him the most.

Johnny Ray was giving me the chance to regain the manhood Dad had torn from my fabric.

My chest swelled.

My father's gaze moved from the closed front door to me standing over him. There was no one left for him to impress. The anger of his wet awakening subsided, and for the first time I caught a glimpse of the broken man inside.

"Wasn't right of you, dumpin' that water on me."

"It's one in the morning, Dad. Works better than an alarm clock."

"Did you even try shakin' me?"

"The way you used to do to me?"

He looked away. "You think I don't know?"

"Know what?"

"I know the things I done weren't right."

"And this is just coming to you now?"

"I knew all along."

"So now that the tables are turned, you think to tell me this. After twenty years? Nothing like a little fear to bring things into focus, huh?" My wounded hand was a ball of fire, but my left was still good. I could do extensive damage if necessary.

"Whatchu want from me, Aramis?"

"An apology wouldn't hurt."

"I'm here, ain't I? Why do ya think I drove myself down to see you?"

"Simple. For the fabulous Johnny Ray Black. Live and in concert."

"I won't deny that's part of it. But reason number one"—he held up his index finger—"was you. When I got word about that shootin' at your shop, well, it got me to thinkin'. You ain't gonna be around forever. Ain't none of us gonna be. And so I figured I owed you an explanation."

"You've been here—what?—two or three days? You said you had things to tell me and that they had to do with Mom. Well, I'm still waiting."

"Just ain't been a good time."

"Can we *stop* the back and forth, Dad? Spit it out!"

Kenny Black's posture changed. I watched it happen—his shoulders and arms slumping, his legs relaxing. He ran one hand over the top of his head, closed his eyes, and exhaled. He'd been the hard-as-nails figure for so long that he seemed relieved to slough off the tough demeanor.

"No big secret," he said. "Just a matter of layin' it all out on the table."

"Go on. I'm listening."

"It's the things I done, the way I was firm with you—"

"There's an understatement."

"When your mother died, I just didn't have any way of dealin' with that. I loved her more than anything on this earth. She was my world. Knowin' she was gone, knowin' I couldn't go back to tell her I was sorry for the things I done and said—it was more than I could bear. And all I've done since is shame her with my deeds. Grief and regret—they can lay a man flat quicker than just about anything."

My throat constricted.

"Thing of it is, I picked you out, Aramis. That's the shameful part. Guess I needed someplace to push all that anger holed up inside of me, and you got the job. Plain and simple."

"That's the way it happened, huh?"

"That's the way it happened."

"Why not someone else?"

He closed his eyes. "Diggin' this up won't do a bit of good."

"Why me? Tell me!"

"Can't leave well enough alone, can ya?"

"Because I was the youngest? The weakest?"

"No."

"The least likely to succeed?"

"Ain't no use in sayin' it, Aramis."

"Gimme one reason, Dad. Just one. Help me understand."

"Told you I was wrong already. What more d'ya want from me?"

I wanted to see him grovel, see him humiliated and on his knees. After all these years, I wanted to feel the power over him that he'd exerted over me. One simple answer. Was that so hard?

In a voice raked with sorrow, my father said, "Okay, ya wanna know why? It's 'cause, from the very beginning, your mother loved you most, and it was too much for this old man to deal with. I never had her love, not fully. Never had me a chance to say good-bye, either. And for them reasons, Aramis, I made you pay."

With the loss of my mother, I'd lost my father too.

Colors shift and blur in my dream, running into one. Through a crimson veil, I see Dad coming toward me. He shakes his head, muttering. His fists are wrapped in gauze.

"Ain't never gonna find it on your own," he says.

"Find what?"

He waves Mom's handkerchief.

I snatch it from him and dash off, pressing the soft material to my face and drawing in its fragrance. Her fragrance. She's near, of that I'm certain.

Still running, I catch sight of her on a riverbank, on her knees.

"Mom!"

Stretching my arms to their limits, I feel the wind create lift beneath me. I need to reach her. I rise from the ground and launch forward, brushing over golden tips of wheat. On pinions of flight, I swoop to her rescue.

Then gravity has its say.

I crash and somersault into the mud, end over end through coffee-tinted earth, catapulting straight past my mother and over the edge. Plunging down. Down. Into liquid nothingness.

Seconds later she, too, plunges below the surface.

Her hair swirls about her face. She brushes it away so that her eyes catch mine.

And she smiles.

obody's dead?" said Johnny Ray. "I figure that's a good thing."

"Is Dad sleeping?"

"Like a baby. So the two of you got things all squared away?"

I shrugged, then pointed at his Tabasco boxers. "You ever change those?"

"Don't see as how it's any of your business, kid."

"We share the same roof."

"If you must know," he said, "I've got eight pair, one for each day of the week."

"And the spare?"

"For emergencies."

"Stop." I held up my hand, which I'd dabbed with burn ointment and rewrapped, and curled away from him into the kitchen.

"Help yourself to the grapefruit juice," Johnny called. "Fresh squeezed."

I swigged it straight from the pitcher, clenched my teeth, shook my head, and uttered one of my tribal grunts.

"That'll wake you up. Good stuff and good for you."

I grunted again. Filled a bowl with cereal. "You're right, Johnny

Ray. Nothing like some fruit to kick off the day." I ate a heaping spoon of Froot Loops.

"A healthy start's always good," he said from the living room. " 'Bout time you listened to your big brother."

Another bite. Crunchy, processed, artificially sweetened, and wonderful.

"Yeah, Johnny. What you said."

Johnny was strumming his guitar, working on a new tune. He played a chord progression that sounded clear and bright, ringing over the hardwood.

He paused to speak. "You heard the news?"

"No."

"Well, Johnny Ray Black is turnin' a new page. Generating some interest in high places."

I gulped down my bite. "Someone on Music Row?"

"Even better."

"Musik Mafia?"

"Along those lines. The independent route's lookin' mighty fine, with room to be yourself, if you know what I'm sayin'."

"What about lookin' the part?"

Johnny laughed. "That's already in the bag, they tell me."

"The things they'll say to make a buck."

He was ignoring me, easing into the lyrics: "Life got brighter when the lights went down. It's been an uphill road to reach this down-home gal. She said we'd never happen; it was just a weekend thing. I said, 'Here's what I been thinking… Let's have a lifelong fling.' "

My bowl and spoon clattered in the sink. I pulled on a light jacket and shoes.

"Catchy. Any particular lady in mind?"

Still gripping a pick in his fingers, he wagged his hand back and forth. "I don't tell my inspiration, you know that. Gotta make the song your own."

"Sarah the bimbo?"

"Don't start."

"Samantha Rosewood?"

His eyes shifted to mine, sparkled, then danced away.

Trees shook in the morning breeze that whipped across the pond. As I headed with hunched shoulders through the park, the chill shoved aside my drowsiness and stirred questions to the surface.

Had I failed my friend Freddy C?

Had he been crying for help all these months, tortured by his own depravity?

If, indeed, he'd done those things to Jessica Tyner and the other girls, he deserved any punishment coming his way. Had he been throwing out clues?

*Shouldn't show my face... If you're smart, you'll get him... Stay outta my hair... I'm not safe to be around... He'll no longer take what doesn't belong to him.*

Tina stood from a bench, motioning at me as her dog yipped.

"Hey," I said.

"Recycling man, he had a plan."

"That wind's cold, Tina. Are you stayin' warm?"

"Hiding and waiting, ceaselessly baiting."

"Are you talking about Freddy C? Did you hear what happened?"

Her eyes met mine for a fraction of a second, pleading for mercy. Then, as though ashamed of herself, she muttered something else and shuffled away with her wooden cart wobbling through dew-soaked grass.

I tried to shrug off the facts: Freddy found outside Brianne's condo with a pair of scissors. Videotaped outside my place hours before I found the clump of hair.

Just one problem: Before taking two bullets, Parole Officer Leroy Parker had wielded scissors of his own. Used them to collect some of Brianne's hair.

Brianne arrived for work with blond hair poking through the back of a pink ball cap. Her eyes were puffy. I hugged her for a long moment, deciding that caffeine-craving customers could pause to remember that we're all human, each one of us.

"Thank you," she said.

I gave her a peck on the cheek. "You sure you're up for work? You can take a day off if you need to."

"By myself? In that hotel? I'd rather be near you."

"Whenever you're ready then."

She headed toward the back washroom.

I turned to the woman at the front of the line. She wore nutmeg-colored mascara and glitter lip gloss and a jogging suit with stripes down the sides. A pedometer hung on her hip.

"Sorry 'bout that," I said.

"Are my espresso shots cold?"

I looked down. "Yeah. I'll pull some new ones. A mocha, was it?"

Using my left hand for everything, I tamped down the espresso and said, "Brianne's condo was broken into last night. She didn't sleep all that well."

"No whip," the woman said. "Make it extra hot."

"Yes, ma'am. And that'll be on the house. Appreciate your patience."

She took the drink and jogged out the door without a word.

No worries. Under control. Just another day on the job.

When the next customer stepped up, I braced myself for more of the same. The man was around my age, African American with tight dreads framing a caramel brown face and sandy eyes. His suit was loose and pinstriped, cut down the middle by a thin gold tie. He raised an eyebrow, told me to shrug off the haters, and tucked a pair of ten-dollar bills into my orange mug.

"Just helpin' a brother," he explained. "We all have our rough days."

At twelve thirty I was supposed to meet with Detective Meade to view video footage and speak with Freddy C. I called Johnny Ray. He has Saturdays off, and he agreed to keep an eye out at Black's as long as he could get a salad.

*On the house? Not a problem.*

Johnny was still en route when the phone rang. I'd just stocked the freezer, and Brianne was helping mop up a customer's spill in the dining area. Brianne pursed her lips and shrugged as if to say, "I'm stuck out here. Could you get that?"

"Black's. This is Aramis."

"Oh, *thank* the Lord. I was hopin' and prayin' to catch ya there."

"Mrs. Michaels?"

"Good mornin', Mr. Black. Ain't interruptin', am I? Don't mean to be a burden."

"Not at all." I peeked at the counter, saw a patron still checking the menu. I thought about her son's killer, now in custody. "Have you talked to the police this morning?"

"Not so as I know. Why?"

"I'm surprised."

"They might've tried callin' me, but the phone's cut off. I'm using my neighbor's mobile phone, on loan. Real sweet of her. Been doin' my best, you know, but I just can't keep up with them bills. Tell me, what's goin' on?"

"Do you think we can talk in person?"

"That's the reason I called. Grown man like you's gotta eat, am I right? Ain't nothin' better than a mama's home cookin'.'"

I stiffened at the sentiment.

"Mr. Black? All's I'm sayin' is, you're without a mama, and I'm without my son. Might be nice for you to come on over and share a meal."

"That means a lot." I cleared my throat. "Thank you."

"There's other reasons too. I'm hopin' for some answers. Been thinkin' on Darrell, so I started goin' through his stuff this morning. Weren't the easiest, but it's gotta be done. A mama's responsibility."

"You're a brave lady."

"I found somethin' might be of interest to ya."

"Yeah?"

"A set of papers, brown and crackly and older than dirt. I'm thinkin' my boy got himself in over his head, and maybe you can help me understand. If I'm readin' right, this here's got the name Samuel Whiteside, signed and dated, real official-like."

"Dated, huh?"

"It's faded bad, but the best I can make out, it says, 'October twelfth, in the year of our Lord, eighteen hundred and nine.'"

"I'm on my way. And I'll tell you the latest on my end."

"No dillydallyin' then. Red velvet cake's goin' into the oven as we speak."

"Land speed records are about to fall."

She gave a cautious laugh—that of a bereaved mother trying to wear a strong face for her little ones. Some who lose loved ones never rediscover that spring of genuine mirth, while others lay their stones of grief in the water's path, creating richer sounds of bubbling, gurgling life.

I believe the spring's out there, a source of heavenly strength.

Each day, in my own fumbling way, I look for it. And I listen.

# THIRTY-THREE

**D**etective Meade would have to wait. I called and left a message at the precinct, then marched home and jumped into my Honda Civic.

Neely's Bend.

With construction-related traffic, the journey took nearly forty minutes. I wasn't followed; I checked my mirrors to ensure against it. That left me with contemplation time behind the wheel.

Neely...with one *L*.

As in Agent James Neely, the man who escorted Meriwether Lewis?

The coincidence seemed too much to push aside. Many family names have changed and dropped letters over the years. Even the owners of Grinder's Stand, where Lewis died, have been listed as the Griners in numerous publications. This is the South, where oral tradition has passed names along without concern for accurate spelling, where secrets have prompted slight permutations for reasons of a personal nature.

I knew I should have an idea what these mysterious documents were, but my mind was too muddled to dredge up the right information.

I turned up Lightning 100, Nashville's progressive rock station, and let the music numb my frustrations with road crews and ever-changing detours.

Maybe it's a trait of my age group or a unique personality quirk, but music tends to occupy one side of my brain so that the other side can get to work. Even as a kid, I did homework better with my ear-phones in and the volume jacked up.

My subconscious released the info and escorted it to the evidence room.

Last night. Leroy Parker's voice: *I told you those papers were the real deal.*

The ICV man: *You said that Michaels kid took the papers.*

Parker: *He did. He swiped 'em from me. I swear it.*

And back in Centennial Park, Mrs. Michaels: *Darrell and Mr. Parker, they found somethin'...a gift from above.*

There was something else. Something that still eluded me.

The Michaels house seemed more dilapidated than I recalled from my previous visit. A shrunken version of a Southern plantation home, the residence only hinted at bygone glory and was in obvious need of repair. I had to wonder how safe the children were, running through the place.

Juniper and maple trees stood guard at the corners, but the house had been overrun by bushes and weeds that spilled over the pebbled walkway. Weather and age had warped the planking, and the pillars at the front porch stood at a discernible slant.

This time Mrs. Michaels willingly opened the front door for me. "How d'ya do, Mr. Black?"

She said it with such unaffected politeness that I thrust out my hand. What was the correct procedure here? I mean, I was raised in the Northwest.

She smiled and looked at the offered hand, wrapped in gauze.

"What happened to ya?"

"Got caught playing with fire."

"Hope you's smarter next time 'round."

"Sorry for the delay," I said. "You know the traffic out there."

"I'm tellin' *you*. Come in, come in." She looked down and patted twin girls on the head. "Where're y'all's manners? Say hello to Mr. Black."

"How d'ya do, sir?" they voiced in unison.

"Mighty fine, my dear ladies," I said in mock chivalry. "And you?"

They disappeared in a fit of squeals and giggles.

Despite the home's rundown condition, Mrs. Michaels had gone to great lengths to make it cozy and livable, and everywhere I looked I saw touches of a mother's love. She gestured toward the dining table. I wondered when it would be best to tell her about the ICV man's capture. Would she want to face the man who'd shot her son?

Mealtime started with fruit tea and a basket of warm biscuits and salted butter, followed by turnip greens, corn, country-fried steak, and fried apples.

Hearty fare. Delicious and satisfying.

Throughout, I joked with the kids, getting to know each of them by their nicknames. The youngest were wide-eyed and curious, the older ones quiet and less apt to laugh. Darrell's death was a reality still settling. Like dust, this type of tragedy is never completely swept away; it sits quietly until stirred by simple words or memories, and on good days it dances through sunlight as a reminder that warmth and hope still exist.

"Now why don't y'all go play upstairs," Mrs. Michaels told the children. "Do as you're told, and you'll be gettin' yourselves some cake when it's ready."

Although they grumbled, reluctant to leave their guest, they no doubt dreaded the boredom of adult conversation. They crawled over and around me before pounding up a creaking staircase with white banisters.

"Thanks for the food, Mrs. Michaels," I said. "Sure hit the spot."

"You saved yourself some room, didn't ya?" The smell of the cooling red velvet cake wafted through the house, even as she prepared the frosting. "This was Darrell's favorite, you know that? Always had a sweet tooth, that one."

I felt honored by this gesture. And sugar? I hadn't had any since breakfast.

Guilt tugged at me as I basked in this hospitality while Brianne held things down at Black's. I reminded myself that Johnny Ray was there as a sentinel, and she'd have his helping hand if the situation required it.

"So," I said, "you have something to show me? The papers?"

Mrs. Michaels pointed with a frosting-coated knife. "I moved 'em right there behind ya, in the bottom drawer."

I turned toward an antique secretary desk. "Mind if I…

"Go on, go on. Have yourself a look. It's why you came, ain't it?"

I detected a rueful tone, yet my attention was on the documents. They sat inside a clear sheet protector, yellowed and brittle. Although tests would be required for conclusive dating, there was nothing to make me doubt they had been penned nearly two centuries ago.

"These were in your son's belongings?"

Mrs. Michaels nodded.

"Were they hidden? You know, tucked away somewhere inconspicuous?"

"That's one way of puttin' it. He was my boy, you realize, and he weren't ever a bad kid at heart. Over the years, though, I learnt his ways. He put things where he figured his mama wouldn't know what he was up to. S'pose it was nosy of me, but I done it for his own good, and that's the Lord's honest truth. After I moved the four young uns here from Memphis, that's when I put my foot down, told Darrell and his older sister there weren't gonna be no more of that in *my* house."

Pressing the plastic against the historic documents, I tried to make out the words on the first sheet and detected a date and signature, just as she'd relayed on the phone. I thumbed carefully through the others.

"So when I started goin' through his things this mornin', I figured it was only smart to check his ol' hiding places. Sure 'nuff, found them papers taped in plastic folders on the back of one of his posters. I'd found money there before, and other things. A little bag of powder once, which I was just *sure* was more of them drugs."

"In the news, they said Darrell's PO had been giving him clean reports."

"Uh-huh. Mr. Leroy Parker. And what'd I tell ya 'bout that man?"

"That he's dishonest," I said.

I'd reached the last document. It was a personal letter.

Mrs. Michaels continued. "Had my doubts about him from the get-go. Know what I think? He was usin' my boy to help him with this Lewis nonsense."

"You still think it's nonsense?"

"Don't rightly know, Mr. Black. Just know I don't trust that Mr. Parker."

"He's dead now. He attacked a lady last night, and she shot him. Twice."

Mrs. Michaels dropped her chin, then leaned over the kitchen sink on both arms, her dimpled back pressing against her blouse. My hand was still on the letter. "God rest that man's soul," she murmured, "for things he done and for things he ain't that he shoulda."

Seemed to be a fitting eulogy. She must've thought so too, because when she turned back, she had shirked off any sympathy or shock and had chosen to help me in my search. She scooped up a magnifying glass from atop the desk, lowered herself into the seat beside me, and moved the instrument over the top paper.

"See for yourself, Mr. Black."

I dropped one arm under the table and leaned closer, peering through the glass. In ink scratched across fibrous parchment, the spidery signatures came to life. One belonged to Justice of the Peace Samuel Whiteside, the other to a doctor whose name was indecipherable.

I thought of my brother's comments at the memorial site in Hohenwald: *A coroner's inquest was never even filed… Papers like that were the personal property of the justice of the peace, but these just disappeared… Whoever had them could've just thrown them in a box and stuffed them in an attic.*

This was that inquest!

These pages could rewrite the history books. Here, in black and white, the coroner's conclusion was that Governor Meriwether Lewis had unequivocally and without question been murdered. His death was a result of multiple gunshot wounds—with bullets from separate weapons. Furthermore, he'd suffered knife wounds and a slit across his throat. The trajectories of the bullets suggested an attacker, or attackers, standing over the governor. And, most telling, Lewis's own hands had no trace of gunpowder upon them.

"A gift from above," I whispered.

"Mr. Black?"

"Do you have an attic?"

"I ain't never been in it, not that I'd fit up there if I tried."

"Didn't your son and Mr. Parker say they found something that was a gift from above? What if these papers were originally hidden up there? Maybe Darrell was looking for a new spot to stash his paraphernalia and—"

"Stash what?"

"Never mind. I think Agent James Neelly stole this inquest to cover his guilt, and he held on to these other documents as leverage against his superior, General Wilkinson."

"You done lost me completely."

"How old is this house?"

"Built before the war. For a time Union bigwigs used it as a headquarters and even added on out back. Built themselves a stable for their horses." Mrs. Michaels rolled her eyes in dramatic fashion. "Least that's what the real-estate fella told me, but they ain't got no record of the original owner."

"Neelly moved here. Maybe even built the place. Then he concealed the papers and took his secret to the grave."

"The grave." Mrs. Michaels quivered at that, then said in a voice husky with grief, "And that's where this all oughta stay, don't ya think? My son got mixed up in this and got hisself killed for it. Spanish gold? Murder? No more, not in my house. We put this back where it came from and leave the dead in peace."

"What about the truth?"

"This here's my home, Mr. Black. And my family, my kin. I don't bother no one, and they don't bother me. Sure, I see we got a mystery on our hands, but it's *our* mystery, and I reckon I can live with it stayin' that way."

"What about the Lewis family?"

"What of 'em?"

"Don't they deserve to know the truth about their forebear? He was an American figurehead. The schools should be teaching kids what really happened. It's possible I'm even a descendant."

"No." Mrs. Michaels pulled herself to her feet and returned to the cake, where she sliced tall slabs and laid them on plates. "What's done is done," she said, "and it ain't *my* job to step in where the Lord's already been."

My hands trembled at the thought of letting this go. She'd called me here, letting me in on a secret and finding a measure of understanding regarding her son's death. Was there any way I could go against her wishes on this? No. This was her family and her home, a place of refuge from the things life had thrown her way.

And overriding all else, this is the South, where outsiders ought not tread.

I'd already waited too long. With this host of revelations still spiraling through the air, she deserved to know that at least one mystery had been solved. Darrell's murderer had been apprehended and booked into the county jail.

She was handing me dessert and a fork.

"Mrs. Michaels?" I set the utensil down and took her hand.

She searched my eyes, then took a deep breath and sank into her chair.

# THIRTY-FOUR

t was a despicable thing to do.

Sharply aware of the document rolled and tucked into the sleeve of my jacket, I still had the nerve to take this sweet woman's hand in mine. It was a genuine act of compassion, even if my motives were muddied and my methods questionable. Nevertheless, as Mrs. Michaels and I talked and dipped forks into moist slabs of red velvet cake, self-loathing settled in my stomach.

I was wrong. Not an easy pill to swallow.

"Thanks for the great meal," I told Mrs. Michaels as I left the house in Neely's Bend. "We'll talk soon. At least we know that man's behind bars."

She gave a grudging nod, her eyes still teary. "There's *some* comfort in that."

"Your kids are the greatest."

"Ain't no question. Thanks for comin' out, Mr. Black."

I knew I would never reveal the secrets contained in the Michaels home, not against her wishes. The truth of Lewis's death would remain undisturbed.

Yet I still had my own heritage to consider. My mother.

Had Dianne Lewis Black lost her life for the sake of these things?

With this as my justification, I had removed the final document from the protective sheath and discreetly concealed it.

The letter was signed by Meriwether Lewis.

My ancestor? I needed to know before anyone else died.

I headed back toward I-24 and eased into a gas station. With the car idling, I unfurled the two-centuries-old parchment and gripped it with the edges of my shirt to protect against fingerprint oils and corrosives.

Although the words had an archaic feel, I could hear among them the faint echo of hidden gold and untold conspiracies.

I couldn't resist reading.

Mother,

It is with much distress I write, as it is not certain or even of strong likelihood that I shall survive this night's indications of intrigue. I believe even now there are agents expediting a course of violence aimed to hinder, or with all finality, dispose of my being.

Hesitance and a measure of alarm have accompanied my good servant Mr. Pernier and me throughout the day, and we are now encamped at Grinder's Stand within a short distance of the Natchez Trace.

Two of my packhorses were said to have bolted during last evening's immense thunderstorm display, burdened down as they were with my collection of documents and valuables. This circumstance has dissuaded our pestiferous escort Agent Neelly from maintaining our company as instead he rides in

pursuit of the missing animals; it is my belief that Neelly has
intended to pilfer the documents from the journey's outset,
for the service and protection of the one who appointed him.
With courses of treason apparent on the part of these individ-
uals, and with such concerns bearing upon my every thought,
I have done as I saw fit.

I wish therefore to divulge matters pertaining to my exe-
cution of certain duties personal and political in nature. The
dangers presiding are certain and imminent, and I must force
upon you this notion: Spare your soul, and turn your eyes
from greed.

At my own hands, a large procurement of gold has failed
to arrive safely in the good graces of the aforementioned traitor, finding instead a circuitous route to a grave of earth and
stone. It has been joined therewith by specific receipts and
letters attesting to his path of personal indulgence.

Alone in my knowledge of this, I find it necessary to
demand a forthright and full confession from the one whose
conspiracies have become odorous to all in proximity. I have it
in my power here to record that all is in order, should that day
present itself. Together in their earthen grave, Spanish gold
and documentation forge a verdict both irrepressible and just.

As for my own person, I have relinquished all further
hope. It is too late to introduce a remedy, and I bid adieu to
my family and to you also, whom I hold in highest regard.
This letter shall be sealed and assigned delivery by the hand
of my good Mr. Pernier, for he has agreed to pay you a visit
and will be attended by a riding crop from my own collection. You have in previous encounters laid eyes upon this

whip and may find its newly embroidered patterns of some aesthetic value.

Take heed, I have penned one other letter of disclosure but foremost wish to procure your attendance to this matter. Should news of my demise reach your ears, you will need the whip to discern the bearings of gold and grave.

I am with every sentiment of love and respect,

Your Son,

Meriwether Lewis

I digested the letter with a sense that fate was spying over my shoulder. My mother must've been familiar with these words. Had she obtained the "other letter of disclosure"? How else would she have known to mouth a warning so specific?

*Spare your soul, and turn your eyes from greed...*

*You will need the whip to discern the bearings of gold...*

Greed. There it was, driving its slaves forward, cracking the whip.

How did the Bible put it? "The love of money is a root of all kinds of evil."

If my mother was indeed connected by blood to Meriwether Lewis, Darrell and Parker's search would've led to Portland. Darrell, being a parolee, was confined to the state of Tennessee—except by official request, which he would've wanted to avoid—so Parker became the solution to that obstacle.

Parker poked around. Asked questions about me. Probably used threats to pressure my incarcerated father for answers. He then crossed swords with my old ICV ties and found himself in a reluctant alliance, sealed by promises of gold and documents that could fuel anarchist fires.

Yes, it was all conjecture. A theory. But it fit.

Darrell Michaels had become a puppet. Resentful and ravaged again by his meth addiction, he hid the papers from the others to pursue the treasure alone. And who should he find standing last in the line of Lewis males?

Yours truly. And right under his nose in Music City.

He must've believed it was a sign.

I can see Darrell that crucial Thursday morning, cookin' and tweakin', preparing to face me with his demands for the whip. Perhaps he believed God had led him to this point and the treasure would soon be his. Maybe his intentions were noble; maybe he had his mom and siblings in mind.

He overlooked the competition and paid the price for it.

At least as he lay dying, he had the decency to try to warn me.

# THIRTY-FIVE

No, I'm not angry."

"You sound angry, Brianne." And she did, even through the cell phone.

"I'm hurt. Why do you do this to me, leaving me on my own? You've been gone for over two hours."

"I'm trying to wrap things up as quickly as I can." I'd already secured Lewis's document at the safe-deposit box used by Black's. Now en route to the downtown library, I took the Broadway exit. Only a few blocks to go. "Has Johnny Ray been helping you? He's still there, isn't he?"

"Of course he's here, you doof."

"Doofus."

"You are so not funny. It's been crazy, everyone wanting their precious coffee for the first chilly day of fall. People've been asking about you. A couple of days ago they seemed worried. Now it's like they're a little annoyed. At least Johnny's kept them entertained with his guitar. He's been taking requests and passing the hat around."

"Johnny Ray to the rescue."

"I suggested it. He did try to help behind the counter—I'll give him credit for that—but the man doesn't know the first thing about what goes on back here."

"Like our kiss by the freezer?"

"Would you stop? I know what you're trying to do, and it won't work."

"I'm just trying to say I'm sorry." I paused. "You've stuck with me since all this craziness started. I really appreciate it. I do. Sometimes I get so focused on my own stuff that I end up comin' off like a jerk."

A tearful tone entered her voice. "You know, the only reason I came to work this morning was to be near you. After last night…I've got all these thoughts running through my head. I'm so scared about what'll happen."

"The detectives said you had every right to protect yourself."

"Self-defense."

"Exactly."

"But it feels like it'll still be there, like this mark on my record. What'll people think of me?"

"They'll think you were a brave girl who—"

"Girl?"

"Lady. A brave, beautiful lady who defended herself at all costs. You're strong. That's part of what drew me to you."

"Really?" Her voice lightened.

"You don't let things stand in your way. Think of how you took the job in the first place, even after the shooting. Not to mention how you kept insisting that I have dinner with you." I slowed and put on my turn signal. "Not that I'm complaining."

"Better not be." She was sounding more playful.

"I didn't know how to deal with it at first, the whole employer-

employee thing. We still need to be careful, I guess. But your persist-
ence broke through."

"As if it was all my doing. Who was it, mister, that threw me
against the wall and kissed me, huh?"

"You know you liked it."

"I'm leaning against that very wall now."

In midturn, I caught the curb of the parking garage and nearly
dropped the phone as the Honda bucked.

"Aramis?"

"I'm trying to drive here."

"Are you coming back this way anytime soon? Did you already
have your meeting with that detective?"

"Not yet. A quick detour and then that's where I'm headed." As
I pulled into a spot beneath the concrete structure, the phone crackled. "I'm about to lose you."

"Just don't stay away too long, or I'll have to see what your
brother's plans are for the evening. He *is* kinda cute in his hat."

"Yeah? Well, he tans twice a week. Mine's real."

"I'll keep that in mind."

Since the beginning, Lewis's letter had been the catalyst. An American icon defending his country against treason, a secret trickling down
through generations, and then a chance discovery by a parolee in his
mother's Davidson County attic.

The ghosts of our nation's past had stirred.

Did it still exist, this old riding crop hiding a map to a cache of
gold? Was the Spanish bullion still out there? And did my mother's

handkerchief contain a similar map, embroidered the day before her death?

I'd held the material to my cheek many times, rubbed the silk between my hands, and traced her initials with my fingertips. The other pattern was intricate, with indigo thread winding about a thicker, turquoise one; yet I'd never seen anything like a map in its details. This was heady stuff. If true, it would give deeper meaning to Mom's death.

And my own survival.

The Nashville Public Library system includes a first-rate collection of reading and research materials. If the twenty branch libraries throughout the county are glittering crown jewels, then the downtown branch is the practically flawless diamond at its center.

The resources are extensive: the Metropolitan Government Archives, with more than five million records on microfilm; the computer lab; the Center for Entrepreneurs; the Civil Rights Room; and the Nashville Room, with its numerous genealogical materials. Many library visitors take their lunches from the downstairs café into the center courtyard where a fountain flows in the midst of the shade trees.

At a computer I investigated the genealogy of Meriwether Lewis, from past to present, then did the same with the Black family, starting with Kenneth S. Black and moving back. In the middle, I hoped to find intertwining branches.

No such luck. Two hundred years leaves time for lots of offshoots.

I did learn that Lewis's mother was a famed explorer, with medical training, culinary skills, and a fearless disposition. His decision in his letter to leave such grave matters in her hands was calculated and wise.

It's a matter of record that Mr. Pernier did indeed visit her after Lewis's death, but Mrs. Lucy Meriwether Lewis Marks declared that he must've killed her son, and she ran him off with a rifle.

Did Pernier give her the letter and riding crop? No one knows.

As my confidence in solving this mystery was building, so was my bitterness toward Uncle Wyatt. In a few weeks, we would confront each other once more, making an attempt at getting *The Best of Evil* by doing good.

"Just got word," said Detective Meade. His Titans clock by the door said it was 3:11 p.m. "The incision and residue pattern on Ms. Tyner's hair specimen match the scissors."

"Which scissors?"

"The ones Frederick Chipps was carrying."

"Frederick Chipps."

I chewed on that, having a hard time accepting it as the man's full name. For the year I'd been friends with Freddy C, I'd held on to some romantic notion that the C stood for Crusader, wanting to believe the best about the man.

"We've already contacted a former employer of his in the state of Illinois, as well as the school where he served as custodian. Court and police records will be sent to us to help establish patterns and build a case." Meade leaned forward on both elbows, linking his long fingers as he gazed at me. "Is there something wrong?"

"Are you sure about all this?"

"The incision patterns, Aramis. His are the very blades that cut Ms. Tyner's hair, implying related and far more serious crimes."

"What about Leroy Parker?"

"He was a public servant, caught up in suspicious activities that are now under investigation. The man's dead. I'd say he paid the price for his impropriety."

"I watched him chase Brianne with a pair of scissors."

"A different pair than those matching the Tyner specimen."

"He was *chasing* her. He cut a chunk out of her hair!" I pushed back in my chair, causing it to thud against the detective's bookcase.

"Mr. Black, I understand you've been under a great deal of stress." Detective Meade rose from his seat and made a quarter turn to adjust a framed photo of his wife on the wall. He was establishing authority, while softening its confrontational aspects. When his coal black eyes reached mine, he showed no fear or hesitation or prejudice—a man I'd rather have on my side than not.

"Stress? Yeah, you could say that."

"But," Meade said, "you must maintain your objectivity, even as I must."

"I'm just a cranky man who's had a very long week. Sorry. Don't mean to take it out on you."

"My mother used to say, 'If you're truly sorry, Son, you'll change your ways.' "

I rocked my neck to the left, to the right. Heard it pop.

"And," he continued, "I'm willing to change mine. For reasons I'm sure you can understand, I'm not presently free to discuss the record of Parole Officer Leroy Parker. I am, however, open to being wrong. In fact, I think it's an attribute of any detective worth his salt."

I looked past his shoulder at the photo of his family in front of the Parthenon.

"You're a good dad, I bet."

"Do my best." He rapped his knuckles on his desk. "Okay,

Aramis, let's have you take a look at that video. There's no mistaking Frederick Chipps in the footage, but you might pick up something we missed."

I followed his upright stride into a small, darkened room.

"The tape's been touched up by our digital department," he told me as footage of the brownstone's parking lot filled the monitor on the table. "Still not the greatest, but we can play it over if need be."

Freddy C was a primary suspect in the Rasputin Rapist case. If he'd planted the hair specimen in my mother's ebony box, I guessed it would have been to frame me. I doubt he would have known the value of the handkerchief.

Where was the handkerchief now? Was it another one of his trophies?

The thought of his salty hands on it made me queasy.

"Detective, wait." I jerked upright in my seat. "Pause it right there. Yeah. Now zoom in to the left."

"What do you see?"

I stabbed my finger at the screen. "That car, the one Freddy's climbing out of—that's not his. I don't think he even has a driver's license."

"Maybe he was sleeping in it, staying warm."

"It's a white Camry," I said. "Same car Leroy Parker drives."

"Drove," Meade corrected me.

"So what was it doing in our lot?"

Detective Meade zoomed in, creating a large image of the car's rear bumper. Together, he and I read the license plate aloud.

"BHT 588."

# THIRTY-SIX

Despite the concerns of his court-appointed attorney, Freddy C agreed to speak to me. He claimed I was a friend. I stiffened at the word, no longer trusting its cozy sound.

He shuffled in, bearded and scraggly. The small opening in the glass partition flattened and filtered our voices, but it couldn't alter visual impressions. He didn't look well, and the way his eyes avoided mine reminded me of my encounter with Tina in the park this morning: *Hiding and waiting, ceaselessly baiting.*

Ten minutes. That's all we were allowed. No time for small talk.

"Freddy C."

"Artemis," he said.

"You don't look so hot. Is it true you were on Brianne's property?"

With no hesitation, he nodded his head up and down.

"Why? What were you doing with scissors?"

"Not what they think." He smoothed his beard. "Not what they think at all."

"If you don't tell me, they can think whatever they want and put you away for a long time. Do you understand me...Frederick Chipps?"

His chin bobbed as he mumbled something, and I told him to repeat himself.

He said, "They told you, didn't they? About Chicago."

"You were acquitted. What's there to tell?"

"Wasn't me, no sir. But no one believed me. No believers. The news, the reporters—they made me into a criminal."

"Are you?"

"What?"

"A criminal. Is that what the C stands for? Chipps the Criminal?"

Freddy bumped his forehead into the partition, disturbing his swept-back strands of hair. He bumped it again, and a voice crackled through an overhead speaker with instructions not to touch the glass.

"You are my friend," he said. "My friend. I need your trust, need your help."

"Friends tell the truth, Freddy."

"No one believes, not even you. But I fight it. I do. Fight it my own way."

"Fight what?"

"Crime," he said. "I fight crime."

"Freddy."

"You must believe, Artemis. This is why I chose you to help. He is not much of a man, but he is very bad. He does bad things. I saw him. Saw him in the park and at the Alumni Lawn."

I checked the clock.

"I followed him," Freddy went on. "Hid and waited in the shadows where he could not see, but I saw. A true man would be strong and in control, isn't that so?" His eyes met mine for the first time, waiting for verification.

"Sure. A true man."

"He was weak. Used a Taser to bring 'em down."

"What're you saying? The rapist used a Taser? You watched this happen?"

Freddy's eyes lit up. "Yes. I baited him. He kept his things in his car, in a padded case, always ready. But I took one of them."

"One of what?"

"The hair. Her hair."

"Jessica Tyner's? You took the hair from his case and put it in my room?"

"You, Artemis. They will believe you."

"You broke into my house."

"No one home. The bathroom window was open."

"That was wrong. You can't do that sorta thing."

He nodded. "But you wouldn't believe. No one believes me. Not after Chicago. I gave it to you so they can catch this man who isn't a man. Not really, is he?"

"And this hair was supposed to clue me in?"

"An anonymous note. I left it to explain."

"I didn't see any note. I saw a stinkin' clump of hair. Even if this is all true, you had no right to take my mom's handkerchief."

He shook his head. "Silky and white? I saw it, but I didn't touch. Freddy C does not steal from friends. Never from a friend. I left a note. This bad man was watching you too, Artemis. Following. And I was worried. We have to catch him. I wanted the police to see, so I took his scissors."

"From the case in his car? A white Camry, am I right?"

"Yes, yes. They can match his scissors. We got ourselves a problem, gotta solve it quick. I've seen him outside her place."

"Brianne's?"

"From your shop, yes. He's followed her home. Not a safe man."

I lifted my hand and leaned close to the glass. "Listen. He's dead, Freddy. We caught him in Brianne's condo last night, and he must've gotten himself a new pair of scissors. He was shot. He's gone for good."

Our time had almost expired. Freddy was chewing on his upper lip, contemplating this recent turn of events.

"Gotta go," I said. "I'll try to help you get outta here, okay?"

"Artemis." He looked up. "Thank you. You're a friend, and friends trust."

"Yes, we're friends. Me and Freddy C." I pressed my fist to the glass. "C for Chipps."

"No." His eyes swung up. "C for Crime-fighter."

Detective Meade leaned against a stone pillar, his tongue working at his cheek from the inside. Although his face was its usual mask of apathy, the lines of exhaustion cutting at the corners of his eyes and lips attested to his pledge of making the world a better place for his family.

Every boy, in his desire to be the dragon-slaying hero, looks for a role model. A mentor. Athletes, actors, rock stars. The challenge is finding a man who can show you how to navigate the daily struggles— with less adventure and smaller paychecks.

As I approached the detective, I had a glimpse of such a man. I realized I hadn't perceived my father in such a light for more than twenty years.

"You're looking mighty pensive, Aramis."

"Yeah. Just thinking."

"You realize, don't you, that anything you tell me about your visit in there is hearsay? Inadmissible in court, off the record, and not to be repeated."

"Thanks for bringing me to see him."

"How's Freddy looking?"

"Like he could use a shower and some sleep. Pretty much like you and me."

Meade raised one eyebrow to study me, before letting that comment slide.

"One question for you, Detective."

"Let's hear it."

"I know that during an investigation it's normal to withhold facts about a serial rapist or murderer. To weed out prank callers and false leads, right? So tell me. Did the Rasputin Rapist use a Taser at all? To subdue his victims? Was that part of his MO?"

Detective Meade's head whipped toward me. Okay, it didn't whip. It turned. By the Meade standard, though, it was worth noting.

He said, "That was three questions, Aramis, and the answer is yes. If anyone asks, I never specified which one."

I made two quick calls, including one for dinner reservations at Layl'a Rul. The restaurant splashed onto the scene in 2005 and continues to be one of Nashville's premier dining experiences, serving Moroccan food with whimsy and panache.

I broke the news as soon as I entered my shop.

"Dinner's on me," I told Johnny Ray and Brianne. "You two have saved my backside, and I owe you big time."

Johnny folded his arms. "Lemme guess. Hardee's?"

"Hey. I do like their burgers."

"The Monster Thickburger is disgusting—"

"Disgustingly good."

"You're a lost cause, kid."

Head down, Brianne was wiping the mahogany with meticulous care. "I don't know. Anyplace sounds good after the day we've had."

Her glance at my brother told me I wasn't included in the sentiment.

"Can anyone spell Layl'a Rul?"

"The Moroccan place?"

"That's the one. Have you ever been there, Brianne?"

"Only dreamed about it."

"Like I said, it's on me."

Johnny tipped his hat. "The man's got the shovel in hand."

"And he's starting to dig his way out," Brianne said with a grin.

We tackled the closing procedures as a team so we'd be ready to leave minutes after locking the door. It was only as I went back to the freezer to stow the last items that Brianne warmed up to me. This time, she initiated the kiss.

# THIRTY-SEVEN

f I had a teddy bear and a penchant for thumbsucking—which I don't, just so we're clear on that—I couldn't have slept any better that night. No dreams. No flashback sequences darting through my head. And with the shop closed on Sundays, no need for my alarm.

I did have a faint warmth still playing along my lips.

Or maybe it was the late-morning sun now prying at my window blinds.

I'd been running on all cylinders, propelled by sugar and caffeine and a need to understand the mysteries unfolding around me. In a span of forty-eight hours, most of these issues had been resolved.

Lying on my side, cradled by a sag in the mattress, I refused to risk this transcendent period of rest with any movement. I kept my eyes closed and went over the facts again.

1. Darrell Michaels's killer was sitting in the county jail—*no more mochas with whip for you, pal.*

2. Freddy C was also in a cell—*but you'll be out soon; just hang in there.*

3. Leroy Parker was dead—*so much for your string of sexual assaults and manipulations.*

True, there was an ICV thug still at large. But my time with the anarchists had revealed, ironically, that most of them have no direction without some leadership. He'd probably tucked his tail and run back to Oregon.

Mom's handkerchief was the unresolved item on my list.

With the filming of *The Best of Evil* in nine days, I'd confront Uncle Wyatt in person and find out why he thought he had the right to steal it.

"Aramis?"

"Uhhh."

"You awake?" It was my dad's voice.

My eyelids peeled open, blinking twice before I registered the time. I couldn't remember the last time I'd stayed in bed past noon.

"One second."

I thrust aside the covers and hobbled to my dresser.

"Aramis?"

"Coming."

I pushed stiff legs into jeans, then got my bandaged hand tangled in my T-shirt as I pulled it over my head. I slipped a striped button-down shirt over my shoulders and scooped up my laundry basket.

I opened the door. "S'up? I was gonna do a load of clothes."

"Musta been tired, boy."

"A little." I edged past him.

"You don't fool me. Plain as day, you just rolled outta bed."

"What?"

"Your T-shirt," he said. "Must be one of them new styles, huh?"

"Yeah."

I didn't check until I was standing in front of our laundry closet, but I'd put the silly thing on inside out and backward. Real convincing. And what was I trying to prove anyway? Hadn't I wasted enough years in that fruitless endeavor?

"You really wear 'em like that nowadays?" Dad was standing at my side. "Never can figure you kids and your clothes."

"It's an antistyle."

"Reason I woke ya is 'cause I'll be headin' out soon, back to Bowling Green."

"Thanks for coming, Dad."

"About what I said. You know, the other night?"

It was pitiful watching him squirm, and I turned to the chore of detergent and washer settings. My expression remained blank.

"I didn't do ya right in them years afterwards."

"After Mom died." I'd say it if he wouldn't.

"I wanna tell ya, before I go."

"You already told me. I was special to her, so I was a curse to you. She died, so you made me pay. You hurt inside, so you turned that outward against the smallest one in the house. Does that cover it? Yep, that about does it."

"Aramis." He clamped a hand on my shoulder and turned me toward him. "I'm sorry for them things that happened."

"They didn't *happen*. You *did* them."

"And now your old man's doin' different. Tryin' anyhow."

"A little late, Dad. But thanks." I turned on the washing machine.

He pulled me back around, and for a moment I thought I was going to level him in our hallway, the same way I had Uncle Wyatt. My elbow bumped against something firm.

"What's that?"

He held the object to his chest. "A book."

"A new hobby? Good for you."

"Years ago I found it in your mother's things, and I been thinkin' you might appreciate it. Somethin' to read on the plane when ya go out west for that show."

I tilted my head to read the spine. *The Three Musketeers.*

"Ever read it?"

"No."

"When she was a teenager, she got this from…a friend of hers. Was one of her favorite books, the way I hear it told. Aramis, I know it used to bug ya how your name was the odd one out. Shoulda told ya earlier, but… Well, here, maybe this'll help ya understand."

He pressed the hardcover book against my chest, and I took hold of it.

"How's this gonna help?"

"Your namesake—he's one of them musketeers. He was your mother's favorite, so she named you after him."

I felt my throat tighten. I wanted to thank the man for this gesture, but my voice had switched off. I threw out a stiff handshake. My father reached out, noticed the thin medicated wrap, then carefully took hold of my wrist instead.

"You have a safe flight out there," he said.

"You too." I shook my head. "I mean, driving back to Bowling Green."

"Chew gum, boy. Helps with your ears. That's what they say."

"Gum. Got it." I cleared my throat. "So, see you next time."

"Next time?"

"Just…you know, Dad. Next time you come to stay with us."

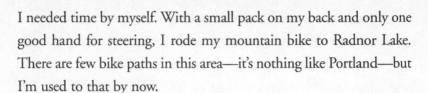

I needed time by myself. With a small pack on my back and only one good hand for steering, I rode my mountain bike to Radnor Lake. There are few bike paths in this area—it's nothing like Portland—but I'm used to that by now.

I turned on Twelfth Avenue and followed it until it became Granny White Pike.

In Nashville, if you follow any road long enough, it'll change names. My theory is that it was a Civil War strategy to confuse the Union troops, and experience tells me it would've been an effective one. Even though I'm from Oregon, I'm still considered a Northerner.

I've been lost here more than once.

Radnor Lake State Natural Area is surrounded by some of the highest hills in the Nashville Basin. The natural habitat covers 1,125 acres and is home to geese and heron, turtles, frogs, snakes, and other mammals. One time Johnny Ray and I saw an eight-point buck twenty feet off the South Cove Trail. He stood stone still, and I almost missed him among the foliage. Then he loped off with three does and a fawn trailing.

I locked up my bike at the visitor center. Dropped a donation in the box. Paying to keep it beautiful, to keep the developers away.

I took the Lake Trail, nodding at passersby, then hiked up along the Ganier Ridge Trail, the road less traveled. I wanted to be alone. Didn't feel like spouting off niceties.

And I wanted to look through my book.

I settled down on a bench and took in the view of the lake where it peeked between the trees. The leaves were rich with yellows and

reds, covering the ground in a flaming blanket that deadened footsteps with a soft whisper. Late October is a perfect time to enjoy the
scenery here, and I sat for a few minutes in silent awe.

With head back, gazing through the leaves' fire, I spoke to the sky.
"Lord, I spend so much time focused on myself. This is awesome out
here. Thank you."

Could've said more, but words were inadequate. If God is real, if
he knows the thoughts in our heads and intentions of our hearts, he
knew what I meant.

From my pack, I pulled a water bottle, a Snickers bar, and my
mother's novel.

*The Three Musketeers* by Alexandre Dumas.

I cracked open the worn cover and the smudged pages, relishing
the image of Dianne Lewis Black with this same book—her hands
holding and turning, her eyes reading, her imagination engaging. I
kept my head down so I didn't have to acknowledge the infrequent
hikers in this back section of the park.

My namesake. Aramis.

I flipped through, trying to find references to the man. I discovered he was a musketeer, stout and amicable, with dark eyes and rosy
cheeks. One passage in particular tethered the thoughts I'd had floating around for the past few days, the past year really: "To be obliging
and polite does not necessarily make a man a coward.… Aramis is
mildness and grace personified. Well, did anybody ever dream of calling Aramis a coward? No, certainly not, and from this moment I will
endeavor to model myself after him."

Who would want to model themselves after my mildness and
grace? Sure, I'd been changing, trying to get a grip. Still, though, I had
a thing or two to learn. Just ask Uncle Wyatt.

The whisssh of leaves and crackkk of a twig brought me out of my contemplation. In my peripheral vision, I spotted black high tops on a hiker still fifteen feet from me.

The guy from the alleyway. I knew right away.

Leaving the book on the bench, I jumped up, chest out, one foot slightly in front of the other. The bruises from our previous encounter were still healing, but he'd had the advantage of stealth and surprise that time around.

"Bring it!" I said. "This time I see you comin'."

# THIRTY-EIGHT

 sudden realization.

"Striker?"

The same ICV goon who'd held a gun to my forehead in a warehouse off Burnside Avenue.

Now he was in jeans and an oversize Slipknot T-shirt, providing ample room to hide a large-caliber gun. His hand was resting on a silver-handled cane made of thick black wood. I could hear him wheezing from the ascent.

"Smoking'll do that to you," I said as my eyes searched the area.

He mumbled a few cuss words at me.

I spotted a fallen limb and armed myself with it. "Should I beat you down now? Or wait till you're ready?"

"Just...want a few...answers."

"Yeah. Right. You could be more creative, at least. Did you use that same cane on me in the alley? When you hit me from behind? Coward."

"A walking stick, holmes. Ain't...nothin' wrong with that."

"Well, you need it apparently. Caught your breath yet?"

He curled his lips at me, but there was little hostility left in him. He lifted one finger from the cane's handle and pointed. "What's wrong...with your hand?"

"This? Training on a speed bag. Forgot to unwrap it."

The man stood taller. "Don't mean ya no trouble."

"Why the cane then?"

"Insurance."

"Dude, turn around and go back to Portland. I've had enough problems since your crew showed up. I just wanna live a normal life. A less violent one anyway."

"What you just said. I seen some messed-up things."

"Now your leader's in jail. That other guy's dead."

"Messed-up," he said again. "And the gold? It don't even exist. Just a lie to keep me goin'." He shook his head, jabbed the cane into the dirt. "That whole life. A friggin' joke, ya hear me?"

"I hear you."

Beneath three crisscrossed scars, his eyes had a lost look in them. "Ya coulda done it."

"Done what?"

"Popped me in the face. Had my Glock, had me down."

"That's last year's news."

"And I was 'bout to kill you. Then…" He ran a finger beneath his scars. "Next thing I know—bammm—I was out like a light." His grim chuckle faded until he was staring me in the eyes again. "Why didn't you do it?"

The guy was earnest in his desire to understand, and it threw me off guard. I'd figured the man had run back to Oregon, to the old life. Instead, he was here looking for an escape route.

Staring at him now, I didn't see an enemy. I saw a victim. A captive.

"Wanna know the truth?"

He was nodding.

"When that fixture fell, it was a sign. It was a second chance, a chance to do things right. To honor my mother maybe. Couldn't exactly start a new life by putting a bullet in your head."

"Now what am I s'posed to do?"

"What do you mean?"

"My next step, homey." The cane stabbed at the leaves.

"Don't have any easy solutions. Get off the streets. Change zip codes, and leave the old ways behind. If you're really searching, you'll find a God who cares about you. The God of peace. Still trying to figure it out myself, but that's the way I see it."

The man set down the cane and lifted his shirt. I saw a gun.

"Hey!" I hefted the branch in my hand.

"Easy, easy," he said. "Just puttin' it on the ground."

I was on guard, coiled and waiting.

He kept his eyes on me as he crouched down. "I ain't used it since."

"Since the warehouse?"

He nodded. His fingers ran over the Glock's smooth metal before letting it go. With a soft thud, the weapon landed on the overlapping twigs and leaves. He stood, toed it away from himself, and then turned to face the trail ahead.

He'd gone a few steps before he looked back over his shoulder.

"Don't got no use for it. Do with it what ya think."

Blame it on Samantha Rosewood. A few months back I had gone to church with her.

Repent.

That's what I learned. According to the minister, the definition has to do with making a 180-degree turn and charting a new course.

All I can do is tell it to you the way it happened. As I watched Striker walk away, I felt as though I was witnessing a miracle. No amount of yakking at a person can make him do what he did. I've had friends who wore the proper clothes, learned the church lingo, but went wild once they left home.

The heart. It's all about what's in there.

So, yes, I saw it as a miracle. No water into wine—though that would've been pretty cool—and no walking on water. This was a no-frills miracle.

Twenty minutes later at the lake's edge, I made sure it was clear both directions and then threw the Glock as far as my left hand was capable. The gun plunged to the bottom of Radnor Lake.

A business supper, that's all it was. Our usual Sunday evening meal before the new week at Black's. Seated in Fleming's Prime Steakhouse and drinking my one glass of full-bodied Shiraz, I found it easy to maintain the front.

"It's a beautiful color," Sammie noted.

"Yeah." I lifted the glass so that the candlelight pulsed at the center, warm and glowing red. "Looks like a little heart."

"It does."

I swirled the wine. "Now it's a beating heart."

She lifted her gaze, and her pupils trapped the same warmth inside.

I set the glass down so the little heart would stop beating.

"You're turning into quite the romantic now, aren't you, Aramis?"

"Me? Never."

"I've seen the way you and Brianne Douglas are with each other."

"Brianne?" I played dumb. "From work?"

"Oh, don't be silly. As long as it doesn't interfere with business, as long as those boundaries remain in place, far be it from me to come between the two of you."

I hadn't yet thought of it that way, the two of us: Aramis and Brianne Black.

"How'd you find her anyway, Sammie?"

"Find Brianne? She found me."

"She has a way of doing that."

"Mr. Black, you *are* taken with her, aren't you?"

"Hey. You gonna answer my question or not?"

"Actually, Brianne's father and I are acquaintances. He's quite the philanthropist. Spent much of his life overseas."

"Yeah. Brianne said they traveled a lot when she was a kid."

"He and his wife worked with charitable organizations, donating their time and money to help the poor and neglected. Some wonderful endeavors, I'm told. Then, during the early nineties, they lost everything in a scam. They thought they were investing in the plight of Kosovo orphans."

"And some fat cat took it all."

"Precisely."

"That stuff makes me mad."

"Don't share this with Brianne, but Mr. Douglas approached me about a job for his daughter. He thought she needed a place to get her feet wet and work her way into the business world. He didn't want her thinking he'd pulled strings for her, though."

"Well, she's done a great job. Bright and full of energy."

"And a doll."

"Considering everything she's been through recently, she's hung in there. She's been very reliable at the shop."

Sammie was holding her knife with such delicate grace that I wasn't sure she'd be able to cut through butter. She seemed to have no trouble, though, slicing her sirloin into manageable bites. As she cocked her head slightly to the right, her auburn hair slipped over her shoulder and plunged in a shimmering waterfall to her toned upper arms.

Sammie stayed in shape playing tennis regularly and shooting rounds of eighteen at the Governors Club. I could see why my brother was attracted to her, even if she wasn't the type to go diving into a quarry pool or backpacking through the Rockies. "What is it you see in Johnny Ray?"

"Your brother?"

"Now who's being silly?"

Sammie touched her mouth with her cloth napkin, raised a quizzical eyebrow.

When Brianne made such a face, her freckles hopped across her nose and down onto her cheeks, cute and playful. When Sammie did it, her lower lip twitched at the corner, and her long lashes seemed to curl just a bit more.

Cute and playful. That was a better match for me.

Still. Sitting across from Sammie was enough to give me second thoughts.

"Johnny Ray," Samantha was saying, "is a gifted individual."

"And to be able to say I knew him when."

"You *should* be proud, Aramis. He's worked on his guitar playing, polished his songwriting, and he has… How should I describe it?"

"A fake tan?"

Another raised eyebrow but no comment.

"That intangible quality," she said after finishing a bite. "Yes, he's handsome in his hat. And when he's onstage, the audience wants to listen, hangs on his every word. Honestly, I think he'd have them on the edges of their seats even if he were doing a commercial for a hair-restoration product."

"You know, men who wear cowboy hats do have more problems with that."

She gave a weak smile.

"In fact"—I threw in the clincher—"Tim McGraw's getting pretty thin on top."

"And," Sammie said, killing me with her kindness, "look at the lady he married. Faith Hill."

Ouch. These Southern women and their subtle jabs.

# THIRTY-NINE

N ag, nag, nag," I told Johnny.

"Would it kill you to try some fresh mango? Picked 'em up at Wild Oats last night, and I can just hear 'em callin' your name."

"Gotta run. Maybe next time."

The toaster gave a satisfying popppp, and I snagged my breakfast goodies. Fast food for the walk to work. I knew Johnny's obsession with my eating habits was just his way of showing affection for the little brother in the house.

A drizzly Monday morning.

Midway through the park, I paused for my ten minutes of silence, huddled close to the Parthenon's soaring stone walls, hoping to stay as dry as possible beneath the columns and decorative roof. Halfway around the structure, I saw a familiar figure crouched beside a bag of empty cans.

"Hey," I called out.

He turned and waited for my approach.

"Freddy," I said. "The crime-fighter."

He smiled, showing yellowed teeth. His hair was combed back neatly, and his beard was trimmed. Beneath his outer coat, layers of shirts and sweaters showed no concern for color coordination. Function over fashion.

We shook hands, and he told me he'd been released the previous day. The police apologized for the misunderstanding, recommended he not approach other people's property with scissors in hand, then provided a hot meal and coffee before delivering him to Centennial Park.

"What'd you think of the jail cell?" I asked.

"Wasn't bad, wasn't bad. At least it was dry. Not that I'd wanna live there."

"You like your freedom."

"Better than most."

"Krispy Kreme?"

He smiled again. "You betcha, Artemis."

"Aramis," I said.

"Say what?"

"Never mind. Let's get moving before it really starts coming down."

On the east side of the park, near the band shell, we spotted Tina and her dog. She was glad to see Freddy. She joined the glazed-doughnut parade, muttering rhymes as she brought up the rear.

Later that morning Detective Meade filled me in on the phone.

Leroy Parker's fingerprints had been lifted from the scissors found in the possession of Frederick Chipps. Tests were being run to match Parker's DNA against previously collected evidence in the sexual assault cases. Three of the women had already identified Parker from random assortments of photos; each of them had been Tasered.

Meade explained that authorities had previously received anonymous notes giving veiled clues about the rapist. After examination, the notes had been dismissed as hoaxes; the smell of sweat and alcohol, as well as the shaky writing and poor grammar, had further discredited them.

Yesterday morning, sitting in his cell, Mr. Chipps had provided a sample of his handwriting. His own shaky handwriting.

Freddy C was a free man again.

The FedEx driver arrived in the middle of our morning rush.

"You can just set it there." I waved him to the counter, pulling his usual order of espresso shots while steaming the next customer's skim milk.

"Need your John Hancock on this one."

"You sure?"

"They paid for signature confirmation. That's the way it's gotta be done."

I signed, then handed over his drink. "Two shots of rocket fuel."

"Attaboy."

"Drive safe."

It was well after eleven when I had a chance to open the envelope. Brianne was looking past my shoulder, playfully grabbing for it.

"Okay," I said finally. "Stop."

"You're no fun."

"Just let me open this, please."

"I can't look?"

"Maybe. But can you cover the counter?"

"Sure thing."

In the envelope were my plane tickets and an information packet. The television show's logo filled the front page. Sharp and simple, red and gold, it incorporated the predictable horns and angel wings around the title *The Best of Evil.*

The subtitle read *When Good Things Happen to Bad People.*

Was Uncle Wyatt a bad person? Maybe not. Did I wanna do something good for the man? Not really.

I'd heard nothing from the coproducers about Uncle Wyatt's dream or unfulfilled wish. I was focused instead on the confrontation and the small victory of watching him squirm under the scrutiny of my questions.

I hadn't thought much about the fact that I'd be a party to some kindness shown him. Perhaps I'd overreacted to his failure two decades ago, but I wasn't sure that made me a candidate for bighearted favors. Of course, I'd already signed the papers. There was no backing out now.

Once I had the handkerchief, it would all be worth it.

"Not fair," Brianne said when she saw the tickets.

"What can I say? I'm going to Hollywood, baby."

"How long will you be gone?"

I checked the tickets again. "Three days. Not too bad."

"Who's gonna cover for you? I can't run this place all by myself. Well, maybe I can." She gave me a wry grin. "But I sure wouldn't want to. I don't want to completely lose my mind."

"I talked with Sammie about it last night."

"Last night?"

"Dinner. Our usual business meal."

"Business," Brianne repeated.

"She'll hire someone from the temp agency. A former Starbucks worker or something." I flashed a furtive look around the shop. "Just don't tell any of our regulars. We don't want them jumpin' ship."

"Oh, they're loyal. Look at what they've put up with already."

"Thanks for rubbing it in."

"I'll have help—that's the good news."

"Is there bad news?"

"You and Samantha sharing a candlelight dinner, and—"

"How'd you know? About the candlelight?"

"Aha! See?" Brianne wiggled her finger at me. "As if you'd find a classy woman like Samantha in any other setting. She's got the money, the looks… She can have things on her own terms, can't she?"

"She's not stingy. She's one of the most generous people I know."

"Why shouldn't she be? She got it the easy way. Old family money."

Brianne went back to her busywork, straightening, cleaning.

"These Hollywood types might really like me," I said. "What if I get an acting role outta this?"

"That's so not funny."

"Oh, come on. You'd love to say your boyfriend is a star."

She brightened. "Aramis, that's the first time you've used that word."

"Boyfriend, boyfriend, boyfriend."

"Girlfriend."

"We're pathetic, you know that?"

"I know it sounds corny," started Brianne, "but I've never felt this way before. Always wanted to, just never really…ignited. You know what I'm saying? My other boyfriends were losers."

"There were others?" I slapped my hand against my chest in pretend horror.

"All right, Aramis. Very funny." She put her hands on her hips and tried to imitate my voice. "There's work to be done. Gotta keep an eye on the counter."

"Yes, ma'am. Right away, ma'am."

Detective Meade stopped in Black's four days later.

"What can I get you, Detective?"

"A cup of your darkest coffee will suit me fine. To go."

"Got French roast brewed. Or…I can whip you up my own little concoction."

"Long as it's legal, Aramis. Just keep it between the lines."

"And something to eat? Your order's on the house."

"I'm not allowed gifts on the job. I'll pay."

He scrutinized the display of bakery items and pointed to a fudge brownie. After ringing up his items—at the employee discount—I followed him to the door. I turned once, to let Brianne know I was coming right back.

She was mouthing something.

*What?* I mouthed back.

*You're looking good.*

Woulda thrown my rag at her, but we had patrons at the tables.

When I turned back, Meade was taking the first swig of his drink. His lips pressed together, twisting one way and then the other, and his eyes bulged.

"That'll curl the hairs on your chest, huh?"

"Don't have any hairs on my chest." He took another swig. "Now tell me what's in this concoction of yours."

"Let's just say it involves espresso shots, coffee, and a couple drops of lime."

"You're trying to poison me, Aramis."

"It's what I drink to start the day."

Meade grimaced. "Well, I was just checking in with you. I know you have that TV show over the weekend, but let's plan on getting together when you return. We're gathering data for our case, and we need to be sure everything's lined up. The district attorney's office will also be contacting you to coach you through a mock trial. Just to be sure you're prepared to face Mr. Kellers and his lawyers."

"So that's the murderer's name?"

"The name of the accused, Aramis. But, yes. Trey Kellers. He still swears he never shot Darrell Michaels."

"Does he also swear he never tagged me with a Taser?"

"He's confessed to the other charges but not to the homicide. You're our primary witness since no one else interviewed actually saw him draw the weapon."

"I still can't believe that."

"Most everyone had their heads down, reading their daily papers, working on laptops. A few were looking around but didn't see it actually take place. Your employee there—she witnessed the man lifting his arm but never spotted the weapon."

"I can talk to her. Jog her memory. I mean, a little white lie wouldn't hurt."

"Mr. Black, my job is to uncover the truth. Not to create it."

"Sorry. It was a joke."

He didn't laugh, didn't smile. "Kellers is refusing to plead guilty or to plea-bargain. This thing may drag out."

"They're all innocent, so they say."

"Same song and dance, yes. But he admitted to owning a revolver, and he's submitted it for evidence." Meade looked at me. "Which is a funny thing. I figured you must've had your facts turned around."

"Where're you going with this, Detective?"

"The day of the shooting we found an ejected shell casing on the floor over here near the window. You're the only one who saw the weapon drawn and fired, yet you stated it was a revolver."

"I know what a revolver is. That's what he had, no doubt in my mind."

"Absolutely. So then, where did the shell come from?"

"Wait a minute. When you fire a revolver, it holds the shell in the chamber. An automatic expels the shell after it fires." How could I have missed that?

"Now we're tracking."

"And I'm completely lost, Detective."

# FORTY

S howtime, boys and girls.

I boarded the plane at Nashville International amid the hoopla of friends, family, a few of the espresso shop's customers, and a camera crew from a local news channel—everyone wanting to brush shoulders with destiny. Even Mrs. Michaels showed up, with all four children bouncing along.

"You go get 'em." Johnny Ray punched my arm.

"I'm gonna wear this for you," I said, holding up a T-shirt. "Let's hope they don't edit it out or make me change it."

Kinko's had provided the technology; I had provided the design. "Johnny Ray Black" it read in gray letters over a black Stetson, with silver spurs hanging from the two *y*'s.

"Thanks either way, kid," he said. "It's the thought that counts."

The cheers of my new fan club died out as I headed through security checks and long airport corridors. Alone, I felt a wave of anxiety. I don't like flying, don't like the idea of being thousands of feet in the air in a metal tube.

I found my place on board, shoved my carry-on bag under the seat in front of me, then buckled in. Started chewing gum.

I was ready.

I pulled Mom's copy of *The Three Musketeers* from my bag. I hadn't opened it since that day at Radnor Lake, saving it for this flight. I wanted time to feel the pages, breathe in the scent of musky paper and ink, enjoy every word.

I also hoped to connect with my mom's favorite character and my namesake. Perhaps I'd get some insight into the way Mom thought. I had some six-year-old's impressions of my mother, but there's only so much you can understand at that age. So much hidden behind the eyes of every person.

"Almost to the best part," the man next to me said.

I looked down at the book, opened to the title page. No, he meant our impending liftoff.

I smiled and nodded like I was in full agreement.

Show-off. Sitting there with legs stretched out and crossed casually, peering through the window with childlike wonder. Beaming with anticipation.

Didn't he understand the laws of gravity?

The plane taxied, then turned and faced the runway while an attendant said something about preparing for departure. Like I could really do anything—a helpless victim, at the mercy of a jet-lagged pilot.

"I love this part," said my seatmate. "The raw power."

I was reading intently, or pretending to. A seasoned flier. Calm and cool.

"It's like an elevator."

For the second and third times I read over the title page.

"Or a roller coaster."

I wondered how to pronounce the author's name.

"Yessss! We're off!"

"Dumas."

The man of boundless joy turned to me and asked, "What'd you call me?"

I rolled up my sleeves and leaned back, feeling much better now that we were in the air. I let his gaze slide down my arms and over my tattoos.

"The author of this book," I explained. "Not sure how to say his name."

He read the title page, panned over my tattoos again, and said, "I think you just about had it. Those French and their strange pronunciations."

I was still on edge, still working with a hair trigger some days. I chided myself and thought of the verse that says, "Do your part to live in peace with everyone, as much as possible."

With Uncle Wyatt? Not likely.

I turned my attention back to the book, scanning over the table of contents. There in front of me, in black and white, I read these words: "Chapter Four: The Shoulder of Athos, the Baldric of Porthos, and the Handkerchief of Aramis."

If I'd been at all uncertain that Mom's handkerchief was a clue before, I was now convinced. I flipped straight past the first three chapters and started reading. I had a gnawing feeling that soon it would all be very clear.

I arrived in Los Angeles in one piece, much to my relief. From the plane, I'd taken in the enormity of LAX and hoped someone would be waiting at the baggage-claim area.

There he was. Greg Simone holding a sign with my name.

"Greg. Hey there."

"Aramis." We shook hands. "Welcome to North Tijuana."

"What? Oh, I get it."

It was all coming back to me. Growing up on the Pacific coast, I made my way up and down Interstate 5 numerous times, from Portland to San Diego, even into Tijuana. Some of those trips were for reasons not worth mentioning. I also have memories of a visit to SeaWorld with Johnny Ray and our girlfriends. I seem to recall that when we returned, I no longer had a girlfriend, and my brother had a new one.

People talk about the good ol' days, and I think, *No thanks. I'm done with that.*

Greg Simone was apologizing for his joke. "That was inappropriate of me, and rude really."

I stepped toward the conveyor belt. "Here's my suitcase, and I have just this one duffel bag. Let's get outta here."

" 'Outta here' is a relative term."

I stared at him.

"We have one more plane to catch. A smaller one."

"How small?"

"A Cessna Grand Caravan. It comfortably seats eight. We told you we'd be shooting at an undisclosed location, if you remember our agreement." He tilted his head, hoping for an acknowledgment, but got nothing from me. "It's a short flight, just a hop and a skip into the San Bernardino Mountains. An absolutely incredible setting, just perfect for your segment."

"Let me guess. Big Bear Lake?"

He snapped his fingers. "Hollywood's back lot. You know, *Magnolia* was filmed there, *The Parent Trap,* oh, and that show *Bonanza.*

Now there's an oldie but goodie. No green screens, all real locations. So you've been to Big Bear?"

"Only heard about it."

"It's an alpine community about a hundred miles from here, nestled around a lake. Don't suppose it'll be too cold yet, but the higher peaks have a dusting of snow from last weekend. The town itself is around six thousand feet, and some of the surrounding peaks reach nine."

"Well, the packet did say to bring a winter coat."

"Not everyone reads those. Good man, Aramis."

I decided not to tell him I'd left my coat at home. I'd figured a Windbreaker would do.

I was wrong.

Carla Fleischmann met us at the airport in Big Bear. She was the clock watcher, schedule keeper, all-around tough lady. She'd left the tight skirts behind, settling on a ski outfit and puffy down coat, and with dark sunglasses holding back her red hair, she showed off a flawless forehead and shaped eyebrows.

A couple more years, and she'd be using Botox to maintain the look.

"Hungry?" she inquired from the front seat as Greg and I climbed into the shuttle. "Or do you prefer getting to your cabin first?"

"I'm starved," I said. Then in a whisper to Greg, "And don't you say a word."

"My lips are sealed."

I'd lost my lunch in flight.

"Grizzly Manor," Carla told the driver. "Aramis, you'll like this place. Their motto is 'Send more tourists… The last ones were delicious.'"

"Sounds…delicious."

"It is. Don't worry, hungry man."

She was right. I ordered Big Bear's Revenge—with a name as fitting as that, how could I pass?—and dove into a mess of chili, cheese, and onions. After dinner, we stopped at the Brewed Awakening Coffee Company, where I got a double latte.

By the time we reached the resort, I was feeling the effects of the two-hour time change.

The cabins were generously furnished, with fireplaces, fourposter beds, and huge windows facing the water. Lodgepole pine and white fir trees stood between the dwellings. In the shadows of the mountains, the lake was brooding and mysterious. The sunlight shining between two peaks slipped away in a blush of pink and gold.

"Tomorrow," Carla Fleischmann warned me. "Bright and early."

"What time's breakfast?"

"Don't worry, Aramis. You'll be well taken care of." She slapped my cheek in playful condescension. "We'll eat on location. We leave at five thirty."

"In the a.m.?"

"Welcome to Hollywood, where time is money. Now go get your beauty sleep so you'll be ready for the cameras."

# FORTY-ONE

**B**ored?"

"Me? Never." Shivering in my Windbreaker, I pushed myself away from a fir tree and gestured toward the lake below. "Talk about a view."

"I told you it was incredible," Greg said.

"Are we ready for the next scene?"

"Hurry up and wait. It's the name of the game in this business. The kid should be here any minute, on his way up from the airport."

"The one who's playing me?"

"That's right." Greg Simone pointed toward a Fleetwood RV parked down the hill. A woman in Levi's and a yellow sweater was descending the steps, long, shiny, black hair pulled over one shoulder in a thick braid. "Here comes your mother."

*My mother?* My mouth went dry.

"Oh," said Greg, "and here's the kid at last."

Before the shuttle van had even stopped, a stout little tyke bounded from the sliding door and whooped once in excitement. They'd found a University of Oregon sweatshirt for him—just like the one I wore at that age. A production assistant corralled the boy and directed him toward the woman in the Levi's. He nodded. Skipped toward the lady. Even from my place up the slope, I could hear his words.

"Hi, Mom."

The little actor's voice was so genuine. So warm.

I cupped my hand to the back of my neck, took a deep breath.

"Aramis, are you shaking?" Greg questioned.

I gave no reply.

"You are," he said.

"Just need a heavier coat. It's cold up here."

"You sure you're ready for this?"

"I'm fine. I'm good."

His finger jabbed my shoulder. "I told you to bring warm clothing. Wait here, and I'll go find something for you." He returned with a dark blue parka. "This should solve the problem."

Without a word, I slipped it on.

Down the hill, mother and child paced hand in hand while the cameras rolled.

Carla Fleischmann had broken it all down for us. The hourlong show, she explained, would be divided by commercials into an introduction, two main segments, and a finale. Each started with a lead-in and a recap of events; each ended with a teaser. In the finale, one of the wrongdoer's dreams would be fulfilled—with the help of the person wronged. Me.

An act of sacrifice. Reconciliation.

Because of weather and production costs, portions of the filming were shot out of sequence. As the day progressed, I wondered how it would all translate to the screen, but my worries were put to rest when I was allowed into a production trailer to watch the dailies and some of the mixing. Then, with a pair of headphones, I listened as a male narrator recorded the show's introduction in a voice-over booth.

This was it. This would go out to millions of viewers. He delivered the words in low, even tones.

*"The Best of Evil…When Good Things Happen to Bad People.* Tonight's story is a gripping drama of a family torn apart by violence and misunderstanding. One woman—shot down at a riverside. Two men—relatives by blood and enemies for years. Will they find redemption amid heart-wrenching loss?"

Later, with my hands raised against the glare on the monitor, I heard the same narration accompanied by theme music as the camera panned the majestic beauty of the San Bernardino Mountains, snow sprinkled and lined with towering firs. A bald eagle soared over a deep blue lake. Then the camera dipped, zooming through tree branches to a river white with rapids where the child actor skipped alongside the woman with flowing hair and graceful strides.

The narrator began speaking again: "As a young boy, Aramis Black shared a deep love with his mother. She read stories to him, and they took nature hikes together."

The mother and child were shown only from behind, through a filtered lens that gave the scene a surreal, aged look.

"By all accounts, she was a hard-working woman. Is that the way you remember her, Aramis?"

The scene faded to reveal my adult face.

"Yeah. She cleaned houses for a living, so her hands were always dried out from long hours of scrubbing. Her last birthday I think I gave her some skin lotion."

The narrator said, "You loved her. That's evident in your voice."

"She was everything to me."

"And how old were you the last time you saw her?"

"Six years old."

"That's a tender age for a boy to watch his mother die." The man's voice was deep and full of empathy. "Will you ever forget the images of that horrific day?"

On film I stiffened. "Never. I think of her daily."

"And who have you blamed for that life-shattering tragedy?"

"Wyatt Tremaine, my uncle."

The shot segued to a stretch of tall reeds. The camera moved through the stalks with the motion of a running child until the reeds thinned and revealed the black-haired woman at a riverbank. A man was grabbing at her. Pushing. Shoving. Pointing a gun.

I turned away from the monitor.

"What do you think so far?" Carla wanted to know.

The sound of a gunshot tore from the speakers behind me, and I flinched.

In the distance, visible between the reflection of wind-driven cumulus clouds, a familiar face moved behind the large side window of the Fleetwood. Uncle Wyatt was in there. Hiding. Awaiting our final confrontation.

"Let's do my next scene," I said.

Carla studied my face. "I like it. You hold that intensity, Aramis. We'll be ready to roll in a few minutes, soon as the lighting crew's set."

The slow pace of the filming process tested my patience through the remainder of the day. I was relieved when lengthening shadows and dropping temperatures ended Saturday's session in the woods above

Big Bear Lake. I had pizza alone in the cabin, watched the end of an NBA game, and lamented the inability of seven-foot basketball players to make free throws.

Anything to take my mind off stirred recollections.

Covered by a thick eiderdown comforter, I drifted into dreamless sleep and woke up needing to remind myself where I was.

Carla Fleischmann knocked once before using her own key to enter.

"Hey." I turned from flames crackling in the huge stone fireplace. "How about a little privacy here?"

"No such thing in show biz."

"It's only six. I thought the schedule said—"

"Change of plans." She zipped her white ski coat. "Storm's moving in by midafternoon, so we need to wrap things quickly."

I adjusted my boxers. "Lemme get dressed."

"Today's the day, Aramis. Are you ready to face Wyatt Tremaine?"

On the monitor, Wyatt looked harmless in peglegged jeans and a button-down shirt. This was my uncle. And yet a stranger to me. Where had he been all these years? Why had he moved to Hohenwald? Had he known all along about Mom's secrets? About Meriwether Lewis?

As the camera tagged along beside him, it revealed deep lines in his middle-aged face. The segment showed him walking through a small town, his boots clicking on the sidewalk. He looked back over his shoulder—a man running from unseen ghosts.

Narrator: "Meet mild-mannered Wyatt Tremaine. For years he's carried the shame of what happened that day at the riverbank. Could he have saved his sister's life? Did his actions goad the killer into pulling the trigger?"

The camera pulled back to reveal the narrator strolling alongside my uncle.

"Your nephew holds you responsible, Mr. Tremaine. Fair? Not fair?"

"The boy's entitled to his opinion, I s'pose. Don't take no joy in what happened. That's a fact."

"How did that day start? Did you suspect the trouble to come?"

Wyatt gazed far off. Natural light revealed shadows beneath his eyes.

"I was out workin' with my tractor," he said at last. "Saw someone wavin' me in from the porch, had a call from my sister. She tells me a man's just pulled up in her driveway, yellin' at her, plannin' to kill her."

"And what did you do at that point?"

"I went to her straight off, hopin' to get there in time."

The shot switched to an old Chevy kicking up dust. Wyatt's face was visible through the driver's side window as the car slid to a stop before a humble farm dwelling that represented my childhood home. Wyatt, viewed in slow motion, ran to the door and through the house. Empty. He vaulted back down the front steps and raced through the reeds toward the river that glistened in the background.

There. A little boy. Crouched in fear on the ground.

The child actor.

But it was me. I could taste the mud in my mouth all over again.

Wyatt shoved the child down, gagged him with a cloth, and said, "Don't you make a noise, you hear? Not one peep."

Shadowy and muffled, seen through the curtain of reeds, the

attacker yelled threats and brandished a gun. Standing, my uncle entered the fray.

The narrator appeared on-screen again, standing on the deck of a lodge, with the sound of the wind playing softly through the Jeffrey pines. I was at his side.

Narrator: "Why did he restrain you the way he did, Aramis? You blame him for your mother's death, but was he simply trying to protect you?"

"Yeah," I said. "That's exactly what he was trying to do."

"Why then do you hold him responsible?"

"I got loose. My mom had already been shot in the leg..."

The camera went back to the river as a thundering gunshot brought a woman to her knees in obvious pain. The narrator and I continued the voice-over while the scene played out with the child actor stumbling through the reeds.

"I ran forward," I explained, "yelling at the man to stop. And he did."

"He stopped?"

"Yes. When he realized I was her child, his entire attitude changed. He turned toward me and told me he could see I was a good kid. He was gonna let her live. Except my uncle didn't get it. Didn't pay any attention and tried to jump the man."

"Was he wrong, Aramis, to try to protect your mother?"

"The gunman warned him. Said if Wyatt moved another step he would kill my mom. But that didn't stop my uncle from trying to be a hero."

"And what was the result?"

Even softened by the voice-over, my bitterness was thick.

"My mother was murdered."

The music came back in with a teaser for the next segment. Then the show's logo swiveled into view. I kept my eyes on the monitor. Fixated.

The following scene opened with a recap as the camera swept past a sign that read Welcome to Hohenwald. Zooming in toward a green John Deere tractor, the lens found my uncle at the wheel. He was plowing a field, jostled by the ruts, talking in his easy manner.

"Aramis never knew, and it weren't my place to tell him the truth. I know the kid blames me, and I figure that's the price a man pays sometimes. There were things in our family, things people wanted to get hold of, and I was just tryin' to protect my own, that's all."

"But," the narrator interjected, "the protection came too late."

Back to the riverside, through the reeds, with white water in the background...

Gunman: "Dianne, you didn't tell me you had a son."

Wyatt: "He's lying. I don't know that kid."

The gunman turned to the child again, and my uncle launched forward.

The sound of a shot shook the monitor's speakers, then the camera spiraled down, jolted, turned up into the merciless sky—mirroring my mother's journey. A montage of her body followed: dropping into the white water, plunging under the surface, bobbing up, then disappearing for good until all that filled the screen were the rapids, depleting their energy into darker, deeper pools below.

The narrator, back at the lodge: "Did you ever learn the gunman's identity?"

I pushed my fingers into my thick hair. Shook my head. "Never."

"Would it ease your mind if we were to tell you that your mother's killer was brought to justice for this ruthless act?"

A barely perceptible shiver. My eyes dark green, uncertain.

The narrator sat me down at a table on the lodge's deck and spread open a file of paperwork and photographs. One photo in particular grabbed my attention. I took hold of it. On the screen, the face of a murderer became clear. Not an actor. The actual man. Darkly tanned with bleached blond hair. I could still see that malevolence roiling through emerald eyes before he fired the fatal shot.

Narrator: "This man was arrested by the Tennessee Highway Patrol fifteen months after the murder. He was pulled over for a traffic violation outside Nashville. There were warrants for his arrest in four states. Eventually he was convicted of murder and armed robbery and spent nearly two decades in the state penitentiary near Salem, Oregon."

"The Oregon State Pen?" That got my attention.

Back in the field at Hohenwald, on his tractor...

Uncle Wyatt: "I saved Aramis's life. That's the thing he ain't never understood. He wanted nothin' to do with me, so I just up and left. By then, the truth was all topsy-turvy anyhow. Didn't lay eyes on my nephew again until just this year. Hoped to talk to the boy, make some sense of it all. One look at me, though, and he popped me hard across the face." Wyatt wiped a hand over his chin. "Funny thing how he got that anger inside him. Just like his daddy."

Seated across from me at the lodge, the narrator gave me a woeful look.

"What do you want?" I demanded.

"Your uncle claims he saved your life. Why do you think he'd say that?"

As my hands wandered through the stuff on the table, the narrator's voice-over joined the music: "Aramis Black came here blaming his uncle for his mother's death but instead caught a glimpse of the killer and the justice rendered. Wyatt Tremaine came to face his nephew's pain and to reveal, finally, his reasons behind his attempt to save the life of Dianne Lewis Black. When we return, one last surprise. And an opportunity for two long-estranged men to get the best of evil by doing good."

I turned from the screen. "One last surprise? What're you hiding from me?"

"Time for action," said Carla Fleischmann. "The crew's ready to go."

"But I—"

"This is what you came for, isn't it? The chance to confront your uncle, to know the facts, to put all this to rest. I came to produce a show that'll resonate with viewers. Genuine emotion is what I want. Your real-time response. This way, you don't need to act. All you need to do is be yourself."

Be myself? The sound of that worried me.

The narrator and I took our seats at the deck table, circled by cameras and lights and microphones and cords. Greg Simone floated in the background. The photos from the file were spread out before me in a casual pattern.

I was frozen. A still-life painting.

After all that had happened to bring me to this point, I decided it must be for a reason. I was meant to be here. Now. The moment of truth.

*God, please don't leave me hangin'. I need you.*

Carla and Greg called out commands. The woman who had played my mother looked on.

She was smiling at me. Our eyes locked.

And then the cameras were rolling. Take one, two, three...

After a few miscues, we worked out the issue of nerves. On the fourth take, the narrator said to me, "Aramis, I'm sure you'd like to know what happened to your mother's killer. He served more than nineteen years for his part in her death. It was lung cancer that ended his life. Nature took its course. Prison officials tell us he had found some measure of peace, though he insisted on mailing something out in the days before he passed. Something that belonged to his son."

I felt disconnected from my own body. My head was nodding.

Something mailed? From the penitentiary in Oregon?

"Apparently," the narrator continued, "he thought you should have it."

"Have what?" I heard myself ask.

"A gift from your mother. That's what he told the authorities. If it's any sort of justice, you and your uncle outlived the violence of Mr. Richard Lewis."

"Lewis?" My head snapped up.

"Your biological father." From my left, Uncle Wyatt approached the lodge and joined us at the table. "Your mother's first husband. She left Richard after he got to beatin' her. Then she married your brother's father, Kenny Black."

I glared at him, felt my fists clench.

"My sister was young and foolish, and for a short time she went back to Richard. I knew it was trouble, tried talkin' her out of it. She wouldn't pay no mind, and she got pregnant with you. Didn't never tell no one who the father was, but I knew. You're a Lewis. She wanted to pass on the family secrets."

"Family secrets?" the narrator said, nudging him on.

Wyatt looked at me. "I figure you know what I'm talkin' about."

I met his glance.

He turned his attention to the file on the table. "At the river that day, Aramis, I knew the man'd kill you once you told him who you were. Your mother, she'd taken an heirloom. Didn't trust Richard with it, didn't trust his intentions. Richard knew she'd try and hide it."

My mind was reeling. I cast the idea aside, then edged up to it. Prodding. Piecing it together.

My darker skin. The handkerchief in the mail—from the state pen.

Kenny Black. I'd never felt close to the man. Could it be true? Had he known all along I wasn't his son? Had he raised me, provided for me, while bearing that burden in secret?

"Richard woulda killed the both of you," Uncle Wyatt was saying. "He knew Dianne woulda passed on the heirloom to you somehow. I could see the realization in his eyes, the way he was talkin' to ya, butterin' ya up for information. It was the thing I feared most. The reason I tied ya down in the first place."

Ready to explode, I kept my voice low. "What're you saying? If I'd stayed down, none of it would've happened? Mom would've survived?"

"Not my place to say."

"You have the gall to come here and point the finger at *me*?"

"No, that's not it."

"You scum!" I hissed across the table.

"Just tryin' to tell ya why I done it. With every ounce of my being, Aramis, I threw myself out there to save her. I did. And for what? I lost my sister in the act."

"My mother."

"Lost you too."

"If this is all true, why didn't he kill me also?"

Tears glistened in Uncle Wyatt's eyes. He was shaking his head. "Richard knocked you 'round so hard I thought sure you were dead. I wrastled with him, kicked the gun into the river. I had him, but he somehow managed to get up and get away. I knew your mom had thrown the whip in the river—to spite him, to keep him from gettin' something he didn't deserve. But I was sure she'd left a clue somewhere, somehow. Well, when the police continued with their investigation, and you told them how her handkerchief got stolen that same day, then I knew. Richard musta gone back to your place and searched the house before spotting your tree fort. Musta made sense to him that she would give the handkerchief to you. 'Course we both know now that they caught him on down the road."

"In Tennessee."

"It's in the blood, boy. In the family. I moved out to see what I could see."

With a bitter grin, I said, "Is that why *you* stole Mom's handkerchief?"

Wyatt opened his hand to reveal the thin silk. "This whatchu want? I took it, and that weren't right of me. I admit that. Your brother gave me a key to get in, figured you'd never allow it. I found it with a note, somethin' or other 'bout calling the cops before someone got hurt. That worried me. All I was wantin' was to track down what your mother died to protect. You gotta believe me on that."

"Why should I trust you?"

"Because I'm your family, Aramis. Your uncle."

I huffed.

"Hear me out. Johnny Ray figured it was time you let go of the past. Well, I needed to do the same. So I got this fool idea how I could win you back."

"How?"

"By findin' the family treasure, to prove what kinda man I was."

"And what'd you find?"

"Found I'm still missin' some part of the clue. Here, take it." He slid the material into my hand. "I'm leavin' it to you. Now that you got your mother's silk handkerchief, now that you know what you're lookin' for, you just might have a fightin' chance. It's the best an ol' man can hope for."

# FORTY-TWO

Looking back, I can see it all so clearly.

My trip to Big Bear Lake had opened the door and let in some light.

It wasn't until I was shown government records from the Oregon penal system that I fully embraced the identity of my biological father. When the ICV thug told me he had talked to my father, he'd been referring to Richard Lewis. I'd funneled my anger toward the wrong man.

I also now understood the years of discord between me and Kenny Black.

No wonder he'd turned against me. A child not even his own.

The show wasn't scheduled to air until February. Of course, I'd signed confidentiality agreements with nondisclosure clauses, never realizing how hard it would be to keep my mouth zipped around my brother and Brianne.

A long time to keep quiet. And just long enough to process everything for myself.

It was in this interim period, between the show's production and airing, that I was handed the last piece of the puzzle.

Johnny Ray pestered me with questions for the full fourteen weeks leading up to the broadcast. Can you imagine the tools of torture at his disposal? Think country twang and cryin'-in-your-whiskey songs.

That first week back in Music City, I tried to put my foot down.

"Johnny, I'm moving outta here if you don't quit."

"You'd never leave your big brother."

I thought of the secrets he'd kept from me. I wanted to say hurtful words but restrained myself.

"Come on, Aramis. Spill it."

"Not gonna happen."

Brianne's methods were more subtle.

That first week back, tired from my travels and still filtering all that'd occurred, I reached 2216 Elliston Place and stared at the door to Black's. The routine was wooing me, but some things would never be the same. Not in this lifetime.

The door opened. "Are you coming inside, Mr. TV Star?"

Brianne stood before me, keys in hand. She recognized my pleasure in seeing her again and rewarded it with a long embrace. We closed the door behind us, and she locked it while giving me a kiss.

"Can't say a word," I responded to her questions. "Gotta wait a few weeks."

"Fourteen. Oh, how will I survive till then?"

"One day at a time. As a wise detective once told me."

"Detective Meade?"

"The only detective I know."

"He's been waiting to see you. Are you going to tell him what happened?"

"Maybe," I kidded.

She leaned into me and purred against my chest. "Not fair in the slightest. If you can tell him, then maybe you could just *whisper* it to me."

"Sorry. If I violate the nondisclosure clause, it'll cost me big bucks."

"Tell me this at least." She kissed my neck. "Did you punch your uncle again?"

"Naughty, naughty."

"Or maybe he punched you. You would've deserved it, actually."

"Hey. Whose side are you on?"

"Did he steal the handkerchief? Did you get back your mom's gift to you?"

"Okay. Stop. In due time, sweetheart. In due time."

"Sweetheart? I like the sound of that." She pecked my mouth with hers. "So you absolutely can't tell me?"

"Strict orders against it."

"Well," she said, "I'm just glad to have you back."

More than anything else, that made it hard to keep my lips sealed. I looked into Brianne's eyes, and I wanted to share. To open up.

This new feeling scared me a little.

Afraid of commitment?

Well, it's a big decision, choosing who you will spend time with, befriend, open your heart to, and maybe even marry. Till death do us part. It's a huge step. And there are so many things you don't know—about yourself and the other person. All the what-ifs.

Women assume we're afraid of commitment, but it's really something else. We're afraid, petrified, terrified, rather-put-a-wet-finger-in-an-electrical-socket scared of failure. That little boy wanting to be a hero fears losing the fair maiden to the dragon. For some, the dragons

are of their own making; for others, the dragons have nothing to do
with them at all.

Discerning between the two? Avoiding failure in the process?

These are sizable tasks for any boy, even if he is a hero.

Mrs. Michaels was the toughest of all. Without ever asking a question,
she almost had me bursting at the seams with the desire to tell her
about my television experience. I wanted to fill her in, give her a
heads-up. I wondered how she would react.

A few days after my trip to Big Bear Lake, she got me on the
phone at work.

"You ain't runnin' out, are ya?"

"No, ma'am." I always felt a need to be polite around her.

"Reckon I can drop somethin' by real quick. Ain't nothin' fancy."

"Today? Isn't it a bit outta your way."

"I ain't callin' for *nothing*. Got me some shoppin' to do for the
young uns, and being as I'll be in your neck of the woods, thought
maybe I could stop in."

"Swing on by. I'd love to see you."

I'd already taken my break and was sweeping the dining area
when Brianne returned from her lunch. I asked her how it was.

"You ever had their sandwiches over at Piranha's?" she responded.
"Okay, so it was thick and greasy, but it was delicious and stuffed full
of fries."

"French fries?"

"Of course, you big doof."

"I used to be a doof. Now I'm a big doof?"

"It's a step up, I promise you."

Brianne rounded the mahogany bar, brushing her fingers over mine as she went to get her apron. My hand still showed scars, slight puckering, from my counter-Taser skills. The skin was extra sensitive, and her touch felt soothing.

A minute later Mrs. Michaels lumbered through the door in a mood.

"Them drivers, I'll tell *you*. Tried to be polite as could be, but it weren't no use. Stole a parkin' place from beneath my nose, then refused, and I mean refused, to let me out into traffic. They was gettin' on my *last* nerve."

I tried not to laugh, but it took a monumental effort, which ended with a fit of coughing. Brianne rushed forward, still drying her hands on a paper towel.

"Aramis, you all right?"

I nodded. Coughed again. Nodded.

Mrs. Michaels's focus shifted from me to Brianne. "Don't I know you from somewheres? Sweetie, I seen you before, and I just can't place it."

Baffled or surprised—I couldn't tell which—Brianne returned the gaze, started to turn away, then turned back. "Mrs. Michaels? Oh, I remember you now." She leaned over the counter and wrapped her arms around the woman's shoulders. "I know about your son, and I'm so sorry."

Mrs. Michaels's expression was a similar mix, but it changed to sorrow. "Was a good kid," she said. "Just couldn't stay away from that stuff now, could he? Them drugs just pulled my boy back down. Got hisself mixed in with the wrong sorts."

"Everyone makes their choices," Brianne said. "He was trying, I'm sure."

"A good kid."

"A good kid." Brianne looked at me as if to say, I don't know all that she's going through, but every mother needs comforting in a situation like this.

I mouthed, *Thank you.*

Brianne extricated herself with grace and moved back to the kitchen cleanup while Mrs. Michaels gathered herself. Her eye shadow was smeared on one side, which I informed her of quietly so as not to embarrass her any further.

"And here I done forgot why I came by," she said at last. "This is for you."

I looked down at a breadbasket. Peeling back the corners of a checkered cloth, I found fluffy biscuits and a cup of her salted butter. Tucked inside, a handmade card was decorated and signed by all four of her little ones. The gift was small, yet so big of heart. All I could do was squeeze her hand.

"Best be goin', Aramis. And tell Miss Brianne that was nice of her to say them comfortin' words to me. Real nice."

Detective Meade stopped by the next morning and didn't ask a single question regarding the television show. "Why don't you whip me up that special concoction of yours."

"Are you sure?"

"Do I look like I'm playing around, Aramis? One Hair Curler to go, please."

Armed with his cup, he meandered to the window and stared outside before turning back and facing the dining area. I could imagine him replaying the morning of Darrell Michaels's murder in his mind, putting the pieces in place as they'd been given to him by the evidence and the testimony of the witnesses.

He gestured with a nod for me to join him.

Brianne looked at the three people in line, at the detective and me, then back to the customers. She'd been through this before and no doubt dreaded it. What sorta trouble was I being pulled into now?

Sipping his drink between sentences, Detective Meade recounted for me the crucial points of the murder and upcoming trial. He let me know of the record Trey Kellers had compiled in his past, a list of priors longer than my own.

We discussed, again, the revolver versus automatic handgun dilemma.

"One other thing, Aramis. I want to bounce something off you, a little tidbit that turned up in our second round of interviews." He proceeded with the details as I tried to hide my reaction.

The final puzzle piece.

I felt like a crowbar had been slammed into my gut.

"What's bothering you, babe?"

I fielded Brianne's concern with a stoic face. We were at my brownstone on a Saturday evening, watching *My Best Friend's Wedding* from the sofa. Even though I knew Johnny Ray was out doing a show at the Douglas Corner Café, I leaned forward and glanced down the hall.

"Let's not talk about it right now. Okay?"

"If you say so. You mind pausing it while I refill our drinks?"

I hit the button on the remote. Watched her go into the kitchen. She seemed so relaxed—shoes kicked off by the door, parading around in pink ankle socks, giggling at her favorite parts in the movie. The pull and tug between Cameron Diaz and Julia Roberts was fodder for some great comedy, but my laughter was shallow. I was weighing the consequences of relationships.

I thought of the romance between Brianne and me. Thought of the connection that had formed between my brother and Samantha Rosewood. All of us, searching for our places.

How could I possibly tell Brianne what I'd discovered?

How could I ruin this date night?

She set our glasses on the table, then nudged me. "Was that a yawn? Are you getting tired?"

"As a dog."

"Do you want me to go home?"

"Not really," I said. I saw her eyes come alive, then dim again as I added, "But I really should get some sleep, sweetheart. I won't be any fun anyway."

I'd been pulling sixty to seventy hours a week, and she'd been holding steady at fifty. Per the secret request of Brianne's father, I'd been training her on the business side of things, squished together in my cinder-block office at Black's, sharing the chair as we went over inventory issues and payroll, codes and permits—when we weren't sneaking in kisses and cuddling.

The New Testament on my desk had caught my eye a time or two. I'd studiously avoided its reprimanding presence.

"Tell me the truth, Aramis," said Brianne. "Is it the chick flick? You can choose something else if you like."

"It's nothing. Seriously."

"Babe, I know you better than that. Something's bugging you."

The phone rang, sparing me the need to explain.

"Hello."

"Aramis, can you hear me? It's loud in here."

"What's going on, Johnny?"

"I just wrapped up the show, had a good turnout. Listen, me and Ms. Rosewood, we're going out on the town."

"Sammie's there?"

"What'd you expect?"

"Can I talk to her?"

I ignored Brianne's sudden stiffness beside me. With all that was going through my head, I had to speak with Sammie. She was a rock. That's what I'd told her.

Johnny said, "She's already gone out to the car."

"Well, aren't you the gentleman."

"Kid, I can't hear ya in this madhouse. Talk at you later."

"Later."

As though on cue, the phone rang again. This was a call I'd been expecting.

"Was that Detective Meade?" Brianne asked after I disconnected.

"The one and only." I leaned back, arms folded over my head.

"And?"

"And," I said, allowing a smile to tug at my lips, "he confirmed something."

She jabbed me in the arm. "You, Mr. Aramis Black, are impossible. Talk in full paragraphs or not, but don't keep stringing me along." She sipped at her drink.

"What if I said that you and I are going out of town tomorrow?"

Her gray blue eyes studied me over her glass.

"Just you and me, Brianne. Don't let anyone else know. Promise?"

"Promise."

"I think I've finally figured out where Lewis hid his treasure, and we don't need anyone tagging along. At this point, I don't trust anyone. You know what I'm saying?"

"Our secret," she said.

"Our secret."

# FORTY-THREE

Under the pretext of a breezy Sunday drive, I told Johnny I'd be back later.

Brianne and I met at ten o'clock and followed the Natchez Trace Parkway, just as my brother and I had done weeks before. With most people in bed sleeping off their sins—or in church repenting of them—the roads are quiet this time of day.

I was counting on it.

Mom's embroidered handkerchief was in my hands, accompanied by the memory of her words: *I have secrets wrapped in here. Someday it'll show you the way.*

"It's gorgeous out here." Brianne reached into her daypack and pulled out a digital camera. She snapped a picture. "The way the sun's peeking through the clouds."

"Hope they come out," I said, with my mind on more than photos.

The weather in late November was less forgiving than it had been before, but dry leaves still clung in patches on the tree branches, and birds flitted about with unabated zeal. There were no bees in the air this time, and the humidity was normal.

"This is it," I said, leading Brianne from the Honda to the broken-top monument. A surreptitious study of our surroundings revealed no tourists, tagalongs, or malcontents. We appeared to have the place to ourselves.

Good. Just as planned.

"The Meriwether Lewis Memorial. It looks so…barren, Aramis."

"Kinda sad, isn't it?"

She shifted her pack while aiming another picture.

"Right over there." I pointed. "Those cabins are Grinder's Stand, where he was shot and killed. I think he was murdered to cover up General Wilkinson's treason. He died after hiding the gold that was meant to pay Wilkinson for his dirty deeds. And this handkerchief. It's a map, just as you suggested."

Her eyes gleamed. "Babe, are you supposed to be telling me this?"

"You and me. Shh."

"We can run away. Carefree."

"The gold. That comes first."

"It's here? How do you know?"

"The map starts at the cabins and leads back along this old section of the Trace. I checked it earlier, but I wanted you to be with me. Come on."

I took her hand, stood at the base of the monument, then started counting our steps—one, two, three—as we moved toward the opening in the foliage. Nondescript, hardly recognizable as the trail once traveled by presidents and thieves, Indians and missionaries, the gap in the trees drew us into its cocoon of forest noises. With the handkerchief held out in one hand, I continued counting out the steps— ninety-three, ninety-four.

We stopped at the hundredth. I glanced around. The underbrush was thick, and a layer of molding leaves covered compact earth.

"Is this it?"

"My shovel. What am I thinking?" I dropped her hand. "I'll be right back."

"What should I…"

"Just wait. I don't wanna recount the steps."

I hurried back through the trees, curving toward the monument and the parking lot. My heart was beating faster than my footsteps. I opened the trunk, retrieved the shovel, then stood still for a moment. My mind played again over the list of clues and convinced me I was on the right path.

A little more digging. Soon I'd know for sure.

Two minutes had passed by the time I jogged back into Brianne's view. She was pacing, surveying the ground for a sign of some sort. I threw out a laugh and said something about her looking anxious.

"Why would he bury it here?" she said. "Wasn't this like a thoroughfare?"

"Used to be."

"So why here? It doesn't make sense. Are you sure about this?"

"You're bright. I've known that from the start."

"What're you telling me?" Brianne stood rigidly, and the pack slid down her arm into her hand. She gave me a questioning look.

"He didn't."

"Didn't what?"

"Bury it on the trace. He buried it near Memphis."

"I don't understand. Then why come all the way out here?"

"It's been right before my eyes all this time." I waved the handkerchief. "See this embroidery? It's a map, just as we suspected. It shows the pattern of the Mississippi River and its inlets. I figured it out from a book."

"What book? This doesn't make any sense."

"*The Three Musketeers.* Chapter four. Aramis was one of the musketeers and my namesake. Can you believe that? My mom must've intended for me to solve it all along, but now that I have, I can't touch it. That gold has hurt too many people."

"Can't touch it? Of course you can, babe."

"No. I'd be profiting from her death."

"But you said…you and me." Brianne stepped closer to me. Although her hair caught a beam of sunlight falling through the branches overhead, her face moved into shadows. "You're confusing me."

"I told you we'd find out what was going on. I'm doing a little digging."

She reached for the shovel. "Let me try. Maybe it is here."

I pulled away. Even as I did, as my shoulders squared, I saw her posture change too. She stiffened for a moment, then pinched the bridge of her nose and tried to hold back tears.

"You don't trust me, is that it, Aramis? Why are treating me this way?"

"You tell me, *sweet*heart."

"You sound upset. I thought we had a relationship here, built on trust. I've never opened up like this before"—sniffle—"not with anyone, so please don't tell me you're gonna turn on me. I can't watch you walk away. I can't… You said we'd share it. Together."

"Is that the same line you pulled on Darrell Michaels?"

"Darrell?"

"You act like you didn't know him. But you certainly know Mrs. Michaels. When she came into the shop the other day, she recognized you."

Brianne rolled her eyes and wiped away a tear. "I went to the same school as some of her older children, yes. That woman's not all there, though."

"Brianne."

She looked up at me, blinked. Looked off to the side.

"Detective Meade conducted follow-up interviews with the people who were in Black's on the day of the shooting. No one saw the guy point the revolver. No witnesses. We knew that already. What we didn't know was that you used to date Darrell."

"Says who?"

"Trey Kellers."

"Well, of course he would say such a thing."

"No, Brianne. You're not listening. Meade corroborated the report. And then I thought back to what you told me about your old boyfriend, the one who'd been all caught up in church, then fallen into his old ways. It all adds up. And why wouldn't you say anything? What're you trying to hide?"

"Aramis, why are you treating me this way? Let's just go, right now. We'll drive straight to Memphis and get this gold and never come back. Never have to worry again about food and clothes, any of that stuff. Just you and me. It can happen. We can make it work."

"You own an automatic," I stated. "You're not afraid to pull the trigger."

"That man would've raped me. Please don't judge me for—"

"I'm not talking about at your condo. The morning of the Elliston shooting you were there in that window booth. With your mocha. Holding that same daypack." I indicated the bag in her hand.

She pulled it closer.

"You didn't see Trey Kellers shoot Darrell with a revolver because—"

"Because of the angle," she said. "I could've lied and told the cops I saw him shoot. But I saw no reason to lie."

"You? Lie?" My laugh was so acidic I thought it would burn my throat. "You were a few feet farther back. Right behind him. The detectives would've measured it out and known it was impossible to see him from there. That's why you didn't lie. One little truth trying to cover your guilt. You killed him in cold blood."

She was shaking her head.

"You took the shot before the other guy. You were afraid Darrell would tell me everything, weren't you? Or just afraid that he'd take the gold for himself."

"You're scaring me, Aramis."

I stepped toward her. Lowered my voice to a throaty growl.

"Tell me, Brianne Douglas. Why?"

She dropped a hand into her daypack and moved with agility, stepping back even as my arm knocked the pack to the ground. She let the gun settle into her grip, holding it with both hands. Standing tall and skinny, she bit her bottom lip. "Don't move any closer. I'll pull this trigger. You know that I will."

I was trembling with that old rage. "You had me fooled, Brianne. Greed's been your thing from the start."

"At first, maybe, but my feelings for you were real. Even now—"

"Even now? You're pointing a freakin' gun at me!"

"Drop that shovel."

I stared. Daring her. Hoping to discover I was wrong about all this.

"Drop it!" Her finger slithered along the trigger.

"You would really shoot me?"

"I'll do what I have to, Aramis."

I dropped the shovel.

"You don't know how it is," she insisted. "My parents went off to help some faceless needy people while their own daughter was being bounced between boarding schools. I learned to take care of myself. Getting the things I want and need, doing it on my own terms. When it comes down to it, we're all alone in this world."

"We don't have to be."

"You and me? Is that what you're saying? Because that's what I wanted to believe. I should've known." She punctuated her sentences by motioning with the gun—on the edge, rambling. "All you men, you're the same. The businessman who conned my parents out of their money. My dad, who let my mother wither away because he had nothing left for proper treatment. And romance? That's where it really gets ugly."

"I did have feelings for you," I said. "That was real."

"These fickle feelings." She huffed. "Darrell told me he loved me too, but I never loved him, never really loved any of the guys I was with. I hated Darrell for his hypocrisy. His drug habit. Everything about him made me cringe."

"So you killed him for it?"

"I'd broken up with him months before."

"But he came crying back to you, wanting your sweet little kisses and telling you he had a plan. Am I right?"

She blinked again. Fresh tears rolled down her face.

"Cry all you want, Brianne. He let you in on his secret. He thought you might run away with him and live happily ever after. Boy, that has a familiar ring to it. But you hated him. You gave him what he wanted for a night or two to get the information out of him, then broke his heart for the final time."

"He wanted to die."

"I'm sure he did. Once he realized that a little tramp had stolen his heart!"

Brianne's finger was twitching on the trigger of her automatic. She said, "I had to get that parole officer of his to tell me the rest. Leroy Parker was gonna help me. That's what he told me. But he turned on me. In my own condo."

"You let him in that night."

"He and I were going to let Kellers take the fall. All we needed was the information we thought you had. But Parker proved an even sicker man than I thought. He had his own agenda. And Darrell, he was practically dead anyway. He'd stopped helping. Stopped trying."

"Big shocker."

"I don't know if he was going for the gold himself or just trying to clue you in so you could get it before the rest of us. But I couldn't let him do either. Already I thought I was too late. Didn't know how much he'd told you."

"Just enough," I said. "Enough to get me searching."

Brianne nodded. "I waited too long. Should've killed him earlier."

"You'll have a long time to think about it, Miss Douglas."

Brianne spun toward the resonant voice. "What?"

Detective Meade had risen from the underbrush, armed with a police-issue stun gun aimed at Brianne's midsection. He was unflinching, his eyes dark and demanding compliance. Beside him stood a Metro warrant officer.

"I heard it all," he said. "Now let's set down the weapon."

Her eyes watered again, but these tears ran faster. Angry tears. Her cheeks twisted while her gaze slid toward me. She mouthed my name as though I were the guilty one: *Aramis*.

The Taser electrodes took her down even as her finger pulled the trigger.

I never flinched.

*Live by the Sword...Die by the Sword.*

In the heartbreaking, trust-crushing finality of that moment, I accepted that the consequences either way were the result of my own bitter choices, my own blindness.

As the shot shattered the forest stillness, I was still standing. The bullet had gone wide, landing somewhere in the foliage, and my former girlfriend was lying on the dirt, quivering. Part of me wanted to kick her. Part of me wanted to drop to my knees and take her in my arms, calling to God for help, cradling her from the loneliness and greed that had stolen her soul. Her love of money and desire for security had eaten her up inside, turning her empty—incapable of truly offering love. Or receiving it.

I've seen that kind of thing before. I'm sure I'll see it again.

The tearing away of that which I'd hoped and believed in felt like a physical wound. A scream welled in my throat, got caught there. Tears burned behind my eyes, locked up. I've always been a fighter. Lived for years by my credo. For a brief moment, weighed by the cost of this woman's actions, I thought of snatching up her automatic and making her pay for this pain—

*No!*

Instead, I did the one thing that's always been the hardest for me—and simply walked away.

# FORTY-FOUR

Fire marshal codes were being violated, no doubt about it. Under normal circumstances in Black's, I would've insisted we conform to such guidelines.

But these were far from normal circumstances.

After a special preview following the Super Bowl, the pilot for *The Best of Evil* had debuted two weeks ago and taken first place in its time slot. My story was scheduled to run in the third week of the series.

Tonight.

Being on television has never been a personal goal; if I had it my way, I'd be standing like a kid at a parade, cheering Johnny Ray on his road to lasting stardom. Still, it was hard not to feel the excitement in my espresso shop.

Black's was wall-to-wall with people facing the huge flat-screen television on the corner stage. We hadn't advertised the gathering. Didn't need to. Between my regular customers, Sammie and Johnny Ray, Mrs. Michaels and her brood, Tina and Freddy C—looking more claustrophobic than the rest—and a cluster of media sorts, we were fortunate to have oxygen.

On the stage, manning the remote and lending a sense of order, Detective Meade stood with a faint smile.

He was drinking a Hair Curler.

I smiled too as I propped myself on the counter. "No more drinks tonight, folks. The bar is closed. My apologies." This was the night we'd been waiting for, and I wasn't about to miss something while adding froth to a cappuccino.

A tinge of anxiety brushed over me.

What would these friends think of me? How would this affect my relationship with Johnny Ray? And what would Mrs. Michaels's reaction be? Had Carla Fleischmann and Greg Simone done justice to the segment or butchered it in the editing process?

Kenny Black hadn't made it here for the viewing. I thought I knew why.

We all have our blind spots. We might know a man for years before we comprehend the one thing that's emotionally crippled him. Kenny Black had admitted to his frustration after my mother's death, but to a much greater degree now, I understood his vile tantrums. I'd pointed my finger, judged, and scorned, only to discover that my own ignorance was as ugly as the welts he'd inflicted.

It didn't make everything right—on his side or mine—but one shared point of understanding can tap into the wells of grace.

Yes, the past was about to come into the light.

A good thing, of course. But painful too.

---

A thunderous cheer rose as the show's logo filled the screen.

The gold letters glittered as though under a spotlight while angel wings curled slightly around their edges. Then the logo flipped, still gleaming and gold, but pierced by a pair of curled devil horns.

Detective Meade lowered the crowd's noise with his hands, then pointed the remote and notched up the volume. Most of the watchers knew little about my past and sat in stunned silence for the majority of the broadcast. Although some liberties were taken with stand-ins and dialogue, the show captured the essence of the truth.

A hush fell over the audience in the shop.

Tension had settled in as the show reached its finale. All eyes were riveted to the screen. There was sympathy here, yes. Also criticism? Blame? The clip of me planting a fist in my uncle's face had stunned many in the room.

The narrator, in suit and tie, stood against the backdrop of snow-dusted mountains. "And now," he said, "we reach the last portion of our show, the moment of truth when the perceived victim does something good for the alleged wrongdoer. Reconciliation, not judgment." He folded his hands. "Tonight you've seen two men who blamed each other. Both were victims. Both were wrongdoers. If we could grant them their wishes, what would those be?"

Wyatt, his face in the corner of the screen: "I'd wanna bring back my sister, give her the life she deserved."

My face in the opposite corner: "I'd want my mom back. I'd wanna tell her how important she was and all that she meant to me."

The narrator continued. "Neither of these men had a desire to accept magnanimous gestures or gifts from the other. Instead, they agreed to turn the spotlight on someone else. An unexpected party. But, as you'll hear, a deserving one."

The scene segued to the nighttime streets of Nashville. Broadway. Glitz and neon. Dance clubs and music outlets battling barbecue joints for tourist dollars.

A murmur of excitement moved through the crowd in Black's.

It was our city on the big screen. Places we all recognized. Memories dancing in those lights. And those cirrus clouds stretched like gauze and tinted orange.

"Is this a live shot?" I heard a patron ask.

My own anxiety was building as the narrator spoke over the scenes of street life: "This week, a new twist. Our crew is in Music City USA. At this moment, in a shop on Elliston Place, a room full of people is watching this show unaware that they are about to become a part of it."

The cameras were breezing through West End, peeling off toward Black's.

My shop went stone silent. Faces turned.

I'd been waiting for this for months.

"You heard it, folks," I called out. "The show continues *here*. Right *now.*"

The audience went ballistic.

From the shadows in the kitchen, Uncle Wyatt stepped forward. I put my arm over his shoulder and led him through the crowd to the stage.

Feet were pounding on the floor and hands were banging on tables as we experienced the surreal effect of live cameras arriving outside our very door, visible to all on the flat-screen television. The place was in absolute, unabashed, joyful pandemonium. Mrs. Michaels's children were bouncing up and down. Even Freddy C was clapping his hands.

A group of security men built like delivery trucks forged their way into the shop, making a path for lights and microphones and cameras. Greg Simone and Carla Fleischmann followed right behind.

We met on stage, backslapping, hands shaking.

Detective Meade and the Delivery Truck Boys tried to restore order.

Oh the mess I was going to have to clean up.

Carla Fleischmann called out, "Ladies and gentlemen, we are live. We have one detail to attend to if you'll give us your attention. As you know, this nephew and uncle cannot replace what they've lost. After much discussion, though, we came to a consensus on how best to bring some good into the situation."

Light applause was quickly squelched by Carla's upheld hand.

Carla said, "Is there a Mrs. Michaels in the house?"

Everything fell silent as faces turned and eventually landed on the woman at the table with four young children.

There she was.

Her arms were crossed, the skin wrinkled and pinched. Her eyes were made up, overdone with blue eye shadow and dark eyeliner. And there, visible to anyone who was willing to look, sat a gorgeous woman who will stand before her Maker one day and put others to shame when her deeds are called out.

Greg Simone took the microphone. "Mrs. Michaels had no idea a few minutes ago that the evil that has robbed her of so much would come face to face with the generous thoughts of two men trying to do some good. Would you like to make the presentation, Aramis?"

I could see myself on the big screen as I took the stage. I turned to face the cameras and a live, nationwide audience, proud to be wearing the Johnny Ray Black T-shirt I'd made weeks ago.

"Mrs. Michaels." I cleared my throat. Steadied my voice. Trained my attention on her. "My uncle and I know all that you've been through. We've both been affected by your son's death and your loss."

One of the cameras turned to catch her first tears.

I was struggling to finish. "A few weeks back I sent in an application regarding your home in Neely's Bend, and three days ago we got a response from the state commission. Due to the historic significance of your home during the time of the Civil War and due to its period of architecture, the nomination has been accepted."

My voice caught.

Carla slipped in with practiced ease. "We will be funding a complete and time-period-accurate restoration of your home. It will be added to the listings on the National Register of Historic Places."

In overlapping shots, the cameras showed Mrs. Michaels soaking it all in. Too choked up to say a word. She tried to wave them off, to turn the attention in another direction, but her children were infused with the energy in the room—pulling on her and giving her kisses, hamming it up for the cameras.

Carla asked one of the twins, "What can you tell us about your mother?"

"She's a good mama. She makes us good cookies."

The other piped in. "Sometimes she's mean, like when she gets angry."

The first put her hands on her hips and said, "Nah, that's just because you don't clean up your room like she tells you. You just shove it all under the bed 'cause Mama's too big to bend down and look there."

Mrs. Michaels laughed. "That's the Lord's honest truth."

I walked down through the crowd, no longer concerned with cameras or television audiences. I gave her a full hug, and she broke down on the spot.

I tried to hold it in, to be tough. Aramis Black. Cool and collected.

Mostly, I succeeded.

# FORTY-FIVE

For the first time in weeks, I could feel life returning to normal.

"You still mad at me, kid?"

"What? Why would I be mad?"

I stepped into the hall and saw Johnny Ray leaning against the wall in his Tabasco boxers.

"For sending your name in to that show. For letting Uncle Wyatt have your handkerchief."

"That caused me a lot of trouble."

"Darrell and that parole officer of his contacted Wyatt. That's why he called me in the first place. Once he knew they were after that gold, he knew the trail would lead to you. But he also knew you wouldn't listen to him." Johnny Ray scratched at his stomach. "Guess I figured that show might give you a chance to settle a few things all at once."

"You were trying to help."

"That I was."

"You should've asked."

He shrugged. "I knew you needed to know the truth, just didn't know how to tell you."

"You're a good big brother," I said. "Or half brother, I guess."

"After all we been through, you and me," he said, "I don't think it matters."

—⊏⊐—

In this city of fleeting fame and crushed dreams, my fifteen minutes had come and gone. The Elliston shooting was history. *The Best of Evil* was sitting high in the ratings, but I was no longer the celebrity of the week.

And that was fine by me.

Many things had been resolved. I understood the secrets that had penetrated my family and tried to tear us apart; I saw how half truths had driven wedges between us.

I also bore new burdens.

Had my impetuous attempt to save my mother, to be a hero, actually escalated into the violence that took her from me? Had I been blaming the wrong person all these years?

I felt entangled again.

There was also Brianne's murder trial. She would face life in prison. I'd done the right thing, I knew that. But I still had regrets. Why hadn't I seen it earlier? Why had Brianne allowed greed to fill her emptiness? Could I have intervened? No. By the time I was in the picture, she'd already committed her irreparable act.

I thought of Mrs. Michaels and her home.

There, at least, was something to smile about.

—⊏⊐—

Today, during a live animal show at Percy Priest Lake, I saw one of the saddest things I've ever witnessed: a red-tailed hawk with only one wing.

This gorgeous creature. Unable to fly.

I wouldn't have gone to the show if it weren't for Johnny Ray and Sammie. They practically kidnapped me from my safe place on the couch. I protested but without much energy. They'd caught me napping during a televised PGA tournament.

"Headin' out to Long Hunter State Park," Johnny said. "On the other side of the lake."

Sammie drove us in her new Ford Mustang. I thought the car was a bit out of character and blamed it on Johnny's influence. Bringing out her wild side.

I thought of Brianne. Pushed the memory away.

The regrets would take time to fade, but there was no use wallowing in them.

We arrived at the park as a local animal shelter began its presentation. The trees, the water, the wildflowers all filled me with new wonder. Nature seems to do this to me. When I'm hiking along a massive limestone cliff, with a drop-off of hundreds of feet on one side, with vultures and eagles circling overhead, I realize my size. My place.

I feel small. And in some way, this makes me feel larger, more significant.

Proper perspective gives weight to our existence.

"This is what we brought you for," Johnny said. "These animals are amazing."

Sammie stood between us, her hair pulled up in a clip and catching the sun.

An animal trainer took us through an entertaining show, featuring creatures rescued in Middle Tennessee. We saw orphaned possums and raccoons, wounded foxes, a deer, eaglets that had been poisoned and barely survived. There was even a porcupine. We all backed up a few steps in nervous laughter.

The loudest laughs went to a crow with an eye for shiny objects. He frightened a few old ladies with large rings, then bobbed his head repeatedly, welcoming the crowd's responses of mirth.

"Now the highlight of today's presentation," the trainer said. She donned a leather glove, and another trainer brought a hooded bird to her. "This is a red-tailed hawk. A male. It's not uncommon to see these hawks soaring over the lake on a day like today. They are extremely efficient hunters, light and fast, with beaks and talons perfectly designed for capturing prey. You can imagine their grace in the air as they float on the thermals. They truly are works of art."

The bird was turned, giving us a beautiful profile of amber and crimson feathers enhancing his streamlined shape.

"This particular bird was found after a tornado. He was a hatchling, blown from his nest." The trainer turned and tapped the bird's chest, causing it to stretch out its wing. "He was created for flight, and yet he's never once flown on his own. As you can see, he's missing a wing. The other was amputated after his fall from the tree."

On one side, the red-tailed hawk had only a nub. I could hardly register that this magnificent bird was unable to lift off the ground. It seemed so wrong.

The trainer said, "Are you ready, boy? Let's show 'em what you got."

The woman started running, and the hawk, detecting the wind in its feathers, shot out the existing wing and lowered its head, visibly thrilled by the sensation of doing what it was created to do.

In that moment, I felt something so raw and beautiful that I almost burst.

It went through my mind, the image of Jesus with outstretched arms—feeling our pain and seeing our scars, lifting us up.

I pulled sunglasses down over my eyes and listened as the hawk screeched with pleasure, crying out for more. For the chance to soar.

Facing the waters of Percy Priest Lake, I heard them come up behind me.

"We have an announcement," Sammie said. She linked her arm in Johnny Ray's and lifted her chin toward me, trying to see my eyes.

I gave her cautious attention. Was I ready for this?

Johnny was beaming. "You listening to us, kid? Didn't wanna tell you until it became official."

I glanced at Sammie's finger. No ring. "What?" I said. "Let's hear it."

Sammie grinned. "I'll be sponsoring Johnny Ray Black. I'm putting up money for your brother to do his own album, on an independent label. With my connections from years of rubbing elbows with record execs, we've gained the ear of some of the nation's largest radio distributors, signing agreements that'll give Johnny's first single guaranteed rotation."

"Uh. Wow! That's great."

"Is something wrong, Aramis?" Sammie asked.

"I thought, well, that you two were involved. Together."

"Oh, Aramis," she said. "Always the romantic at heart."

Johnny elbowed me in the ribs. "No wonder you've been mopin' around. Mmm, now I see what you've been thinkin'."

"Haven't been thinking anything. Drop it."

"I'm just sayin', is all."

Pretending to be oblivious, in her Samantha Rosewood way, Sammie slipped her arm into mine and linked the three of us. For a woman so light, she managed to lead us back to the parking lot without difficulty.

"Who would like to drive?" She dangled keys in front of us.

I snatched at them ahead of my brother.

Too late.

"Silly boys," Sammie giggled, having switched the keys into her other hand. "You think I'd let some Yankee take the wheel of my car? You'd have to catch me first."

She took off, dashing toward the Mustang and slipping into the driver's seat.

Johnny and I turned and stared at each other.

"Now I've seen everything," we said in unison.

The Mustang peeled alongside us, engine revving. Samantha was smiling, elbow propped in the open window.

"What's keepin' y'all? Can't keep up with a woman?"

"Aramis," Johnny asked later that evening, "did you ever figure out the patterns on Mom's handkerchief? Not that I have any say in the matter, not technically. You're the one with the Lewis blood."

"How long have you known, Johnny? That we were half brothers, I mean?"

"Since we were kids. Why do you think you got the funny name and the darker skin? Not to mention the embroidered map."

"A couple of people died for the stupid thing."

"I hear what you're sayin'. But don't tell me you haven't taken a shot at findin' the gold. Could be lots and lots of money."

"It has nothing to do with the money."

"You *did* find it, didn't you?"

I shrugged.

"I knew you would, kid, just knew it."

"The clue in *The Three Musketeers* gave it away. In the fourth chapter, Aramis solves a problem by suggesting that a particular lady's handkerchief be cut in half. Voilà. There you have it."

"In half? You actually cut it?"

"Had to be done. When I turned the pieces around, the embroidered sections fit together to form a perfectly clear map, if you know what you're looking for."

"Where is it?"

"Still hidden."

"You *are* a half brother, no doubt about it. I'd be diggin' as we speak."

"I can't touch it. It'd be wrong."

"What about for me? I'm not even a Lewis, not by blood."

"It's caused the Lewis family enough grief, I think. If it's any consolation," I added, "I've been putting it all down on paper. I hope to publish the story, the way it's happened. I owe it to Mom."

"She'd like that, Aramis. The way you helped out Mrs. Michaels and patched things up with Uncle Wyatt shows how things've changed. Mom would be proud."

What others who sought the treasure never pieced together was the geographical and seismic influences along the Mississippi River. As I began my search, I came across information about an earthquake in 1811. The quake was so large that many inhabitants along the river claimed the water actually flowed the other direction.

Hyperbole? Old wives' tales?

No. To this day Reelfoot Lake still exists, the result of waters that rolled back and got trapped in a massive area of sunken earth. Considered to be one of the nation's greatest hunting and fishing preserves, Reelfoot is Tennessee's largest natural lake.

During the same quake, the famed Chickasaw Bluffs, on which Memphis was founded, shifted and crumbled in places.

Which set me to thinking.

What if Lewis's gold was disturbed during the earthquake? What if its location migrated a few yards? What if it was covered? Or buried?

Comparing old maps to current ones, I was able to determine where the river's course had shifted. Even five or ten yards would make a dramatic difference. And with some perseverance, I found the spot.

Bars of gold. A hoard of Spanish bullion intercepted on its way to Wilkinson.

"Johnny Ray."

He brushed back his golden brown hair. "What?"

"Here's my promise. When I'm all done with the book, you'll have a clue."

"To the treasure? Why not give it to me now?"

"Nope. Gotta wait. I'll spell it out for you though, using the first letter of each chapter in the story. Once you string 'em together, you can see where it leads."

"Then ya better get to writin', kid. Better do it now."

# ACKNOWLEDGMENTS

*Dudley Delffs (editor and friend)*—for trusting me with the idea.

*Mick Silva, Shannon Hill, and Carol Bartley (editors)*—for making this story so much better.

*Carolyn Rose, Cassie, and Jackie Wilson (wife and daughters)*—for bringing joy into my daily routine, along with lots of hugs and kisses.

*Heidi Messner (my sister) and family*—for being examples in so many ways.

*Shaun Wilson (my brother) and family*—for being faithful friends through the years.

*Jamie White and Louis Harrison (friends and neighbors)*—for traveling with us on this artistic path.

*Sean Savacool (friend and writer)*—for friendship and inspiration as a member of the Tennessee Inklings…a.k.a. the Tinklings.

*Sergeant Joseph Perrigoue and Specialist Holly Perrigoue (friends)*—for going the extra mile to help us do the same.

*Cherilyn Washington, Stephen Vail, and Roosevelt Burrell (management team at FedEx Kinko's)*—for flexibility with my schedule as deadlines loomed.

*Davin Bartosch (friend and co-worker)*—for brisket and unforgettable Belgian Triple.

*Valerie Harrell (friend and co-worker)*—for laughs at work and creative sparks.

*My fellow members of Sta Akra (a group of novelists)*—for forums, e-mails, ARCs, and much-needed encouragement.

*River Jordan, Brian Reaves, Matt Bronlewee, Vernon Buford, Venessa Ng, Karri Compton, and many others (fellow writers)*—for lifting me up with your words.

*Ian Monaghan (brother-in-law)*—for ballistics information and ideas.

*John McClendon (hiking friend)*—for that first visit to the Lewis monument.

*Gary and Joni Morgan (pastors) and Mosaic Nashville*—for a place to follow the threads of God's design.

*Nashville Public Library (Edmondson and Main branches)*—for places to study, daydream, and write.

*Flyleaf, P.O.D., White Stripes, U2, Plumb, Underoath, As I Lay Dying, Audioslave, and Day of Fire (musical artists)*—for sonic energy in the late-night hours.

*Readers everywhere (the ones holding this book)*—for taking time to read my work.

I welcome your feedback at my Web site or e-mail address:

wilsonwriter.com

wilsonwriter@hotmail.com

# ABOUT THE AUTHOR

ERIC WILSON credits his childhood as a missionary kid, smuggling Bibles through the iron curtain, for his becoming a novelist. After writing stories to impress schoolyard sweethearts, he eventually followed his wife's advice to "write what was in his heart" and wrote two supernatural thrillers. *Dark to Mortal Eyes* (2004) and *Expiration Date* (2005) are the first in a planned five-part series exploring the five senses. *Best of Evil* is his first contemporary mystery. He and his wife, Carolyn Rose, have been married sixteen years and live with their two daughters, Cassie and Jackie, in Antioch, TN.

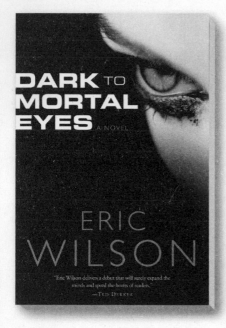 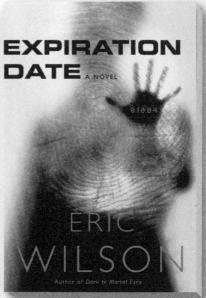